PRAISE FOR THE NOVELS OF
#1 NEW YORK TIMES BESTSELLING AUTHOR
BARBARA FREETHY

"In the tradition of LaVyrle Spencer, gifted author Barbara Freethy creates an irresistible tale of family secrets, riveting adventure and heart- touching romance."

*-- NYT Bestselling Author **Susan Wiggs***
on Summer Secrets

"This book has it all: heart, community, and characters who will remain with you long after the book has ended. A wonderful story."

*-- NYT Bestselling Author **Debbie Macomber***
on Suddenly One Summer

"Freethy has a gift for creating complex characters."

*-- **Library Journal***

"Barbara Freethy is a master storyteller with a gift for spinning tales about ordinary people in extraordinary situations and drawing readers into their lives."

*-- **Romance Reviews Today***

"Freethy's skillful plotting and gift for creating sympathetic characters will ensure that few dry eyes will be left at the end of the story."

*-- **Publishers Weekly** on The Way Back Home*

"Freethy skillfully keeps the reader on the hook, and her tantalizing and believable tale has it all– romance, adventure, and mystery."

*-- **Booklist** on Summer Secrets*

"Freethy's story-telling ability is top-notch."

*-- **Romantic Times** on Don't Say A Word*

Also By Barbara Freethy

The Callaway Series
On A Night Like This (#1)
So This Is Love (#2)
Falling For A Stranger (#3)
Between Now and Forever (#4)
Nobody But You (Callaway Wedding Novella)
All A Heart Needs (#5)
That Summer Night (#6)
When Shadows Fall (#7)
Somewhere Only We Know (#8)

The Callaway Cousins
If I Didn't Know Better (#1)
Tender Is The Night (#2)
Take Me Home (A Callaway Novella)
Closer To You (#3)
Once You're Mine (#4)
Can't Let Go (#5)
Secrets We Keep (#6), *Coming Soon!*

Off The Grid: FBI Series
Perilous Trust (#1)
Reckless Whisper (#2), *Coming Soon!*
Desperate Play (#3), *Coming Soon!*

Lightning Strikes Trilogy
Beautiful Storm (#1)
Lightning Lingers (#2)
Summer Rain (#3)

Standalone Novels
Almost Home
All She Ever Wanted
Ask Mariah
Daniel's Gift
Don't Say A Word
Golden Lies
Just The Way You Are
Love Will Find A Way
One True Love
Ryan's Return
Some Kind of Wonderful
Summer Secrets
The Sweetest Thing

The Sanders Brothers Series
Silent Run & Silent Fall

The Deception Series
Taken & Played

CAN'T LET GO

The Callaway Cousins #5

BARBARA FREETHY

HYDE STREET PRESS
Published by Hyde Street Press
1325 Howard Avenue, #321, Burlingame, California 94010

© Copyright 2017 by Hyde Street Press

Printed in the United States of America

Cover design by Damonza.com

ISBN: 978-1-944417-37-6

One

"I can do this," Annie Callaway told herself as she ventured into the surf, the setting sun dancing off the dark sea in front of her. With each passing minute, the royal-blue sky was changing into a glorious spectrum of oranges, pinks, and purples.

Dusk was beginning to fall on Southern California, but while it was past four in the afternoon, the temperature was still in the high seventies and unusually warm for early December. She wouldn't know Christmas was a few weeks away if it weren't for the holiday decorations on the pier.

As she moved deeper into the water and let it swirl around her knees, she could feel the current, and it gave her pause. She told herself she could handle it. The waves weren't particularly large right now. In fact, only one surfer lingered out beyond the break; most of the other surfers had given up on the day.

She'd seen that lone surfer before, usually from the deck of her apartment on the bluff behind her. He often came out in the late afternoons, and he was never part of the pack, always separate, always alone. He seemed to have an infinite

amount of patience, waiting for just the right wave, and she
had yet to see him get tossed off his board. He always won
his battle against nature, and she found that inspiring.

She wanted to win...*at something.*

After the last two months of being pummeled
professionally and personally, she needed a victory—a
triumph of some sort. She couldn't be the only Callaway
loser.

It was bad enough she'd chosen to be an artist, instead of
following in the family tradition to serve and protect the
community or the world. She really couldn't afford to fail at
something most of her siblings and cousins probably found
trivial. She needed a test, something she could pass,
something she could do...which brought her back to her
latest—probably *bad*— idea to get over her fear of swimming
in the ocean.

If young children could do it—why couldn't she?

She'd grown up across the street from Ocean Beach in
San Francisco, and she'd been in and out of the water without
a second thought until she was about ten. Then everything
had changed. She and her neighborhood friend Kim Watson
had been playing on the beach when a rogue wave had come
in and swept Kim off her feet and out to sea.

She could still remember standing on the shore, terrified
that Kim would not come back. She should have jumped in
after her, but she'd been paralyzed by fear. Luckily, her older
brothers, Dylan and Hunter, had jumped into the water and
pulled Kim to safety, but she'd never forgotten the terror she'd
felt that day. Since then, she'd stayed far away from the
ocean.

Until now...

She took another step forward, her feet sinking into the
wet sand, goose bumps running up and down her body. Two
more steps had her in water up to her thighs. She drew on
every fiber of Callaway courage and finally dunked herself in
the water up to her chin. Her heart skipped a beat, not just
from the fear but from the cold. There was only one thing to

do—start swimming.

She kicked her feet and pulled her arms through the water, feeling somewhat amazed that she was actually doing it. *She was swimming in the ocean!* Her hair was wet. There was salt on her lips. *She was doing it!*

The realization sent a rush of joy through her body. It was going to be all right. This was the first step—one of many she would take to get herself back on track, to prove she could still fight, be tough, and resilient. Callaways might go down, but they always got back up. She could hear her Uncle Jack's favorite mantra in her head as she paddled in and out of the waves, ducking under a larger wave to avoid it breaking on top of her head.

Memories of being happy in the ocean were coming back to her. In her head, she saw her brothers on their surfboards, her sisters playing in the water, her parents and extended family picnicking on the beach. She'd missed those days. She'd let fear take away what had once been pure pleasure.

No more being afraid! She was done with that.

A shout made her turn her head. The surfer was paddling toward her, yelling something, but the wind took away his words. He put up a hand and waved it around in the air.

She didn't know what he wanted. *Was there a big wave coming?* Nothing seemed out of the ordinary. She pushed her hair off her face, wondering what she was missing.

"Get out," he yelled, drawing closer to her. "Shark!"

Shark?

Had he just said shark?

She swiveled around in the water, suddenly seeing dark shapes everywhere, some between her and the beach. *Were they shadows or were they sharks?*

Her heart began to pound and her fear returned in huge, paralyzing waves. She couldn't move. She wanted to scream, but her breath was stuck in her chest.

Finally, she started to kick her feet, but was that making things worse?

The churning water, the terror, almost made her pass out.

Something bumped into her leg.

Oh, God!

And then he was there, grabbing her arm, hauling her onto his board with an ease that seemed unimaginable in the moment.

His body covered hers as he paddled toward shore, and she more than appreciated his hulking, powerful male figure. It seemed to be the only thing between her and a pack of sharks.

When they hit shallow waters, he vaulted off the board, took her hand and pulled her onto the sand.

She sank down in a boneless mess of terror, looking at him through wet strands of tangled hair, her heart beating way too fast, her breath coming in short, ragged gasps.

He squatted down in front of her, and for the first time she saw his face—his ruggedly handsome, masculine face that was square, with angled planes and a strong jaw. He had blue eyes that were bright against his tan skin, and his gaze as it raked her body made her shiver for another reason.

She thought he'd pulled her out of danger... Now, she wasn't so sure.

"Are you all right?" he asked in a gruff voice.

"I—I think so."

"Didn't you hear me yelling at you to get out of the water?"

"I—I didn't," she said, her teeth chattering from cold and fear. She'd been so caught up in her happy little victory moment, she'd lost track of everything around her, but she wasn't going to tell him that.

Looking past him, she saw other people gathering around in a half circle. A Jeep pulled up, and two lifeguards jogged across the sand. The taller one squatted down next to her rescuer, asking them if they were okay while the other moved the gawking crowd back a few steps.

Her rescuer stood up and moved away as the lifeguard peppered her with questions.

She wanted to tell the surfer to wait. She wanted to say

thanks, because it occurred to her that she had not expressed even one word of gratitude. But when the lifeguard finally finished questioning her, and she found the energy to get to her feet, the man who had rescued her was gone.

Her gaze swept the beach and then moved to the water where the beachgoers had turned their focus from her to the half-dozen sleek shapes that seemed to be swimming very close to shore.

For a second, she had thought maybe the sharks had been in the surfer's imagination or hers...but they were very, very real.

She felt sick to her stomach at the memory of something smooth and heavy hitting her leg. *Had it been a shark?*

If the surfer hadn't pulled her out of the water and onto his board, she could have been attacked. She could have lost a limb or her life.

She bit down on her lip as waves of nausea ran through her.

She'd thought she'd given herself an easy test, a way to win, to feel good about achieving something, but she'd almost gotten herself maimed or killed.

Turning away from the sea and the sharks, she walked over to the towel she'd left on the sand. She pulled on denim shorts and a tank top, grabbed her sandals and then headed across the beach to the eight flights of stairs that led up to the bluff, to her apartment, to safety.

When she got to the top of the cliff, she took one last look at the beach. The crowd had dispersed, and she could no longer see any dark shapes in the water. It was over. She should feel relieved, but she was too stressed to breathe freely, the adrenaline surge still working its way through her body.

She walked down the street to the four-unit apartment building she'd moved into six weeks earlier, lucky to have been offered the beachfront sublet by an actor friend of hers, who would be shooting a television series in Boston for the next six months. He'd offered it to her for a steal, asking only that she keep his plants alive.

Climbing the stairs to her second-story apartment, she unlocked the door, and tossed her towel and keys on the coffee table in the living room. The apartment had an open floor plan with a sofa and loveseat facing a big screen television in the living area closest to the front door. A dining area with a long, rectangular table sat adjacent to the kitchen, both rooms facing a wall of windows and a stunning ocean view.

As she moved over to the windows, she thought how beautiful and calm the sea looked now, but clearly there was danger lurking just beneath the surface.

She jumped as her phone buzzed in her pocket, her nerves still on edge. Relief and happiness ran through her as her younger sister Kate's name flashed on the screen.

"You have perfect timing," she said, as she sat down at the table.

"Well, I don't hear that very often," Kate replied. "What's going on, Annie?"

"Not much, unless you count the fact that I almost got attacked by a shark a few minutes ago."

"No! What? Where?" Kate demanded, her voice raising in intensity with each word.

"The ocean."

"Well, I would assume the shark would be in the ocean, but you don't go into the sea, remember?"

"I didn't go into the ocean...until today. I thought it was time to get over my fear."

"What happened?"

"I don't really know. I was enjoying the water, feeling ridiculously proud of myself for actually swimming around in the current when I heard a man yelling at me. It was a surfer. I'd seen him beyond the break a few minutes earlier. He was shouting at me, but I didn't realize what was going on until he got closer to me, and he yelled 'shark.' Then I felt something bump into my leg. I cannot tell you how terrified I was."

"No," Kate breathed.

"Yes." She felt better now that she was talking it out. "I was frozen, but the surfer grabbed me, and pulled me onto his board and got me to shore before the shark attacked. When I looked back in the water, it actually seemed like there were at least three or four sharks out there."

"I can't believe it."

"It's true."

"Oh, Annie, you have the worst luck sometimes."

"Don't I?"

"At least you're not hurt, right?"

"I'm fine. But I don't think I'll be going back in the water for another few decades. I have never been that scared or come so close to dying…I know I wasn't attacked, but when I think about what could have happened when I froze—"

"Don't think about it. And don't beat yourself up for not acting the way you think you should have acted. Maybe not moving was the best decision in that situation."

She suspected her FBI agent sister had had far more dangerous moments than the one she'd just lived through. "Thanks for understanding."

"I wish you weren't so far away. I want to give you a hug, Annie."

"I wouldn't mind a hug," she said, feeling a little lonely. Her family, her friends, seemed very far away at the moment. "But enough about me. How are you? *Where* are you?" While Kate was based in DC, her job took her all over the world.

"I'm at Dulles Airport. I'm on my way to London. I wanted to call and wish you a happy birthday. I know I'm a week early, but I'm not sure what my schedule will be next week."

"It's sweet of you to remember."

"Like I could forget my big sister's birthday. Are you having a party?"

"No. Since I moved to the beach, I'm not really close to my friends." She didn't mention that she'd recently realized how superficial many of her Hollywood friendships had been.

"You're only twenty miles away from your last place,"

Kate said dryly.

"In LA traffic, that's like two hours," she retorted.

"I'm sure your friends will travel. What about that guy you were seeing?"

"Long gone."

"I'm sorry."

"Nothing to be sorry about, trust me."

"Well, you shouldn't be alone on your birthday. Why don't you go home next weekend? Let the folks pamper you for a few days. They're still miffed you skipped Thanksgiving this year. You can catch up with the family, maybe help out with some of the wedding plans, meet the newest Callaway babies..."

It was a tempting thought. She'd skipped Thanksgiving because she hadn't wanted to go home with nothing much to show for her life. Hopefully, that would change by Christmas, but probably not too far before that. "I can't go home this weekend, but you don't need to worry about me."

"Well, I am worried about you, and so is Mia. You never really told us what happened on your last job or what you're doing now for money."

"I got laid off. There's no big story to tell. But I have an interview this coming week that looks promising. It's at an animation production company and they're looking for someone who wants to wear a lot of hats, bring an idea from seed to completion. They're looking to produce a superhero movie, so I'm trying to think of something that hasn't already been done."

"I'm sure you'll come up with something. You're incredibly creative. Do you need a loan to tide you over?"

"No. I have savings, and my sublet is costing me next to nothing. I'm also getting a paycheck from my teaching gig at the community college."

"I forgot about that. How's it going?"

"Not as bad as I thought." She'd agreed to substitute teach an introduction to animation class for a friend who had to go on maternity leave three months early. While she'd expected it to be boring and not at all her thing, she'd actually been surprised by how much she enjoyed introducing her world of art and animation to young, eager minds. Even though she was only twenty-eight, about to turn twenty-nine, she'd gotten cynical from her years in Los Angeles, and it felt good to be around optimistic energy and big dreams.

There was good in the world, and as her gaze drifted to the window, she thought about the surfer. He'd rescued her with no thought to his own safety. He could have just paddled to shore, but he hadn't done that. He also hadn't waited around for a thank-you, and she couldn't help wishing she knew more about him, but she didn't even know his name.

"Annie, are you still there?" Kate asked.

"Sorry, you got me thinking."

"In a good way?"

"Maybe."

"Then my work here is done. I should get going."

"Hold on. How are things going with you and Devin?"

"Will you hate me if I say perfect?"

She smiled at the happy tone in her sister's voice. "I'll be jealous, but I won't hate you. Any wedding plans?"

"Not yet. We've talked about it, but we're not in a rush. We're very happy as we are. Devin loves running his own investigation firm, and I love being an agent. We don't want to jinx it with wedding plans and me turning into a bridezilla."

"That would never happen. You don't care enough about dresses and flowers to be a bridezilla."

Kate laughed. "That's true. And Mom is thankfully distracted by Dylan and Ian deciding to have a double wedding in February that she's not bugging me at all."

"The way things are going, I'll be the last single Callaway standing."

"With Hunter still single, I don't think that will happen," Kate said dryly.

"True."

"I'll call you when I'm back in the States. Stay away from

sharks."

"Don't worry. I am not going anywhere near the water. Talk to you soon." As her sister hung up, she set her phone on the table and then grabbed the sketch pad that had been sitting empty for the past month.

What she hadn't told Kate was that after her last job fell apart, she'd had a severe case of artist's block and a terrifying fear that all her creativity had somehow vanished.

Now she picked up her pen, the surfer's image dancing through her head. He had had strong features, a full, sexy mouth, and startling blue eyes, that had been both bright and shadowed at the same time. It was as if he'd seen too much of something…sun, life, heartbreak…

Her fingers flew across the page as she brought his features to life. For the first time in a long time, she felt inspired…

Two

Saturday morning, Annie woke up early, a new mission in mind. After spending half the night trying to capture her surfer hero's face on her sketch pad, she'd decided she needed to see him again. She told herself she wanted to thank him for saving her life, but in reality, she just felt a compelling need to connect with him again. Maybe it was because they'd shared a life-changing moment together, or perhaps it was because he had the most interesting blue eyes she'd ever seen. Whatever the reason, she was up and out of her apartment before eight, heading down the cliff steps to the beach below and following a path to the pier.

With yesterday's shark sightings, new signs had been put up on the beach, warning people to stay out of the water, and at the moment the surfers seemed to be obeying that directive. There were, however, a lot of people on the beach path, a mix of runners and leisurely strollers enjoying the still perfect weather and getting in a little exercise.

As she neared the pier, she could see lines of people waiting outside the restaurants, probably hoping to get an ocean view table from which to enjoy their pancakes or eggs.

But she wasn't looking for food this morning; she was in search of information.

She took a left just past the pier and made her way to Sonny's Surf Shop. Stepping past the rack of surfboards in front of the small blue building, she found more surfboards and boogie boards inside the shop, as well as wetsuits and snorkel gear.

There were a crowd of shaggy-haired, skinny, sunburned guys gathered at the counter, most of whom appeared to be in their teens or early twenties, and she felt very much out of her element, but she pushed forward anyway.

The group moved to the side, telling the clerk they'd be back later. Then the bald, fifty-something man behind the counter wearing a Sonny's Surf Shop T-shirt gave her a smile. "Good morning," he said. "Are you looking for a board? I'm Sonny; I'm the owner."

"It's nice to meet you, Sonny. I'm not looking for a board, but I am looking for a surfer."

The man stiffened, his dark eyes slanting with suspicion. "You a cop?"

"No, of course not." She found it difficult to believe anyone would mistake her for a police officer.

"Then what's your business with this surfer?"

"I want to thank him. I was in the water yesterday when some sharks came near the shore. He saved my life."

The man's expression suddenly changed. "I just read about that online. You're the girl in the photo."

"What photo?" she asked in surprise.

He picked up his phone from the counter, tapped several keys, and then turned the screen to face her. She was shocked to see herself sitting on the sand with her rescuer right in front of her, his hand on her shoulder, his gaze on her face.

With the lifeguard kneeling next to the surfer, it was clear that the photo had been taken by someone right after she was pulled from the water. She looked like a bedraggled mess, her long hair tangled and dripping all over her face, her eyes wild and unfocused.

"That must have been a terrifying experience," Sonny said.

"Beyond belief," she murmured, unable to tear her gaze away from the face of the man she hadn't been able to forget. He was just as attractive as she remembered with his thick, wavy, dark-brown hair, sculpted face, and blue eyes. He had on a black short-sleeve wetsuit that clung to his broad shoulders and long, lean legs. A knot grew in her throat and an unexpected shiver ran down her spine.

Pulling her gaze away from the picture, she turned to Sonny. "That is the guy I'm looking for. Do you know him?"

Sonny took his phone back. "Sure, that's Griffin Hale."

"Do you know where I might be able to find him?"

"He owns the Depot on 4th Street. He'll probably be there tonight. He's there most weekend nights."

"The Depot?" she queried.

"It's a bar at the old train station. I should warn you— Griffin is not the friendliest guy," Sonny added. "He keeps to himself, likes his privacy, and doesn't hang with any of the other surfers, but from what I've seen of his skills, you're damn lucky he was the one out there yesterday."

"I know. I was very fortunate."

"Do you surf?"

"No, and I don't plan on going back into the ocean any time soon," she said with a firm shake of her head.

"I guess I can understand that you'd be a little spooked now, but if you change your mind, I can hook you up with a nice board."

"I'll keep that in mind. Thanks for your help."

She walked out of Sonny's and paused to put on her sunglasses. Sonny had said that Griffin worked most nights. She'd check out the bar this evening. Hopefully, she'd have a chance to say thank-you to the man who had saved her life.

Griffin wiped down the bar at the Depot, not quite sure

he was ready for Saturday night—their busiest night of the week. He'd opened the Depot two years earlier with his partner Vinnie Price, and it had done much better than they had ever imagined. They'd even started opening up for lunch a few weeks ago, and while the crowd was smaller during the day, they did a steady business between twelve and two, and then again around happy hour and into the evening.

It was a little before five o'clock now, and there were a dozen or so people in the bar. With two bands coming in later, one to play from nine to ten and the other from ten to midnight, the bar would be packed all night and he would need all hands on deck.

As he looked around the room, he felt a sense of pride and accomplishment. With the help of a local designer, he had transformed the train station into a modern bar, while keeping the exposed wood ceilings and old ticket windows with inset iron bars for atmosphere. He'd added vintage train photographs on the walls and stacks of old suitcases strategically placed throughout the bar to make one feel as if they were about to go somewhere fun, even if they never left the building.

He'd also traded the linoleum-covered floors for hardwood, added a stage at the far end of the room for live music and karaoke, a couple of TVs for the big sporting events and brought in a dozen or so round tables that were scattered in the middle of the room with several high-tops for four, adding additional seating.

He set his towel down on the counter as Vinnie came out of the kitchen with two burger plates and headed for a nearby table. Vinnie was not only his partner but also the chef. He didn't usually wait on tables, but apparently the wait staff had yet to arrive.

He smiled to himself as Vinnie, a big, burly, former Marine, former football linebacker, with short brown hair and tattoo sleeves on both arms, delivered two perfectly grilled burgers to two middle-aged guys who'd been arguing over which basketball team—the Warriors or the Lakers—was better. Since the bar was close to Laker land, a staunch defense was being delivered for the home team.

On his way back to the kitchen, Vinnie paused by the bar, giving him a concerned look. "Shari is late again. Second time this week. Said she's having car trouble. Not sure I'm buying it."

"I'll talk to her when she gets in."

"You should do that. I've been getting a bad feeling in my gut the last week."

"About Shari?"

"Not sure yet. Something."

He wanted to dismiss Vinnie's bad gut as being due to the fact that Vinnie was forty-five years old and still ate bacon cheeseburgers like a teenager, but he couldn't quite get there.

While Shari's tardiness didn't particularly bother him, he'd had an itchy feeling down his spine the past week, too. He'd found himself looking over his shoulder one too many times. That was a feeling he'd thought he'd gotten rid of since he'd moved to San Clemente a few years ago, but it seemed to be back. Since he'd never been a paranoid person, he had to take it seriously.

"Probably nothing," Vinnie added, meeting his gaze.

"Probably not. But we'll keep an eye out."

"Always do," Vinnie said, as he headed into the kitchen.

A few minutes later, Griffin was relieved to see Shari Carlan, a woman in her late twenties, enter the bar. Shari had shoulder-length black hair streaked with blue and dark eyes that held a lot of shadows, some of which he knew something about. He knew she had her secrets, but he didn't care. She was a good waitress, and he was happy to see her show up tonight.

"Vinnie was just looking for you," he said.

"I'm like three minutes late," she retorted, irritation in her face.

"Everything okay?"

"Aside from the fact that my fourteen-year-old car is a lemon—yeah, it's great." She pushed through the door leading into the kitchen.

"She's in her usual good mood," Justin Pike said, coming around the bar.

A twenty-three-year-old surfer/student with golden blond hair, a boyish face, and an easygoing smile, Justin was the complete opposite to Shari and brought a fresh, young energy to the bar, which usually resulted in a horde of single women hanging around when Justin was serving up drinks.

"Hopefully, she keeps the mood away from the customers," he said.

"I wouldn't count on it, but I'll keep the drinks coming, so it will all be good," Justin added with a laugh.

Griffin was eleven years older than Justin, and at thirty-four, he sometimes felt like an old man next to Justin. He didn't remember ever being as carefree or as chill. He'd been born with intensity, and the need to take care of himself from a very young age had only heightened that intensity.

"What's going on around here?" Justin asked.

"Not much. Anything new with you?"

"Met a cool girl today."

"That doesn't sound like news," he said dryly.

"She's studying to be a nurse, probably way too smart for me," Justin added with a laugh. "But, man, she was hot. She might come in tonight."

"Great. But remember if she's drinking for free, that's on your tab, not mine."

"Got it," Justin said, not taking offense. "She's worth it."

"You might want to rethink that strategy when you take a look at your next paycheck. You've been buying the ladies a lot of drinks."

"Having fun," Justin said with a shrug. "You should try it sometime."

As Justin finished speaking, the front door to the bar opened, and a man walked in. He wore dark-gray slacks, a white button-down shirt, and a striped navy-blue tie. His brown hair was cut very short, his face cleanly shaven. And he was the last person Griffin wanted to see. But whatever

Paul Daniels had to say needed to be said with a bit more privacy.

He tipped his head toward a table in the corner, then poured two shots of bourbon and walked around the bar, sitting down across from a man who inspired both loyalty and frustration whenever they met up. "Could you look more like a fed?" he asked.

"I didn't have time to change," Paul Daniels replied. He took the shot with a swallow of satisfaction. "Smooth."

"You must be off the clock."

"Almost."

That answer didn't make him happy. "I told you we need to take a break."

"And we did. It's been two months," Paul replied. "Megan is a twenty-four-year-old woman. She's jittery, fragile, and isn't doing well in isolation. She needs people around her that she doesn't have to lie to. It won't be for long—a week, maybe ten days."

"You always say that."

"And I'm mostly telling the truth."

He drank his shot, breaking his own rule about not drinking while working, then said, "Where is she?"

"In the car."

"Alone?"

"Rob is with her." Paul paused, resting his forearms on the table, as his brown-eyed gaze settled on Griffin's face. "She's not any happier about this than you are, but I think this would be a good place for her."

"Where is she from?"

"A long way from here. I'm not worried about danger finding her; I'm worried about her cracking or running. Some people can live a lie with no problems. Others can't."

He knew that better than anyone.

The door opened again, and for a split second he thought it might be the person Paul had brought to the bar, but the woman with reddish-blonde hair and sparkling green eyes was much more familiar and even more disturbing. She'd been very attractive in the orange bikini she'd had on yesterday, but it had been hard to get past the enormous fear in her eyes. Today, wearing white jeans and a clingy blue top, she looked beautiful and back on her game.

But why was she here? He couldn't believe it was a coincidence.

"Damn," he muttered.

"Ex-girlfriend?" Paul asked, raising an eyebrow as he followed his gaze.

"No, but not someone I wanted to see."

"You never want to see anyone. I'm still surprised someone as unfriendly as you decided to open a bar."

Sometimes—like today—he asked himself the same question. But while there were a lot of people in the bar, he didn't have to interact with very many of them.

As the redhead's gaze lit on him, a smile spread across her face. He felt like he'd just been struck by a hot, bright ray of sun. It warmed up places in his body that had gone cold a long time ago.

"I'm going to get Megan and bring her in," Paul said, getting to his feet. "I'll let you deal with whatever this is."

"What?" he asked, a little distracted by the woman making her way across the bar.

"I'll be right back."

He had a lot more he wanted to say to Paul, but his friend was already gone, and the woman he'd pulled out of the ocean yesterday was almost at his table. He stood up, his nerves tightening. He could sense danger from a mile away. He didn't know why this woman was trouble; he just knew that she was.

"I found you," she said, a proud note in her voice.

"I wasn't lost," he said shortly.

"I know. But I was looking for you," she stumbled, obviously put off by his abrupt response.

Good. *He didn't want her to feel welcome.* He wanted to get rid of her as soon as possible. She was too pretty, too curious, too…*everything.*

"I'm Annie Callaway. I wanted to say thank-you," she continued. "You saved my life yesterday."

"Maybe—maybe not," he replied with a careless shrug. "The sharks might not have bothered you."

"They could have killed me."

"Well, they didn't, so it's all good."

"Because of you."

"I just did what anyone would do."

"No one else did," she pointed out.

"I was the only one there."

She frowned. "I'm not here to ask for anything. I just wanted to tell you how grateful I was for your help. I didn't get a chance yesterday. You disappeared really fast."

"I had to get to work. How did you find me?" he asked, suddenly wondering how she'd gotten from the beach to the bar.

"I went to Sonny's Surf Shop this morning. I figured he probably knew most of the surfers. He gave me your name and said you owned this place."

"So much for privacy," he muttered.

Irritated fire sparked in her green eyes. "I don't think he thought he was giving out state secrets."

"Right. Look, I appreciate the thanks. I'm glad you're all right. I need to get back to work."

"It's nice here. Maybe I'll get a drink."

The last thing he wanted her to do was linger, but he could hardly kick her out. "Sure. What do you want?"

"A vodka tonic."

"Got it." He walked over to the bar and made her drink while Justin tended to a group of customers, who barely looked twenty-one, but they seemed to know Justin.

Hopefully, he was checking their IDs in between looking at whatever someone was showing him on their phone.

Annie Callaway slipped onto a barstool in front of him. "I see you surfing a lot," she said. "I live in an apartment on the bluff. You like to go out late in the afternoon."

"It's quieter then." He was annoyed that he'd gotten so

predictable. He hadn't thought anyone was paying attention to him, but obviously he was wrong. He put the drink in front of her. "Here you go."

"Thanks."

"Hey, Ms. Callaway—I can't believe you're here after what happened to you," Justin said, coming down the bar with surprise in his eyes.

"You two know each other?" he asked with a frown.

"She's my teacher," Justin said with a grin. "Introduction to Animation at the community college."

"It's nice to see you, Justin," Annie said. "I didn't know you worked here."

"And I didn't know you almost got attacked by a shark yesterday." Justin's gaze swung from Annie to him. "And you saved her life. Did I not just ask you what was new? And you said, 'not much.'"

"How did you hear about yesterday?" he asked.

"There's a photo online," Justin said. "Cameron just showed it to me."

"What photo?" His gaze swung to Annie. "Do you know something about a photo?"

"I saw it online, too. Someone snapped a picture of us when we got to the beach."

He pulled out his phone. "Where's the photo?"

"Just put in shark attack, San Clemente," Justin advised, moving away to serve more drinks.

He pulled up the photo and inwardly swore. He'd made a point of never having his picture taken, but yesterday he'd gotten careless. "Do you know who took this?" he asked. "Was it one of your friends?"

"No, I didn't know anyone on the beach yesterday. Why are you so bothered by it? It's not a big deal."

His pulse was racing, but he forced himself to take a deep breath. She was right. A photo wasn't that big of a deal—not anymore. And it wasn't like he was named in the article. In fact, his image wasn't even that clear.

"It's fine," he murmured, putting his phone back into his

pocket.

"I wouldn't say fine; I look like a drowned rat. You came across as the hero of the day, so if anyone should be bothered by the picture, it's probably me."

"I'm not bothered."

"You could have fooled me."

"Excuse me," he said, moving back around the bar as Paul entered the room with a young woman. She wore jeans and a tank top and was very thin, with long brown hair and thick-framed glasses that didn't hide the fear or the uncertainty in her eyes.

"This is Megan," Paul said. "My friend, Griffin Hale. He'll hook you up. I'll check in with you tomorrow."

Megan looked terrified, clutching to the over-sized tote bag that she held in front of her like a shield. He didn't want to be dealing with her tonight, but it didn't appear that he had a choice.

He gave Paul a nod, and then turned to Megan. "It's going to be fine."

"I don't want to be here," she said.

"It's a good place for you. Come on, I'll show you where you can put your bag," he added, aware that Annie Callaway was watching them both with very curious eyes.

As he took Megan up the back stairs, he was reminded of his earlier foreboding that trouble was coming. He just didn't know if the danger was connected to Megan or to Annie.

Three

——➤➤◆◆◄——

Annie sipped her drink as Griffin Hale disappeared into a shadowy hallway with a woman who seemed to be a little afraid of him. Their brief exchange with another man had been filled with tension. The woman clearly didn't want to be in the bar, but Griffin had told her she was where she needed to be. *What on earth did that mean?*

She'd always had a big imagination and a lot of curiosity, which had been helpful in her career as an artist and an animator. In fact, it was one of the reasons why she'd moved out of advertising and into storytelling with her art. She thought it would be better to make money off her imagination than just worry herself with worst-case scenarios in her everyday life. Griffin Hale had definitely rung the bell high on her curiosity meter. Not just because of the woman he'd escorted into the back hallway, but because of the way he'd reacted to seeing the photo of them online. He'd also been less than friendly when she'd tried to thank him.

Why? Was he just a reluctant hero? Someone who had acted on impulse and now didn't care for the publicity?

Another dozen questions ran through her head as she

worked her way slowly through her drink. Griffin probably expected her to be gone by the time he came back, but she was in no hurry to leave. She had nowhere pressing to be, and she was curious to see if Griffin would come back alone or if the woman would be with him.

"Can I get you another drink, Ms. Callaway?" Justin asked with a friendly smile.

"You can—a vodka tonic," she said. And outside of the classroom, you can call me Annie. I'm like five years older than you."

He grinned. "Sounds like a good plan. I must admit you're one of the youngest teachers I've ever had."

"I hope you're not missing Mrs. Barker too much," she said, referring to the woman she'd replaced.

"Not at all. She only taught the first few classes, and it was easy to see she wasn't really up for it. Plus, you have more experience in Hollywood, which I like. I'm hoping to do something in the film industry."

"There are definitely a lot of different avenues you can take," she said carefully, not wanting to crush anyone's dreams even though there was a whole lot of negative she could say about Hollywood.

As Justin took her empty glass away and served her another vodka tonic, he said, "So how close were you to the sharks yesterday?"

"Really close. I felt one brush my leg. I have never been so terrified."

"No way. I've been surfing since I was six, and I've never seen a shark."

"Must have been my unlucky day."

"What did you do?"

"I froze. I was actually completely unaware of the sharks until Griffin started yelling at me and paddled in my direction. He got to me just in time. He pulled me onto his board and took us to the beach. I had no idea sharks would come that close to shore."

"They seem to get closer every year, but most of them

won't hurt you."

"I didn't want to stick around long enough to find out."
She sipped her drink, then said, "Did you meet Griffin when
you were surfing?"

"I did. He's not the friendliest dude, but the old man is
damn good on the waves."

"Old man?" she echoed. "What is he—thirty-three, thirty-
four?"

Justin laughed. "Something like that. Anyway, he's a
good guy. He gave me a job when I needed it. He looks out
for people, but don't tell him I said that. He doesn't like that to
get around."

Now she was even more curious about the man. "Did you
see the woman he took in the back a few minutes ago?"

"Nope. Why?"

"Just wondered. She seemed kind of scared."

"Of Griffin?" he asked doubtfully.

"Maybe not of Griffin, but something."

"Well, she's probably just someone else who needs
Griffin's help. They come around here off and on. You want
something to eat? Vinnie cooks up a mean cheeseburger. He
has a special sauce he puts on it that gives it a little kick."

Her stomach rumbled at the thought. "That sounds good."

"Fries?"

"Absolutely."

As Justin put her food order in, she glanced around the
bar, enjoying the atmosphere. She particularly liked the old
train station details. Someone had definitely put some thought
into the décor. *Was that Griffin?* He didn't seem like the type.
On the other hand, she really didn't know anything about him.

As she considered that thought, Griffin came back into
the room alone. His lips drew into a tight line when his gaze
met hers.

"You're still here," he muttered.

"Justin said your cook makes a mean burger. I just
ordered one. Everything okay?"

"Why wouldn't it be?" he challenged.

She licked her lips, realizing her nosy questions were not going to make her more welcome at the bar. "Just wondering. The woman you were with seemed in some sort of distress."

"She's fine. Don't worry about her." Griffin paused as a big man came out of the kitchen and put a burger down in front of her.

The man looked more like a football player than a cook or a waiter, but the burger he delivered was amazing. Topped with lettuce, tomato, onions, and some sort of sauce, the juicy quarter pounder made her mouth water.

"Enjoy," the man told her, then tipped his head to Griffin. "Another one? I thought we were done."

Griffin frowned and shot her a quick look, then pulled the man into the kitchen, leaving her with even more questions.

As she ate her burger, her mind swirled with possibilities. When Griffin returned, he moved down the bar, switching places with Justin.

She couldn't help wondering if he was deliberately avoiding her. It had been awhile since a man had treated her so dismissively, but for some reason she didn't think it was completely personal. There was something else going on in the bar tonight, and it had to do with the woman Griffin had taken into the back hallway. She wondered what was back there. *An office? Restrooms? Living space?*

After finishing her burger and her second drink, she decided it was time to find out. There was a band setting up on the stage and the bar was getting more crowded by the minute. Both Justin and Griffin were slammed by orders and two additional waitresses had come on board to help out, but they were also kept very busy. The Depot was definitely the place to be on a Saturday night. She doubted she'd have any further conversation with Griffin tonight.

Sliding off her seat, she moved through the nearby doorway. To her left, she could see a closed door labeled Office and another marked Storage. To her right were the restrooms, a doorway leading into the kitchen, and at the end of the hall was a stairway leading up to a second floor and a door labeled Employees Only.

She had a feeling that Griffin had taken the woman up those stairs. She moved down the hallway, peering up the stairway but unable to see or hear anything out of the ordinary, and she wasn't ready to make her way up the steps. She was already being way too nosy. She obviously had too much time on her hands these days.

"Looking for something?" Griffin asked.

She swung around at the sound of his sharp voice, hoping the guilty feeling running through her body didn't show in her expression. "The restroom."

"You just passed it."

"Right," she said, heading back down the hall.

Griffin stepped in front of her. "What are you really doing here?"

She was confused by his question and the suspicious look in his eyes. "I don't know what you mean."

"You didn't just come here to say thank-you, so what's going on?"

"That *is* why I came," she said.

He folded his arms across his chest, unconvinced by her words.

"Okay, I'll admit that since you took that woman upstairs, I've been a little curious about her. She didn't seem like she knew you or that she wanted to go with you."

"I told you before she's fine. She's upset about something and she came here to get away from her problems."

"Then why did she tell you she didn't want to be here? Why did that man seem to be handing her off to you?"

"You do know this is none of your business, right?"

"When I see someone who might be in trouble, I make it my business. Seems like you do the same thing. You saved me yesterday when you saw a shark circling my way. Maybe I feel the same way about her."

"And you think I'm the shark putting her in danger?" he challenged.

"Are you?" she asked, knowing she was playing with fire, but she couldn't seem to stop herself.

He gave her a long, hard look that sent a chill down her spine. Yesterday he'd been her savior. Today—she wasn't sure who he was.

"No," he said flatly. "I'm not a danger to the woman who went upstairs. But that's all I'm going to say about it out of respect for her privacy, and I'd ask you to leave it alone."

"If you were a danger, I doubt you'd tell me," she muttered.

"If I were a danger, then you should consider whether you want to put yourself in the middle of this."

They exchanged another long, measuring look. She didn't know what he could read in her eyes, but his gaze was completely indecipherable. The only thing she knew for sure was that this conversation was going nowhere.

"I'm going to go," she said.

"Best idea you've had yet." He stepped aside. "After you."

She walked past him and reentered the bar. The noise level had gone up with another influx of people. Despite the crowd, she could feel Griffin's eyes on her as she made her way to the front door.

He didn't trust her. That was fine. She didn't trust him, either.

He might not want to see her back in the bar again, but that didn't mean she was going to stay away. She needed to think about that…

After Annie left, Griffin went upstairs to check on Megan. The door was locked as he'd expected. He gave a three-tap knock, announced he was coming inside, and then used one key for the dead bolt and another for the main lock.

Megan sat on the couch, a knitted blanket wrapped around her thin shoulders, her gaze on a television screen that was playing some sit-com with a lot of canned laughter. He doubted she was watching the show; there was a distant gaze in her eyes, a shut-down expression that he'd seen more than a few times in his life, sometimes in his own mirror.

"Everything okay?" he asked her, perching on the edge of a nearby armchair.

She shrugged and didn't bother to look at him.

"No one came up here, did they?"

At his question, her gaze swung to his, and her wary, fearful look returned. "No. You said no one would come up here."

"And that's true," he said quickly. "I was just double-checking. Did you look at the menu I left you? What would you like from the kitchen?"

"I'm not hungry." Her gaze moved back to the television.

He got up and walked around in front of her, blocking her view. "Okay, here's the deal, Megan. You're going to be here at least a week. You need to eat. To drink. To sleep. You can do all of that, can't you?"

She drew in a breath and let it out. "Do you know who I am, why I'm here?"

"I don't need to know, and you don't need to tell me."

"The agent said that you've done this before."

"I have," he admitted.

"I feel…lost," she whispered.

He could feel her pain in a way she probably couldn't imagine. "You're not lost. You're just taking a time-out from your life. You'll get it back. You'll be who you used to be."

"Will I? It doesn't seem possible."

"It's possible, but none of that happens if you don't go along with the plan. I realize you don't know me, but you're going to have to find a way to trust me."

"Trusting you—a stranger—seems as dumb as anything I've done so far."

"Paul Daniels trusts me. He wouldn't have brought you here if he didn't. He said you've been having a difficult time."

"That's an understatement."

"I can't change what's happening in your life, but I can make the next few days easier for you. It's up to you. I'll bring you up some food, or if you feel up to it, you can come down to the bar."

"How can I be around all those people? I've been in hiding for months."

"Because you can," he said simply. "No one knows who you are, and no one will. Paul brought you here so you could feel normal again."

"Normal? That's not going to happen." She paused. "Who else lives here?"

"I have the apartment down the hall. Only you and I have keys to this place."

"I want your keys," she said.

He hesitated, then took the two keys off his ring and handed them to her. "Here you go."

She took the keys and gave him another suspicious look. "Are these the only ones?"

"Yes," he lied. "So, what's it going to be? Room service or you come downstairs?"

"I don't want to go anywhere."

"Then I'll bring you a burger, unless you don't eat meat?"

"I eat meat," she mumbled.

"Great. The kitchen is busy, so it will be about thirty minutes."

Getting a shrug in response, he headed to the door. "When I come back, I'll knock three times. You can check the peephole to make sure it's me."

After pulling the door shut, he waited until he heard her shove the dead bolt home, then he returned downstairs. He stopped in the kitchen on his way back to the bar and asked Vinnie to make a plate for upstairs.

His partner gave him a look that said he did not want to be a part of this, but the kitchen was too busy for Vinnie to waste time complaining. He did, however, deliver one parting shot.

"You sure you know what you're doing?" Vinnie asked.

There had been a time in his life when he'd been sure about everything, but that was a different lifetime. "Not really, but it is what it is."

As Vinnie turned his attention back to his grill, he returned to the bar, relieved that the pretty and incredibly nosy Annie Callaway was gone. He wanted to believe she had truly just come by to thank him for saving her life, but her actions after that had been very suspicious. She'd been heading upstairs when he'd caught her, and that could have been disastrous.

He definitely needed to be more careful about his encounters with Paul when there were other people in the bar. He'd certainly never considered that someone might think he was a dangerous man out to hurt an innocent woman. Hopefully, he had alleviated Annie's concerns, but he had doubts about that. There really wasn't any reason for them to see each other again, but somehow, he didn't think that was the way it was going to go down.

Four

⟶ ⋙ ⋘ ⟵

Sunday afternoon, Annie was still thinking about Griffin Hale, and her previous bout of artist's block had completely disappeared.

In fact, she'd spent half the night and all morning at her dining room table working on sketches of not only Griffin, but the Depot, and some of the other people she'd seen there—the outgoing and friendly Justin, who had a boy-next-door look about him; the stocky man in the kitchen, whose hands seemed too big and too rough to plate such delicious food; the raven-haired waitress with the gothic look about her, who sneaked a peek at her phone every time she had a few extra seconds to spare; and the waifish woman with the big glasses and the terrified eyes who'd been called Megan.

They'd all captured her imagination. She didn't know where her sketches were going yet, but she felt like she was on the verge of an idea, something exciting, something different, maybe something that could kick-start her career…

But as she glanced at her watch, and realized it was almost noon, she knew that her drawing time was about to end. She was going to have to put her creative ideas on hold.

She'd gotten a text that morning from her younger sister, Mia. Apparently, the twins—Mia and Kate—did not believe she was fine, no matter how many times she told them she was, so Mia and her husband Jeremy had decided to take a day trip to San Clemente from their home in Angel's Bay, which was about three hours north.

While a part of her was not looking forward to another sisterly grilling, she did miss her family, and as someone who loved art and who had not chosen to save lives and fight fires or bad guys like the rest of her family, Mia was the one most likely to understand what she was going through.

Her apartment bell rang, and she jumped to her feet to buzz her sister inside. Then she went to open her door.

A moment later, Mia came up the stairs. Mia had thick, wavy blonde hair and bright blue eyes. She was followed into the room by her husband Jeremy Holt, who had dark hair and dark eyes, and Mia's stepdaughter Ashlyn, who was the spitting image of her father.

"You're all here," she said, giving her sister a tight hug, and then following up with Jeremy and Ashlyn.

"Oh, my gosh, this is amazing," Mia said, heading straight for the windows. "You have an incredible view."

"I love it," she said. "It's a nice change from where I was living in LA. My only view there was of the dumpster behind my apartment building. But I'm trying not to get too spoiled. I only get the place for six months. Then my friend will be coming back." She paused. "Can I get you guys anything— water, soda, orange juice?"

"Water would be great," Jeremy told her.

"Of course." She turned to nine-year-old Ashlyn, who had started to get past her shy nature when it came to the big, often loud, Callaway family. "How about you, honey?"

"Orange juice," Ashlyn said with a small smile.

"Coming right up. Mia?"

"I'm good."

She got drinks for everyone while Mia, Jeremy, and Ashlyn sat down at her table.

"What are all these?" Mia asked, picking up some of her sketches.

"Just some random ideas I'm working on."

"They're really good," Jeremy commented. "Are you doing a graphic novel?"

"No, I'm making a pitch for a job with an animated film company. I have an interview at the end of next week and I need to come with ideas."

"It looks like you have a lot to bring to the table," Mia said. "You're so talented, Annie. Any company would be lucky to have you. I know it's been a tough few months, but I hope you haven't lost your confidence."

She didn't want to admit that until yesterday she'd thought she'd lost a lot more than her confidence. "I am hoping for a turnaround in my career path," she said lightly. "And it's nothing for you to worry about. I hope you didn't drive all the way down here because you're concerned about me."

"Would I do that?" Mia asked with mock innocence.

"It was a nice day for a drive," Jeremy put in with a smile.

She smiled back at him. "You're a good sport. I know Mia wanted to check up on me, because I missed Thanksgiving."

"I did," Mia admitted. "I couldn't believe you didn't come. You don't usually miss the holidays."

"I was busy. I had things to do."

"Like what? You should never be too busy for family."

"I'll make it for Christmas. So, what's new with everyone? How are our brothers?" she asked, changing the subject, as she sat down.

"Ian and Grace, and Dylan and Tori are planning their double winter wedding," Mia said. "They were all disgustingly in love at Thanksgiving."

"You should talk," she said with a laugh. "You and Jeremy couldn't keep your hands off each other the first time you brought him home."

"I'm sure that's not true," Mia said, with a flush of pink in her cheeks.

"What about Hunter?" she asked.

"Who knows? Like you, Hunter seems eager to keep his family on a need-to-know basis. He's still traveling the world. I guess he'll be able to get another firehouse slot when he gets back, if he wants it, but Dylan said he wasn't sure if Hunter wanted to be a firefighter anymore."

"What would he do instead?"

"Who knows? Hunter doesn't seem to confide in anyone these days. Maybe you should reach out to him."

"I'll text him," she said. "Not that he usually gets back to me in under a week, but you never know. What about Mom and Dad? All is well?"

"Yes, they're both doing great. I spoke to Kate yesterday. She said she'd just talked to you and that you were almost attacked by a shark, which seems like information you might have shared with me, too."

"I'm fine. A surfer rescued me, and no harm was done."

"Was the shark big?" Ashlyn asked with wide, curious eyes.

"I saw some shapes in the water after I got out, and they looked big to me," she replied.

"That's scary," Ashlyn said.

"Very scary," she agreed.

"You're lucky someone got you out of the water," Mia said. "I think you should go back to being afraid of the ocean, Annie."

"Trust me, I'm already there."

"I'm glad you're okay." Mia tucked her hair behind one ear and gave Jeremy an odd look.

Annie frowned. "Wait, is something else going on? Is there another reason you came down here besides wanting to check on me?"

Mia gave her a sheepish smile. "There is. You always could read me like a book."

"Well, tell me already."

"I'm pregnant. Jeremy and I are going to have a baby."

"What? Yay! That's so wonderful." She got up from the table and threw her arms around Mia. "I'm so happy for you."

"I'm happy, too," Mia said with a blurry smile.

Annie gave Jeremy a quick hug and then sat back down. "How far along are you? When is the baby coming?"

"I just hit seven weeks. It's probably too early to be making an announcement, but I told Kate yesterday, and then I knew I had to tell you, too, because Kate can't keep a secret."

"That's for sure. Which means you need to call Mom and Dad and the boys, too."

"We're going to make some calls tonight, but since you were close enough to see in person, I wanted to tell you now."

"I'm going to be a big sister," Ashlyn interrupted.

"There is nothing more fun than that," she said, giving her niece a smile. "I love being a big sister."

"I hope I get a sister and not a brother," Ashlyn said. "I want someone to play with."

"Boys can be fun, too," she said with a laugh.

Ashlyn didn't seem convinced, but she was already moving on. Turning to her father, she said, "Daddy, can we go down to the beach and see if the sharks are there?"

"Sure," Jeremy said. "Why don't you two have some sister time, and Ashlyn and I will meet you down on the beach in a bit? Then we can take a walk to the pier and get lunch? Does that work for you, Annie?"

"It's perfect," she said. "When you leave the building, go to the right, and you'll find steps to the beach."

"Got it."

As Jeremy and Ashlyn left, she gazed back at Mia, noting the glow in her sister's eyes. "You're really happy, aren't you?"

"So much, and not just because of the baby, Annie. I love Jeremy and Ashlyn so much; this baby is just going to make our little family that much better."

"Of course, it will."

"And I'm so lucky to have a job that I love, one that will work around my pregnancy." She subconsciously rubbed her stomach as she spoke. "Living in Angel's Bay, I've found a community of friends and support. It's quite amazing, really. You should come up and visit. It's really not that far."

"I will definitely have to do that. You've really blossomed since you moved there and met Jeremy. How does he like working for the police department?"

"It's pretty tame compared to his military adventures, but he's happy with the slower pace of life." She paused. "I like your hair, Annie. It's blonder than it used to be."

"You and Kate always told me blondes have more fun, but I've also been spending more time in the sun."

"I think Kate is the one who has more fun," Mia said with a grin. "I'm glad you've had some time to relax in the sun. I must admit you seem more energized than I thought you would be. You've been a little down the past few months."

"I've been restless," she admitted. "Even before my last company closed, I knew things were going bad; I should have made a move earlier. But almost getting eaten by a shark on Friday kind of changed my perspective. It made me realize I'm not ready to give up, and I don't want to waste my life."

"I guess I should be thanking the shark then."

She grinned. "It's weird. That experience broke my creative block. I haven't been able to draw the last couple of weeks, but last night I spent hours with my sketch pad."

Mia picked up one of the many sketches of Griffin. "So, this guy…is he purely out of your imagination? Because you have quite a few drawings of him."

Mia had always been perceptive. "That's the surfer who rescued me from the shark."

"Oh, really? What's his name?"

"Griffin Hale."

"Is he as attractive as he appears here?"

"More so, I think. His face is complicated and fascinating, angles and planes, light and shadows. He's hard to pin down on paper."

"Well, you've certainly thought about his face. Is he single?"

"I actually have no idea," she said, realizing that it hadn't actually occurred to her that he might have a wife or a girlfriend, although there definitely had not been a ring on his finger. "But it doesn't matter if he's single or not," she added. "He is not interested in me at all."

"Why would you say that?"

"Because it's true. I went to thank him for saving my life, and he acted like I was bringing him the plague."

"Really? That's not usually the reaction you get from men. Maybe he was just shy about accepting thanks."

"He didn't seem shy, just very unapproachable, and very eager to get rid of me."

Mia tilted her head to the right, giving her a thoughtful look. "You like him."

"I wouldn't go that far."

"Then how far would you go?"

"He…intrigues me."

"And apparently inspires your work. You should find out if he's single."

"I have enough problems in my life without adding a man into the mix."

"The right man wouldn't be a problem."

"Then I have definitely not met the right man, because so far they've all been problems." She got up from her seat. "Let's go to the beach and find your awesome family."

"Okay. Then we'll have lunch, and you can tell us more about this rescuer of yours."

"I've told you everything I know…so far anyway."

"Then you are planning to see him again?" Mia asked with a gleam in her eyes.

"He owns a bar. It's possible I might stop in sometime."

Mia laughed. "Not only possible, incredibly probable. I know you, Annie. When you get curious about something or someone, you don't stop until all your questions are answered. Just be a little cautious. I can't imagine why anyone would be rude to you without knowing you, so even if this guy is hotter than hot, make sure you know he's a good guy."

"He did save my life, so he has to be a good guy, doesn't he?"

"I would think so, but hearing the doubt in your question, I'm not sure *you* think so. Is there something you haven't told me?"

She definitely had not brought up the mysterious Megan, but she was going to keep that to herself for now. "I don't know what I think about him. But you're right, I have some questions, and I'm going to get the answers."

"I'm sure you will."

—————

After a two-hour lunch filled with great food and even better conversation, Annie said goodbye to Mia, Jeremy, and Ashlyn at the pier. They were going back to her apartment to get their car, but she wanted to check out the downtown winter arts fair before returning home, so she decided to walk the half-mile from the pier to Main Street.

While San Clemente was one of many beach cities on the Southern California coast, it had more of a small-town feel, and local events seemed to bring out the community in a big way. Today's fair was no exception.

Most of the booths were crowded, and items on sale were quite impressive, with everything from jewelry to photographs, paintings, silk scarves, knitted sweaters and blankets, flower arrangements and homemade quilts. Being an artist herself, she felt a strong connection to the vendors who were not just putting their products on display but also their hearts and souls.

She wished she had a little more cash in her bank account, so she could invest in some of the art, but until she got another job, she needed to watch her budget carefully.

As she reached the end of the street, she paused to dodge

a group of moms with baby strollers and thought about the life her sister would soon be moving into: babies, burping cloths, diaper bags, and car seats. But Mia would handle it all well. She was great with kids and she'd be even better with her own.

Even though Mia was already a stepmother, this baby would be the first new biological Callaway of the next generation. It was weird to think of her younger sibling having a child, but no doubt there would be more to follow soon, with Dylan and Ian getting married.

Just more fun, more family, she thought, trying to get rid of the wistful feeling running through her. It wasn't like she wanted to have a baby right now. That wasn't the case at all. But she wouldn't mind having someone to share her life with.

Shaking her head, she put that thought away. She'd survived a shark attack, and she had a lot to be grateful for. Today was a beautiful day and she was going to enjoy it.

While she was waiting for the crowd to move, her gaze drifted down a side street, and she suddenly stiffened.

A woman sat on a low brick wall in front of a deli, wearing faded jeans and a long-sleeve top, her brown hair pulled back in a ponytail, thick glasses on her face. She looked exactly like the woman from the bar the night before, the one called Megan, the one Griffin had hurried upstairs.

On impulse, she headed down the street. As she drew closer, she could see Megan's shoulders shaking and she pulled off her glasses to wipe tears from her eyes. Clearly, she was in distress, and she was also alone—no Griffin or other guard dog in sight. Never one to ignore someone in distress, she said, "Excuse me."

The woman jerked at the sound of her voice. As she lifted her head, she shoved on her glasses, but they did little to cover the fear in her eyes.

"Are you all right?" she asked softly, not wanting to spook her. "It looks like you've been crying."

"I'm—I'm fine."

"You don't look fine. Can I get you some water or

something?"

The woman shook her head. "No, just leave me alone."

Despite the woman's words, she took another step forward and then sat down on the brick wall next to her. "You remind me of my sister Kate. When I'd catch her crying, she'd always tell me nothing was wrong, and she just had something in her eye. She hated to look weak. I could understand it, because we grew up in a big family where strength is a prized trait. But I told her sometimes tears are good for washing away the bad stuff. And she didn't need to hide them."

"What did she say?" the woman mumbled.

"She usually told me to go away," she said honestly. "But I'm not very good at doing that, not when someone is obviously upset."

The woman turned to her with dark eyes filled with so much pain that it almost hurt Annie to look at her.

"I can't cry the bad stuff away," she said. "If I could, it would be gone by now."

"I'm sorry." She paused, licking her lips uncertainly. She didn't want to spook Megan, but she wanted to be honest. "I saw you last night at the Depot. You went upstairs with Griffin."

"What?" The woman's momentary trust vanished as she stiffened and look around. "You saw me? You know Griffin?"

"I wouldn't say I know him exactly. He saved my life on Friday, but aside from that we've only had a short conversation."

"He saved your life?" she asked in confusion.

"Yes. From a couple of sharks. I was in the ocean. He was surfing. He saw the sharks circling me, and he rescued me before I was attacked."

"That's crazy."

"It still feels unbelievable to me, too, but it happened, and I'm really grateful to him. He put himself in danger for a stranger. Not many people do that."

The woman stared back at her. "No, not many people do."

"Anyway, I'm Annie Callaway. I just moved here a few weeks ago, so I don't know too many people. Sometimes I get a little bored with my own company, and then I go out in public and talk too much." She gave her a self-deprecating smile. "You're apparently today's recipient."

"I'm—I'm Megan," she said, stumbling a bit, as if she wasn't sure she should volunteer even that much information.

"It's nice to meet you, Megan. What do you think of the fair?"

"It's—all right. People are—happy."

Megan's comment seemed a little odd, as if it surprised her that people could be happy.

"Everyone is enjoying the great weather. It's hard to believe it's almost Christmas, and it still feels like summer."

"I know. I miss snow."

"You're not from around here?"

"No."

She waited for the woman to expand on her comment, but she didn't seem interested in sharing any more information.

"I can't do this," Megan said suddenly.

"Do what?" she asked.

"Be someone else. I don't know how to do that. I barely know how to be myself."

"Why do you have to be someone else?"

"Because I have to. But I'm so unhappy, and I don't know what to do about it."

She could hear the desperation in Megan's voice and while she had no idea what was going on, she wanted to try to help. "I don't know what you're facing, Megan, but the best advice anyone ever gave me when I was feeling down is to go out and do something. Take action. Make a decision, even if it's a really small one. It gives you back your power, and the belief that you can change things, that you can control your life."

Megan stared back at her. "Who told you that?"

"My mom. She's pretty wise. Of course, it's easier to give advice than to take it."

"I have to go," Megan said abruptly.

"Wait. Look, if you need a friend, someone to talk to, you can call me. Let me give you my number." She dug into her bag and pulled out a business card she used for freelance work. "We don't have to talk about anything personal. As you can tell, I'm pretty good at keeping up my end of the conversation without much help."

Megan reluctantly took the card. "Okay, but I don't know how long I'll be in town."

"I get that. These days, my plans tend to be minute by minute."

"Megan!" The sharp male voice brought them both to their feet. "Why the hell did you run off like that?" Griffin asked. Then his gaze moved from Megan to her, and his blue eyes glittered in the sunlight. "You! What are you doing here?"

She swallowed hard, caught off guard by the anger in his gaze. "I was walking through the fair and I saw Megan."

"And you decided to introduce yourself."

"As a matter of fact, I did," she said evenly, not intimidated by his gruff words. She had three older brothers. She could hold her own.

"Megan, let's go," he said.

She instinctively put a hand on Megan's arm, drawing the woman's gaze to hers. "If you don't want to go with him, you don't have to."

"What are you saying?" Griffin asked. "You have no idea what you're getting into the middle of, Annie."

"I know you're pissed off, and Megan is upset. I'm not going to let you hurt her."

"I'm not trying to hurt her; I'm trying to protect her."

"What do you mean?"

"I can't explain, but that's the truth. Ask her," he said, tipping his head to Megan.

"He's right, Annie," Megan said. "Thanks for your help, but I need to go with Griffin." She slipped out from under Annie's grip.

"I'm parked at the corner. Meet me at the car," he said, pointing to the dark-gray SUV.

Megan hesitated. "Thanks, Annie. You're a nice person."

"I think you are, too."

As Megan left, Griffin shot her a dark look. "You need to mind your own business."

"Well, that's not going to happen any time soon," she snapped. "I don't know what's going on, but if you hurt Megan, I will hunt you down."

"You don't even know her," he said in amazement. "Now you're her defender?"

"I know she's in trouble. I just don't know if you're the trouble."

"I'm not. I'm trying to help her. She told you that."

"Well, you don't seem to be doing a very good job. She was crying her eyes out a second ago."

"That's not because of me."

She gave him a speculative look. "Who is Megan to you, Griffin? Why did that man bring her to your bar? Why are you watching out for her? What's going on?"

He ran a hand through his hair. "That's a lot of questions."

"I'm just getting started."

"I agreed to look out for Megan and to give her a place to stay for a while."

"That sounds like a simple answer for a complicated situation."

"What do you think is going on?" he challenged.

"I have no idea, but I'd really like to know. Megan seems sweet. I'm not so sure about you," she said with a frown.

"Hey, I saved your life, remember? I'm the good guy here."

"You were good to me on Friday. Since then you've been an ass."

His jaw dropped. "Maybe I should have let you fend for yourself with the sharks. You probably would have taken a bite out of one of them."

As he planted his hands on his hips and glared at her, she could feel the air sizzling between them. There was a lot of anger and irritation…and something else. She hadn't felt this riled up by a man in a long time. She told herself it was because she really didn't like him. But she'd never been a good liar.

"I'm a little braver on land," she said. "And I am glad you didn't leave me to the sharks. You did save me, and maybe I want to pay it forward."

"With Megan? She doesn't need you to save her."

"Because you're going to do that? Who are you going to save her from, Griffin?"

"It's really not your business."

"It wasn't your business to save me, but that's what heroes do."

"So, now you're a hero?" he asked.

"I did make her stop crying. Look, I have no idea what's going on, but I do know this. That woman is in desperate need of a friend, so you better get rid of that scowl of yours. It might be sexy, but it's not comforting. And if you're supposed to be taking care of her and making her feel safe, you're going to need to smile once in a while."

His scowl deepened. "I'm leaving now."

"I'll see you around, Griffin."

He paused. "I have the right to refuse service to anyone who steps into my bar. You might want to remember that."

"But if you did that, you wouldn't be the good guy you just said you were," she retorted.

His jaw tightened, and it looked like he wanted to say something, but instead he just turned and walked away.

She blew out a breath, feeling worked up by their conversation, and even more determined to find out what was going on with Griffin and Megan.

Five

Griffin punched the start button on his car with a little more force than necessary, and it still did nothing to ease his desire to put his fist through a wall. First Megan had taken off on him when he wasn't looking. Then Annie Callaway had lit into him, like he was some kind of a bad guy. If he had been a bad guy, she'd been stupid as hell to say it to his face.

What the hell was wrong with her—sticking her nose in someone else's business? She had no idea what she could be getting herself tangled up in.

He pulled out of his parking spot and sped around the corner, a mix of emotions running through him. He was pissed off and annoyed at Annie's interference, but he had to admit that he also admired her desire to fight for someone she didn't even know.

He needed her to stay out of this, but he didn't think that was going to happen. If she came to the bar, he could kick her out, but would he? He slammed to a stop as the light turned red in front of him.

Megan put a hand on the dashboard to brace herself.

"Sorry," he muttered, glancing over at her. "Why did you

run off? I thought bringing you to the fair would be fun, give you a chance to get some air, but as soon as I turn my back, you're gone."

"I know. I just felt overwhelmed and I had to be by myself."

"If you had to be by yourself, why were you talking to Annie?"

"I was crying. She came over to check on me."

At least Megan's story matched Annie's explanation. "Why were you crying?"

"Because I'm...I'm a mess," she said helplessly. "I feel like a fish out of water. I don't belong here. I don't belong anywhere. I don't know you. I don't know this city. Everything feels wrong."

"You've only been here a day. You have to give it a little time. And it's not forever."

"But that's the thing—I don't know if that's true, if I'll ever be safe, if I'll ever have a life."

"I think you will," he said quietly, hoping that he was speaking the truth.

"But you don't know."

"No, I don't," he said honestly.

He hit the gas as the light turned green, careful not to speed. He didn't think Megan's jangled nerves could take any more stress. "Paul brought you to me because he knew you were coming to the end of your rope, and I understand that. I run a bar where people come and go, and no one questions who they are or how long they'll be there. You can fit in if you want to." He shot her a quick look. She was still pale, but there was a new light in her eyes that he hadn't seen before. "You do have some control over how you feel, Megan."

"Annie said the best way to get control back is to do something, make a change, take action, even if it's just something small."

He frowned. Even though he didn't disagree with Annie's suggestions, he didn't like that she'd felt comfortable enough to give Megan advice. "Annie doesn't know your situation."

"No, but she wasn't wrong. I can't keep living like this. I can't just wallow in despair. I might as well be dead."

"What do you think would help you, Megan?"

"I don't know. Maybe I could help out in the kitchen, wash dishes or something."

"I think that's a great idea, and I'll pay you for your time."

"But is it safe to be seen—even in the kitchen?"

"Paul said you're a long way from home, and only a few people know you're here. I don't even know your real name or where you're from."

"He didn't tell you?"

"No. Paul only tells me what I need to know to keep you safe, and in this case your safety isn't the issue—your sanity is."

Megan let out a sigh. "I do feel a little crazy. Actually, the most normal I've felt in weeks was when I started talking to Annie. She told me I could call her if I need a friend."

"You don't need to call her. You can talk to me," he said, wanting to discourage that idea.

For the first time, a hint of a smile appeared in her eyes. "You?"

"We're talking now, aren't we?"

"I guess, but you're not very approachable."

"I'll work on that."

"I'm sorry I ran out on you."

"I understand. And while I don't believe you're in any danger, I'd still like to keep an eye on you. Can you give me a heads-up if you need to get some air?"

She nodded. "I can do that."

"Thanks."

She gave him a curious look. "Did you really save Annie from some sharks?"

He sighed. "Yeah, and apparently no good deed goes unpunished."

Megan's laugh surprised the hell out of him. He gave her a quick glance. "What?"

"You like her."

"No. What I feel for her is about as far from *like* as you can get."

Megan didn't contradict him, but the voice in his head told him he was a fool for thinking anyone would believe that, including himself.

⟶⟫⟪⟵

Annie spent the rest of Sunday and most of Monday telling herself to stay away from the Depot, leave Griffin and Megan alone, concentrate on herself, her teaching gig, and the new ideas that were nudging at her imagination but not quite fully springing to life. But when Justin asked her to go to the Depot with him after class, because he had something important he wanted to talk to her about, she surprised even herself with a very quick yes.

It was probably completely inappropriate. She shouldn't be having a drink with one of her students. She shouldn't be going to a bar, whose owner had clearly told her she was not welcome.

On the other hand, being at the Depot had helped her get through her creative block, and since the people there were inspiring her new work, she wouldn't mind getting another look at everyone.

And then there was Megan. It couldn't hurt to check up on her, too.

She arrived at the Depot at half-past five. The bar was hopping, with happy hour in full swing. There was no sign of Griffin, and the butterflies in her stomach danced around in both flutters of relief and disappointment. She told herself it was good he wasn't there; she didn't need another altercation like the one they'd had yesterday.

"Let's grab this table," Justin said, motioning her toward a small table for two. "I don't start my shift until six, so I have a few minutes."

"I'm very curious as to what you want to speak to me

about that we couldn't discuss in the classroom."

"We'll get into that. But first, I'll get you a drink. What would you like?"

"I'll take a Chardonnay."

"You got it."

She settled into her seat while Justin went around the bar. He took a moment to greet an older, busty blonde, wearing a clingy blue top and black jeans. She appeared to be in her early forties, and had a brassy, loud laugh. *Another character for her sketch pad,* she couldn't help thinking. That woman probably had a story. She wondered what it was.

In fact, everyone, with the exception of Justin, seemed to have a story, something behind their smiles and the shadows in their eyes. Only Justin appeared happy, carefree, chill... *But was he really? Or was normalcy his disguise?*

She smiled at her wayward thoughts. At one time, she'd thought of becoming a writer, but for her, the story usually came out in art, not in words, and now she was starting to think of Justin as a surfer assassin or a surfer detective or a surfer villain...

He could really be anything except what he probably was, a twenty-something guy with ambitions to surf and draw and live a nice life.

Justin came back with her glass of wine and took the seat across from her. "Here you go."

"Thanks. So, what is this all about? You want some help on your final project? Because I can give you a few tips, but that's really all."

"I appreciate that, and I might take you up on those tips. But I need a favor, and it doesn't have to do with class."

She was actually relieved to hear that. "What does it have to do with?" she asked, sipping her wine.

"The Depot is hosting a fundraiser holiday party here in two weeks. It's for Griffin's favorite charity, Hamilton House."

"I've never heard of that."

"It's a recreation center for kids and teens—mostly foster

kids or children who are living in shelters. They depend on donations, and every year Griffin hosts a party here to gather toys and checks."

"That sounds very generous."

"Griffin is a generous guy. But for this event to be really successful, it needs more publicity, like flyers and T-shirts. I thought I could come up with a design, since I started taking your class, but everything I've come up with is really bad. I told Griffin I would take care of the design and the materials, but I'm running out of time, and I've got nothing. I don't want to let Griffin down. But now it's probably too late to get another artist to work on what we need done by like Thursday."

"Thursday, huh? That's fast."

"I know and there's also no budget for an artist."

"I have a feeling I know where you're going with this."

He gave her a charming smile. "I thought you might want to help out since Griffin saved your life."

She smiled back at him, thinking he did have an innocent kind of guile, something she could play up in her superhero idea. "Pulling out all the stops, are you?"

"Kind of desperate here. What do you say? Do you have a little spare time to work up a design?"

"I could probably help you, but I'm not sure your boss would like it. I'm not Griffin's favorite person."

"You're not?" Justin asked in surprise. "Why not?"

She thought about that. "I'm not sure, but I think I make him uncomfortable."

"Oh, right, because he saved your life and you keep wanting to thank him," Justin said, with a nod. "Griffin hates when people compliment him or show him gratitude. Don't take it personally."

She thought it was more than that, especially after their encounter yesterday, but she wasn't going to tell Justin that.

"And I know Griffin will appreciate your help on this. It is for the kids, after all," Justin added.

She made an impulsive decision she'd probably regret.

"Okay. I'll do it. But you're going to have to tell me what Griffin is looking for."

"He doesn't know. He said he wants the design to reflect the bar and the spirit of the holidays and the kids. Does that help?"

"Not really."

"I'm sure whatever you do will be great. The event is a week from next Sunday. It's at three in the afternoon. There will be a toy drive, music, presents, food, Santa, that kind of thing."

"I'll do some thinking. I might have more questions."

"Feel free to ask away. And as a thank-you, I'm going to buy you dinner."

"You don't have to buy me dinner, Justin."

"It's the least I can do. The special tonight is Vinnie's chicken tortilla soup. It's amazing. But if you want something else, that's fine, too."

"I'll take the soup."

"I'll put your order in."

As Justin left, Megan came into the bar from the back hall. She hesitated for a moment, looking a bit panicked by the number of people in the bar. Her gaze darted around the room, but when she saw Annie, the tension in her face eased, and she made her way over to the table.

"You're back," Megan said. "I wasn't sure you would be."

"I wasn't sure I would be, either, but I'm friends with Justin, the bartender, and he wanted to talk to me about something."

"I haven't met him yet."

"He's the cute blond. I'm sure you'll like him." She paused. "You look better today."

Dressed in baggy jeans and a loose-fitting top, Megan still had a waifish look, but she had put on some lip gloss, and her eyes seemed brighter, energized, making her appear more youthful than she had the day before.

"I feel better," Megan said. "I took your advice. You said the best way to change your mood is to take some sort of action. I decided that I might as well be productive while I'm here. Griffin told me he could use help in the kitchen and in the bar, so I'm going to do what I can—for a few days anyway."

She couldn't help wondering what was coming up in a few days, but Megan was talking more than she had the day before, and she didn't want to shut her down with too many questions.

"I'm not sure I'll be good at it," Megan added. "I've never worked in a bar."

"You'll be fine. If you wait tables, I can tell you that a bigger smile will get you bigger tips, but don't take crap from anyone, especially guys with too many drinks in them."

"You've had experience?"

"I waited tables in college and a little bit after that. Tips can be good."

"I don't even know if I can smile anymore, but I'll give it a shot."

"You can do it. Just think about something or someone that makes you happy."

Her words had the opposite effect than she'd intended, and she frowned as she saw dark shadows pass through Megan's eyes. "I wish I could help," she said impulsively. "Don't you have any family you can ask for support?"

"No," Megan said shortly, following up with a firm shake of her head.

"Well, you have my number if you ever want to talk."

"I better get to work." As Megan got up, she almost ran into Justin, who had a tray in his hands with one large bowl of soup. "Sorry," she said. "I didn't see you."

"No worries. I'm a good dancer," Justin said with a smile. "Didn't even spill a drop." He set the soup down on the table, then added, "I don't think we've met. I'm Justin."

"Megan," she said. "Griffin asked me to help out tonight."

"Great. We can always use more help."

"I'll see you later, Annie," Megan said, as she moved

toward the kitchen.

As Megan left, Justin turned to her. "Anything else I can get you right now? I need to get ready for my shift."

"I'm good, and I will pay for this myself. I'm your teacher, so you can't say no."

"Well, if you put it like that…"

"I do. I'll start thinking about some designs tonight."

When Justin went back to work, she picked up her spoon and dug into the thick soup. It was filled with chicken, tortilla strips, vegetables and cheese, and it was as good if not better than the burger she'd had two nights ago. No wonder the Depot was always crowded. They didn't just have drinks; they had really exceptional food.

While she ate, she pulled out her notepad and started doodling. Instead of focusing on her cast of superhero characters, she thought about Christmas and the train station and the kids Griffin wanted to provide toys for.

She didn't really know what he wanted; he probably didn't know, either.

She could do the usual holiday stuff, but she wanted something better than that, more personal, more intriguing. Playing around a little more, she drew elements of the train station, wondering if she could tie in a theme of trains, change, new adventure.

"What are you doing?" Griffin's question drew her head up. He was staring down at her notepad. "What are you drawing?"

"Justin asked me to help him come up with a design for your holiday event—for flyers and T-shirts." She licked her lips. "I'm an artist."

"Yeah, I can see that," he said in his usual gruff tone. "But Justin was supposed to do it."

"And he feels guilty that he might not be ready to actually do what he told you he could do. He has some talent, but he's a beginner."

"I can't pay you, Annie."

"I wasn't asking you to. It sounds like it's for a good

cause." She was happy he hadn't tried to throw her out of the bar, which based on yesterday's conversation might have been a distinct possibility. "I'd like to help out. But I will need more information about it, especially the charity aspect. I'm not familiar with Hamilton House. Could you tell me something about it?"

He stared back at her, indecision in his eyes. "I told Justin I'd take him to Hamilton House tomorrow."

"Can I come along? It would be helpful to see the place, meet the kids."

"I suppose," he said with a sigh.

"What a fantastic invitation," she said dryly. "For someone who's doing you a favor."

"Someone who I didn't ask."

"Justin asked me. Same thing."

"It's not at all the same thing. I was going to go at three thirty tomorrow. The place fills up after school, and I thought it would be good for Justin to see it when it's busy, when the kids are there."

"I can do it then."

"You don't have a job?"

"I teach on Mondays and Wednesdays and I'm currently interviewing for some other jobs, so I have a little time."

"All right."

Since their conversation appeared to be over, she expected him to leave. Instead, he took the chair across from her and after a momentary hesitation, he said, "Why are you getting so tangled up in my life, Annie?"

Her jaw dropped at the blunt question. Looking into Griffin's amazing blue eyes made her even more uncomfortable.

Why was she getting so tangled up in his life?

She probably should at least know the answer, even if she didn't want to say it.

"I wouldn't say I'm entangled. I'm in between jobs and I'm new to the area, so I have more free time than I normally do. Your bar is nice. Don't you want people to come here?"

"You're not helping out with the event because you think you owe me for saving your life, are you?"

"No. I'm grateful for that, but I don't think I owe you anymore."

"Why not? I saved you from sharks."

"And you've made it clear you're not interested in hearing thanks, so I'm done saying it."

"Good." He paused. "Then let me ask you another question."

"And here I thought I was the nosy one."

He ignored that pointed comment. "Do you think I'm holding Megan against her will, that I'm hurting her in some way?"

"It crossed my mind on Saturday night," she admitted. "But Megan told me yesterday that you're helping her, and since she's moving freely around the bar tonight, I guess I believe her. I still don't understand what's going on."

"Not everything is your business."

"I know that."

He shook his head, an odd look in his eyes now. "You're..."

"A caring, kind person," she offered when he couldn't seem to come up with a word.

A gleam entered his eyes, and it sent a different kind of shiver down her spine.

"We'll go with that for now," he said. "I guess I'll see you tomorrow."

"I guess you will," she said, as he got to his feet.

As Griffin walked away, she couldn't take her eyes off him. She'd thought he was attractive the first time she'd seen him. Then his bad attitude had cast a darker glow around him. Tonight, she'd almost gotten a smile, and her mind had changed again. Who knew what she would think of him tomorrow...or what he would think of her...

Six

Tuesday afternoon, Griffin was regretting his impulsive invitation to take Annie to Hamilton House. *Wasn't he just inviting more trouble?*

Not that Annie seemed to need an invitation to pop up in his life. At least this way, he wouldn't be surprised by her sudden appearance; he wouldn't feel blindsided, like he had every other previous time that he'd run into her. Today, he would control the situation. At least, that was the plan...

But he had a feeling when Annie was involved, things just happened.

And the last thing he needed was unexpected things happening.

Megan came up to the bar with an order for two draft beers. While she'd spent most of yesterday in the kitchen, today she'd decided to help out waiting tables, and he was amazed at how much her entire attitude had changed since she'd found a purpose in her life. He didn't know if it was their conversation that had helped her turn the corner, or if it was what Annie had said to her, but at this point he was happy to see her feeling and acting as normal as she could possibly be under the circumstances.

"I have to take off for a few hours," he told her. "It should be pretty slow until about five. Danielle will be manning the bar while I'm gone. And Vinnie is in the kitchen if you need anything."

"It's been pretty quiet since the lunch crowd left," she said, as he filled two mugs with beer. "I'm sure it will be fine."

"You're doing a good job."

"Thanks."

As the door opened, both he and Megan turned their heads.

Annie breezed into the bar, and he sucked in a quick breath. He'd thought he'd been ready to see her again, but as it turned out—he wasn't. Every time he saw her, he noticed something new. The first time at the beach, it had been her big, green, terrified eyes that had drawn him in. When she'd come to the bar, he'd realized her dark-blonde hair was actually streaked with red, and that those fiery flames matched her personality, a personality that was becoming more and more vibrant every time he saw her.

And, of course, he'd be a liar not to admit that he'd noticed her bikini curves that first day on the beach, but today dressed in slim-fitting black jeans and a sheer silky top that hinted at some lacy camisole beneath it, she looked even sexier, her pale, slightly freckled skin glowing, her eyes bright, her full lips parted in a tentative smile.

Dammit! What the hell was he thinking inviting her to go with him to Hamilton House? He wanted to spend less time with her—not more. He wanted to forget about her, not get closer to her. He needed to make this just about business. She was going to do a design for him. He was providing a research opportunity. It wasn't a date—definitely *not* a date.

Not that he really knew what a date felt like anymore. It had been a while since he'd asked anyone out. Maybe too long. Perhaps that's why he was having such a strong physical reaction to a woman who had already proved herself to be way too curious about his life and his relationships. He valued privacy and personal space, and Annie seemed to have no respect for either.

But she was here, and it was too late to back out on today's outing, no matter how much he wanted to.

"Hi, Megan," Annie said. "Griffin."

He gave her a nod, then watched as Annie gave Megan a hug.

Megan seemed a bit surprised by Annie's affection, which was understandable since Megan had been living in an alternate reality the past few months. But she also seemed very happy to see Annie.

"How's your day going?" Annie asked Megan.

"Pretty good. I haven't messed up any orders."

"That's fast. My waitressing days were filled with a lot of messed-up orders."

"I thought you said you were an artist," he interrupted, not sure why he was challenging her, but there was something about Annie that made him nervous, so he kept going on offense, thinking that was the best defense.

"I am an artist, but in college, I was also a waitress. I've actually had a lot of different jobs. But you probably don't want to hear about all that." She cleared her throat. "Are you ready to go?"

"Yes," he said, coming around the bar. "Let's do this."

"See you later, Megan," Annie said.

"If you want to eat dinner together, I'll be here," Megan said, an uncertain note in her voice. "But only if you want to. I know you were here last night. You probably have other stuff to do."

Hearing Megan's shy invitation, he felt conflicted over what he wanted Annie to say. If she said yes, she'd be helping him out with Megan, but she'd also be spending more time in the bar.

"I'd love to eat with you," Annie said. "It sounds great."

"Okay, great. I'll see you later."

Annie turned to him. "Are you driving?"

"Yeah, my car is out back." He led her out of the bar, down the hallway, and through the back door to employee's lot.

As he always did, he made a quick scan of the area before flipping the locks on his SUV.

As Annie buckled her seat belt, he started the car, checked the rearview and side view mirrors and then backed out.

"You seem more cautious than I would have thought," Annie commented, as he pulled into the street and drove past the front of the bar.

"What?" he asked, his gaze still skimming along the cars parked near the entrance to the bar. None of them appeared to be occupied; that was good.

"Are you looking for someone or something?" she asked.

"No," he said shortly, irritated that she'd caught him and more annoyed that he was losing his once excellent covert skills.

"There it is," she said with a sigh. "The scowl. It's back. Is it just me who brings it on, or is it everyone?"

"It's you."

"Most people like me."

"You'll have to introduce me to some of those people some time."

"You already know two of them—Justin and Megan."

"Justin wants a good grade, and Megan doesn't have any friends here," he couldn't help pointing out.

She made a face at him. "I can scowl, too, you know."

He almost smiled, but somehow he held it back. "I'd look in the mirror before you try that again."

She sat back in her seat and folded her arms across her chest. "Let's talk about Hamilton House."

"Great idea. What do you want to know?"

"Justin told me that they offer help to underprivileged children, many of whom are in foster care or living in shelters."

"Yes, and there's also a focus on helping kids whose

parents are incarcerated. There's a huge generation of children growing up with parents who are in jail."

"That's sad. How did you get involved?"

"I heard about what they were doing, and I decided to volunteer."

"Very generous."

"I don't do that much."

"If you did, you wouldn't admit it. I don't know you very well, but I do know that you do not like to brag about anything heroic."

"Because I'm not a hero," he said flatly.

"All evidence to the contrary."

"Fine. I was a hero when I saved you from the sharks, but that's it. That's where it ends."

"What about Megan? You're helping her in some way."

"That's called being a friend."

"Megan isn't your friend."

"She's not yours, either, but you seem to want to help her," he returned.

"That's true," she admitted. "I do want to help Megan. She seems like a lost soul. I know you're not going to tell me her story, but I wish I knew what was going on with her."

"It's not my story to tell."

"You're right," she said, surprising him with her answer.

He'd thought she'd pester him all the way to Hamilton House with questions about Megan.

"So, what's *your* story?" she continued.

He inwardly groaned. He should have anticipated that would be her next question. As he stopped at a light, he glanced over at her and saw the smile in her eyes. She knew he didn't want to talk about his personal life, but she didn't care. And there was a part of him that kind of liked her gutsy curiosity.

"My story is too long for this short trip," he said.

"Give me the highlights. We'll start with something easy. Are you from San Clemente?"

"No."

"Want to give me a section of the country?"

"Midwest."

"Not a lot of ocean waves to ride in the Midwest."

"Nope."

"What about family? Brothers, sisters, parents?"

He thought about her questions and decided to give her enough to keep her happy. "Mom died young. Dad is a mechanic. No siblings."

"Does your father still live in the Midwest?"

"No, he doesn't."

"How often do you see him?"

"Rarely."

"What about extended family?"

"I have one grandfather still alive. He's doing all right." As he thought about his grandfather, he felt a little sad. If there was one person in his life who he missed, it was that old man.

"Do you see him?"

"No. What about you? What's your story?"

"Well, it has a lot more people in it than yours. You really don't give much away, Griffin."

"How many people are in your family?"

"I have two parents and five siblings in my immediate family."

"That is a lot. Where are you in the order?" he asked curiously. "Wait, let me guess."

"You're not going to be able to guess."

He thought for a moment. "Let's see. You're bossy, so you could be on the older end. On the other hand, you tend to push yourself into things that don't involve you, which might suggest you're on the younger end. I'm going to go with middle—three or four."

She frowned. "I am not that bossy or that pushy."

"Am I right?"

"I'm fourth," she admitted, a grumpy note in her voice.

"Bingo."

"I have three older brothers and two younger sisters—

they're twins."

"I knew it. You boss your sisters around, but you're also looking for a little attention, so you can stand out in the crowd."

"I only boss them around when they need it," she said defensively. "But these days, there is very little bossing. They're both settled in their lives. Kate lives in DC. She's an FBI agent and her boyfriend Devin is a former agent turned private investigator. Mia runs an art gallery in Angel's Bay and is married to Jeremy, an ex-soldier turned cop. He has a daughter from another relationship, but Mia just told me yesterday that she's pregnant, so it looks like their family is expanding." She took a breath. "Kate and Mia are really wonderful people. I miss them."

He could hear the genuine affection in her voice. "What about your brothers?"

"Dylan is the oldest; he's a firefighter. So is Hunter, who is third in our line-up. Firefighting is the family business, by the way. My grandfather, my father, my uncle, and a bunch of cousins are all firefighters."

"What about your other brother?"

"Ian is a scientist. He's brilliant and his IQ is off the charts. I have no idea what he actually does, but I know he helps people. My family is amazing, not just my siblings and parents but my cousins as well."

"But?" he asked, hearing an odd note in her voice.

"But there are a lot of overachievers in the family. Callaways are born to serve and protect. We're raised with the idea that we need to give back. We need to do something that helps people. Most have followed in that tradition, but there are a few of us who haven't."

"Like yourself."

"Yes. Being an artist is who I am, but it's not really the Callaway way."

"Does your family give you a hard time?"

"That's the thing—they don't. And if I told them I sometimes feel out of step with everyone else, they'd say I was crazy."

"You might be crazy," he said lightly.

She smiled. "I might be. Sorry I rambled on. I tend to talk too much, especially when I'm nervous."

"Are you nervous?" The question came out before he could stop it.

"A little. You're not the easiest person to be around, Griffin. I don't know what I did to piss you off."

He let out a sigh. "You didn't really do anything."

"Then why all the annoyance?"

"I'm a private person, and you don't have much respect for boundaries."

"That might be true," she conceded. "But I'm interested in people, in things. I'm an observer. It feeds my art."

And her words only reminded him that keeping her at a distance was a good idea. It just didn't seem particularly practical considering how close they were right now. He decided to change the subject back to her family. "Where does your family live?"

"Aside from Mia, most are currently in San Francisco. Hunter is traveling the world, so I don't know where he calls home these days."

"How did you end up here?"

"I went to UCLA for college. After that I got a job in LA doing graphic design for an advertising agency for a few years. It paid well but it was not what I wanted to do with my art."

"What did you want to do?" he asked curiously.

"Work in film, animation specifically. I eventually got hired by a production company to do just that. I learned a lot and the company had some success, until the past year when we couldn't come up with an idea that would get us funding. Eventually, the group disbanded, and I found myself unemployed. Since then, I've been freelancing and looking for another permanent job. A friend of mine offered to sublet me his beach apartment in San Clemente for six months, so I decided to come a little farther south. I have a job interview on Friday that looks promising, so hopefully something will come of that. And once again, I've told you more than you want to know."

He actually preferred when she did the talking, but he was starting to feel badly about not paying her for her time. "Maybe you should be charging me for this job."

"Oh, no, I'm happy to donate my time. It sounds like a great cause, and it will be fun, too. I'm not destitute. I have savings. My parents raised me well. My dad used to say for every dollar you spend, you should put two in the bank. I can hear his voice in my head whenever I'm looking at some really expensive but super cute shoes."

"And the winner is—your dad's sage savings advice or the shoes?"

He glanced over at her, and sucked in a breath as her mouth dimpled in a deliciously sexy way. "I can't lie— sometimes, it's the shoes."

He couldn't stop the smile that crossed his lips.

Annie's eyes widened in surprise. "Wow! Your lips can go up instead of down—shocking."

He shrugged. "You finally said something amusing." He pulled into a parking spot. "And we're here."

—➤➤◄◄—

Annie was shocked to have gotten a smile out of Griffin Hale, but that moment had quickly passed, and as they walked into Hamilton House, she could feel him retreating. The man couldn't seem to decide how he felt about her, and she wasn't quite sure how she felt about him, either. For the moment, she decided to focus on getting the information she needed to create some great flyers and T-shirts for the holiday fundraiser.

Hamilton House was located in a renovated warehouse in a neighborhood that was a mix of industrial, retail, and lower income housing. It felt a bit barren on the outside, but once she entered the building, she was greeted with warm, bright colors in the reception area and the sound of music and laughter coming from what appeared to be a dance studio. A middle-aged woman at the front desk got up to welcome them. She had brown hair and brown eyes and wore a purple shirt that said *A book a day keeps the boredom away.*

"Griffin, it's good to see you," she said with a warm smile.

"You, too," he replied. "This is Annie Callaway—Deb Johnson. Deb runs this place."

She shook Deb's hand. "It's nice to meet you."

"Annie is going to design the flyers and shirts for our holiday event," Griffin added. "I thought she might get some inspiration if she could see what you're doing here firsthand."

"Of course, and if I can help in any way, please ask. The kids loved this event last year, and I know they're going to feel the same way this year. It's a special day for them," Deb said. "We really appreciate everything Griffin does to not only help us bring in important donations but also make the kids feel special."

She could see Griffin shifting his feet uncomfortably at Deb's glowing words. He really hated gratitude.

As the phone on the desk began to ring, Deb moved away to answer it. "I'll let you show Miss Callaway around, Griffin. Feel free to go wherever."

"Deb seems nice," she commented as they left Deb to her call.

"She is nice and very good at running this place. It's actually more than just a job to her," he explained, as they walked across the lobby toward the dance studio. "Deb's father, Mitch Hamilton, started the place fifteen years ago after his son Ethan, Deb's younger brother, overdosed. He felt guilty that as a single father, he hadn't been able to provide a safe place for Ethan to spend his time after school."

"That's sad, but it's good that something positive came out of it. Is her father still around?"

"No, Mitch passed away two years ago, right after I got involved here. Deb has a loyal group of supporters but she was worried about money, so I thought a holiday event would help a little."

They paused outside the studio, and she smiled at the eight little girls, who couldn't have been more than eleven or twelve, doing some kind of salsa dancing. The music was fast, the smiles were big, and the laughter was infectious.

"That looks fun," she said. "I loved taking dance class when I was young, but I wasn't very good, especially at ballet. That was way too structured for me. And the ballet teacher was kind of mean."

"You were probably talking during class," he said dryly.

She rolled her eyes, unwilling to admit that was true. "Let's keep going."

For the next hour, they went through the Hamilton House. Annie saw kids playing basketball in the gym, getting help with homework in a computer lab, and painting in an art class, which was, of course, her favorite part of the building.

Griffin introduced her to quite a few people, all of whom seemed to genuinely know him and like him, which told her he spent a fair amount of time at Hamilton House beyond a once-a-year holiday event.

"What did you think?" he asked as they returned to the car.

"It's a great place for kids. Everyone seemed very happy. I think you're doing a good thing with the fundraiser."

He nodded. "It's important to keep the doors open and the lights on."

"I agree." She turned sideways in her seat to look at him. "But there's always a little mystery surrounding you."

He glanced over at her, but she couldn't read his expression, because he'd hidden his amazing blue eyes behind a pair of aviator sunglasses, which only made him more attractive, and her heart beat a little faster.

"I don't know what you're talking about. I just showed you everything there was to see."

"You did, and I saw how many people greeted you by name. Boys gave you high fives, girls gave you hugs, adults looked at you with respect and affection. There's no way you just host a party a year and drop off toys for Christmas. What else do you do there?"

"I volunteer on occasion."

"Doing..."

"I coach basketball games. I've helped some kids with reading, getting on the computer, that kind of stuff."

"How did you get involved in the first place? How did you hear about them?"

He sighed. "You have a lot of questions, Annie."

"Want to give me some answers?"

He hesitated, then said, "I didn't grow up with a lot of money. After my mom died, there was no one home when I got out of school. My dad also drank a lot. Sometimes he came home to make dinner; sometimes he didn't. I had a bad few years and I got into some trouble."

"What kind of trouble?"

"Teenage stuff, not jail-worthy, but not great, either."

"Did some place like Hamilton House save you?"

"No, there was nothing like that around where I lived. My grandparents stepped in after a time. I actually went to live with them when I was sixteen. They set me straight, but a lot of kids don't have grandparents or anyone to help them out like that."

She was beginning to see where some of his hard edges had come from. "And how did you find Hamilton House?"

"Vinnie brought me here one day. He knew Deb from his childhood, and that's how I got involved. But it's not really a big deal. I don't spend a lot of time here. Others do far more than I do for this place."

As usual, Griffin was downplaying his actions. She knew better than to try to get him to admit that volunteering was a good thing and maybe even a little heroic. He seemed to dislike it whenever she tried to give him any kind of credit.

"Did you get any inspiration?" Griffin asked, as he started the car. "For your designs?"

"I did. I loved all the colors. It was like walking through

a rainbow, but I don't want to do a rainbow, because that's not quite right. And it doesn't feel like Christmas." She paused. "I also liked the motivational quotes etched on the walls and over the doorways and running under the windows. I need to find a way to incorporate the holiday spirit, the idea of giving back, helping someone less fortunate and also have a design that entices people to participate or to put on a shirt..." She realized she was once again rambling. "Sorry. My ideas are usually pretty messy in the beginning. My vision won't come alive until I start drawing. I usually go through several drafts, though, so I'm going to need a day or two."

"I wish I could give you more time than that, but I thought Justin was working on this for the past week. I didn't realize he was just working on a way to get out of it."

"His optimism was a little misplaced, and then he didn't want to let you down."

"I get it. I'm just sorry to put you in a time crunch, but I need the designs by Thursday or the printer can't get the flyers or shirts done in time."

"I'll make it happen. I'll work on it after I have dinner with Megan."

His scowl came back at her words. "I forgot about that. You're eating at the Depot, right?"

"I think so. Although, I guess we could go somewhere else."

"Eat there. My treat. It's the least I can do for your help."

She didn't know why he wanted them to stay in, but she could only assume it had something to do with whatever trouble Megan was in. It certainly didn't have to do with any desire on Griffin's part to keep her close. While he'd unbent a little, he still had a lot of walls up, and she knew only a tiny bit more about him now than she'd known before they got in the car.

"Where do you live?" she asked curiously.

He shot her a quick look, then said, "Over the bar."

"So, Megan is staying at your place?"

"No, there are two small apartments upstairs. They were

originally offices for the train station, but I turned them into living spaces. Originally, Vinnie was going to take one, but then he decided he didn't want to sleep where he worked."

"How did you meet Vinnie?"

"Through friends. He's a great partner. He runs the kitchen; I run the bar."

"Who designed the interior? It's really charming and warm. That wasn't you, was it?"

"You don't think I can be charming and warm?"

"I think you could be—if you wanted to be. But that doesn't seem like something you want to be."

"We got off on the wrong foot."

"Did we? I think our first meeting was absolutely perfect, but that's because you saved my life. Our second meeting—not so much."

"I was having a bad day, and you walked in on the middle of it."

"And was Sunday a bad day, too? Monday, as well?" she challenged.

"Okay, let's call it a bad week. You kept popping up when I was not expecting it. Can we go from here?"

"Sure," she said, liking that he was willing to acknowledge he hadn't been the most welcoming person in the world to her. "But I can't guarantee that I won't pop up again when you're not in the mood to see me. I don't have the best timing. I don't know what it is, but if there's a chance to walk in on someone or something at the worst possible time, I seem to do it."

He gave her a curious look. "Besides me, who else have you walked in on?"

She drew in a breath and let it out. "You have your secrets; I have mine."

"Boyfriend?"

"I'm not going to tell you."

"Husband?"

"No. I've never been married. And I'm still not going to tell you. See how it feels when the shoe is on the other foot?"

"Yes." He paused. "I'd like to say I'll be more open, Annie, but that probably won't happen. So, we both know where we stand."

She actually had no idea where they stood. There had been some nice moments between them, but Griffin seemed to take one step forward and two steps back when it came to her. However, there was no more time to discuss it, because he was pulling into the parking lot.

As she stepped out of his car, her phone rang. It was the number for the production company she was going to interview with on Friday. "I have to take this," she said. "It's about my interview."

"I'll leave the back door open and meet you inside."

"Thanks." She answered her phone. "Hello?"

"Annie Callaway?"

"Yes?"

"This is Diane Bartlett. I'm calling from Dorsey Productions about your interview on Friday. I wanted to confirm the time with you—eleven thirty."

"That's what I have down."

"Excellent. Mr. Dorsey is also requesting that you come with art to go with any pitches you want to make."

"Okay. Do you know how much detail he wants?"

"He said that's up to you, but he'd like to see enough to understand the project."

"I can do that."

"Then we'll see you on Friday."

"Thanks." As she slipped her phone into her pocket, she realized just how much work she had to get done in the next three days. Not only did she have to come up with designs for Griffin's holiday fundraiser, she needed to hone in on the art for her pitch.

Well, at least she was at the Depot. She could have dinner with Megan, soak up more atmosphere, and then go home and start drawing. She didn't know what her idea for the pitch would be, but the characters from the bar were driving her artistic vision at the moment, so she was going to ride that wave and see where it went. *Hopefully not into the jaws of a shark*, she thought with amusement, wondering if the surfing metaphor had something to do with Griffin, who seemed to be constantly on her mind.

As she walked across the lot, she saw Megan come out the back door with a bag of trash.

"Vinnie is giving me all the fun tasks," she said, pausing by Annie.

Annie smiled. Despite her complaint, Megan didn't look all that unhappy about her chore. "New girl always gets the trash—at least that's what I was told every time I started a new job," she said, as she walked with Megan to the dumpster at the end of the lot.

"That's exactly what Vinnie told me," Megan returned. "How was your field trip with Griffin?"

"Informative. Hamilton House is doing great things for a lot of kids. I'm happy to be a part of the fundraiser."

"Vinnie told me a little about it," Megan said. "It sounds like fun."

"Maybe we can brainstorm some ideas over dinner."

"I don't know how creative I am these days, but I can try."

Annie's phone beeped with a new text. She stopped walking to read it, while Megan dumped the trash into the dumpster.

It was a text from her brother Dylan asking if she'd really been attacked by a shark. Apparently, Mia and Kate had decided to share that information with the rest of the family. She'd text him later when she had more time, because she knew it was not going to be a one text and done kind of response.

As she put her phone away, she heard the roar of an engine, and the squeal of tires. A dark sedan came spinning around the corner at a high rate of speed. Instead of racing down the street, it made a sharp turn, launching into the employee parking lot with a shrieking scream of the engine. Her jaw dropped as the car headed straight toward them.

She instinctively turned and shoved Megan toward the side of the building, then she dove out of the way, hitting the ground hard with her hands and her knees. The car missed them, but smashed against the side of the dumpster before spinning around, ready for another attack...

Seven

Annie looked over her shoulder, seeing a hooded figure behind the wheel. He revved the engine again, but before he could go after them, Griffin and Vinnie came running out of the back door and into the lot.

The driver pumped the gas and sped past them, spinning back out into the street before racing out of sight.

Her heart was pounding against her chest, her breath coming short and fast, fear hitting her in huge, debilitating waves. She wanted to stand up, but she wasn't sure she could get to her feet.

What the hell had just happened?

She glanced back at Megan, who was sitting on the ground, her arms wrapped around her knees, her face white as a sheet. "Are you okay?" she asked.

"They—they found me," Megan said, her teeth chattering.

"What? Who?" she asked in confusion.

Megan stared back at her, but she didn't answer. She was retreating inside herself. The light was going out of her eyes. She was rocking back and forth as if she were a child, as if she were somewhere far, far away.

"Annie," Griffin said sharply, as he and Vinnie reached them. "Are you all right?"

"I think so."

He held out his hand to her, and she was happy to have his fingers curl around hers as she stumbled to her feet. She felt a little light-headed from the adrenaline rush and her inability to take a deep breath.

Vinnie squatted in front of Megan. "How are you doing, Megan?"

"They—they found me," Megan said. "They found me. They found me."

Annie frowned as Megan's words went around in a terrified circle. "Who found you, Megan?" she asked.

Griffin's gaze narrowed at her question, and he exchanged a pointed look with Vinnie, then said, "Let's all go inside."

"Good idea," Vinnie said. "Let me help you up, Megan. Come on, you can do it." He grabbed Megan's hand and pulled her to her feet.

While Annie still wanted an answer to her question, she was more than happy to leave the parking lot.

After entering the building, Griffin led them up the stairs. She was finally going to see what was up there. He stopped at the first door and looked back at Megan. "Do you have the key?" At her blank look, he added, "Check your pocket, Megan."

At his firm command, Megan reached into her pocket and pulled out a chain with two keys. Griffin grabbed it and let them into the apartment.

"Is this your place?" she asked.

"No, it's where Megan is staying."

That might explain the simple, stark furnishings. The apartment was comfortable but impersonal.

Megan sat down on the couch, drawing her feet up underneath her. Vinnie pulled a blanket off the back of the sofa and put it around Megan's shoulders. Then he said, "I'm going to make some tea."

As Vinnie moved into the kitchen, Annie sat down on the couch next to Megan and gave her an encouraging look. "It's going to be okay," she told her.

Megan stared back at her through dull eyes. "No, it's not. You have no idea, Annie."

"No idea about what?"

"I don't think now is the best time for questions," Griffin interrupted.

"You don't?" she asked with annoyance. "It seems like the best time to me, considering I was almost run over a few minutes ago."

"I'm sorry," Megan said. "I'm really sorry." At the end of her sentence, she got up from the couch, walked into the other room and shut the door behind her.

Annie was surprised by Megan's abrupt exit. She looked up at Griffin. "Do you think one of us should go in there and talk to her?"

"Let's give her a minute," he said, sitting down next to her. "I know you have a lot of questions, Annie, but first tell me what happened."

"I was looking at a text on my phone. Megan was throwing a bag of garbage in the dumpster. The next thing I knew, a car came racing around the corner, so fast it looked like it was on two wheels. I thought it would go down the street, but it turned in to the lot and headed straight for us. I pushed Megan out of the way and dove for cover. I think the car hit the dumpster and then turned around again." She shook her head in bewilderment. "I didn't know if he was coming back at us, but then you and Vinnie were there, and he drove off."

"Did you get a look at the driver?" he asked, his gaze intent on her face.

"I saw a hood, I think. I didn't see a face. I don't know; it happened so fast. I'm not even really sure what kind of car it was."

"It was a Ford Taurus."

"Did you see the license plate?"

"There was no license plate."

"Are you sure? Doesn't there have to be a plate?"

"There's supposed to be, but there wasn't one."

"We need to call the police."

"I'll call who needs to be called," Vinnie said. "The kettle is on. There's tea in the cupboard. I'll make the calls downstairs after I check the security camera."

"You have a camera on the lot?" she asked.

"We do," Griffin said with a nod. "But without a license plate, I'm not sure we'll have much more to go on than we have right now."

"I'll let you know," Vinnie said. "Call if you need me."

As Vinnie left the room, her gaze narrowed. She was still feeling light-headed, but she wasn't so fuzzy that she wasn't aware something was off in the way Griffin and Vinnie were reacting to the situation. "What did Vinnie mean when he said he would call who needs to be called? Isn't that the police?"

"Sure," Griffin said. "Don't worry about that. Are you feeling all right? You didn't hurt yourself when you jumped out of the way?"

"My knees sting a little, but I'm fine. I'm certainly doing better than Megan." Her gaze moved to the bedroom door and then came back to Griffin. "She said they found her. Who was she talking about? Don't tell me you don't know or you can't say."

"I don't know, Annie. I am telling you the truth. I don't know who tried to run you down."

Her lips drew together. "But you do believe it was deliberate, and that Megan was the target, right?" She could see the truth in his eyes.

"Probably."

"Why? Who is she? Why are you protecting her? You owe me some answers, Griffin. Or I can ask the police some of these questions. Maybe they can get answers out of you."

"Is that a threat?" he countered.

"Do I need to make it one?" she asked, not backing

down. "You can talk to me or you can talk to them."

"All right," he said slowly. "I will tell you what little I know so that you don't put Megan in even more danger."

"How on earth could I do that?" she asked in bewilderment.

"Megan is a valuable witness in a criminal case. She's been in witness protection for the last ten months."

Griffin's words shocked her to the core. She didn't know what she'd expected to get as an explanation, but it hadn't been this.

"Are you part of her witness protection?"

"Not really," he said.

"What does that mean?"

"The man you saw in the bar Saturday night, the one who brought Megan to me, is a US marshal. He's been in charge of Megan's protection. In the time that she's been with him, there have been no incidents, no threats to Megan's life, no indication that her whereabouts had been discovered. But Megan was starting to go stir-crazy with the isolation, the lack of conversation with anyone besides the marshals protecting her. She ran away twice. They were afraid she'd manage to escape at some point and not only would the case lose its prime witness, but Megan could get herself into more trouble."

"So, they brought her here? To you? Why?"

"I've been friends with the marshal on her case for more than a decade. I've done him favors in the past, giving his protectees a place to work and live until they no longer need to be in hiding. When cases go on for almost a year, people have to find a way to have a life, or they can't survive."

"But aren't you putting yourself and everyone in the bar in danger?"

"He doesn't bring me anyone too high profile and definitely not from this area. Megan's case is important, but more on a local level than a national one, and she's a long way from home. Witnesses have to live somewhere."

"I guess. Is Vinnie calling your friend and not the

police?"

Griffin met her gaze and gave a small nod. "He'll talk to Paul first and then we'll go from there. I did warn you to stay away from Megan. You should have listened to me."

"You could have been more forthcoming, Griffin."

"I really couldn't. I wouldn't have told you now if your life hadn't been put in danger by the mere fact that you were standing with Megan. I'm sorry about that."

"You don't sound sorry," she couldn't help saying, seeing the angry light in his eyes.

"I told you not to get involved with Megan. I asked you not to come back to the bar, but you did."

"Because Justin wanted my help, and you didn't turn it down."

"I should have. You were nosing around the bar from the second you stepped into it. I knew you were going to be trouble. Every time I turned around, there you were. And now look where we are."

Anger ripped through her. "You're acting like this is my fault. And it's not."

"Dammit, Annie. Why do you have to be so..." He waved his hand in the air in frustration.

"What?" she demanded. "What is wrong with me now?"

"This," he said, framing her face with his hands and pressing his mouth on hers.

She was so stunned by the kiss, she parted her lips in surprise, and that only made the kiss get hotter. Griffin's mouth was possessive, demanding, filled with anger, desire, and conflict. And she reacted with the same mix of turbulent emotions. She felt overwhelmed, consumed, and hungry for more. Every taste of his lips was a tease, and she wanted the hands that were running through her hair on her body—all over her body.

It was crazy, ridiculous. How could she want someone who didn't even seem to like her very much?

But he was kissing her like he needed her, like he couldn't get enough.

She needed to push him away. But he tasted so good, and the heat between them was filled with an electric connection that felt impossible to break.

But she had to break it. She had to come back down to earth.

Finally, she pulled away, her breasts heaving as the blood rushed through her veins. She stared at Griffin, wondering why he didn't look as unsettled as she felt. "Why—why did you do that?"

"There's always a question with you."

"And I want an answer. Why did you kiss me? Was it to stop me from asking questions?"

"I kissed you because I've been thinking about it since I met you."

Her jaw dropped in shock. "No, you haven't. You've been pissed off at me since I showed up in the bar."

"I've been pissed off at myself," he corrected. "Because as much as I wanted you to go away, I also wanted you to come back."

She had no idea what to say to that.

"My life is complicated," he continued.

"Everyone's life is complicated."

"That might be true, but I like things simple, and you are not simple, Annie Callaway."

She didn't know what that meant either, but then the past hour had been filled with one confusing moment after the next. *Was he complimenting her or insulting her? Who knew?* She tucked her hair behind her ears as she tried to slow down her heart with some deep breaths.

"Do you want me to apologize?" he asked.

"God, no. And, just for the record, I think you're a lot more complicated than I am."

"I shouldn't have kissed you."

"I just said don't apologize. It happened. It's…fine."

"It was better than *fine*," he said, a gleam in his eyes.

Her cheeks heated up again. She cleared her throat. "So, what now? What happens with Megan?" she asked, desperately needing to change the subject.

He blew out a breath. "Megan," he said, as if he'd almost forgotten about the woman in the next room.

"Yes. Megan. Let's talk about her."

"The marshals will come and get her, and move her somewhere else."

"If whoever is after her found her here, they might find her again."

"They might," he said evenly. "But the marshals will do everything they can to protect her."

"She's really scared."

"She is," he agreed. "But hopefully this won't go on much longer."

"She'll be safe after she testifies?"

"She should be. Once she tells her story, there won't be any reason for anyone to try to shut her up."

"What about revenge?"

He shrugged. "It's not impossible, but that's not usually the case."

She tilted her head, giving him a thoughtful look. "So, the Depot is like a halfway house or a hideout or an underground railroad," she added, her imagination taking flight.

"Whoa! Let's just call it a place for someone to work for a few days before they go somewhere else."

"And how appropriate that they're working at a former train station, a place where people used to come to catch a train on their way to somewhere else."

"I hadn't thought of it that way."

And now she couldn't think of it any other way. Her superhero idea suddenly coalesced in her head. She could use Griffin and Vinnie and the train station for her story pitch. She had a desperate urge to find a pen and some paper.

"What is going on in your head?" Griffin asked, giving her a wary look. "I can see the wheels turning."

She wasn't about to tell him her idea. He'd only shut her down, and right now she wanted no limits, no barriers, no walls. "Just thinking about everything." She paused as Vinnie returned to the apartment.

"Can I speak to you in the hall?" Vinnie asked Griffin.

"Yeah."

As Griffin went to speak to Vinnie in private, she stood up and walked over to the window, which faced the employee parking lot. Since they'd come upstairs, the sun had gone down, and the lot was filled with dark shadows, only one light near the entrance and another near the back door offering any illumination. There were three cars in the lot, one of which belonged to Griffin and the other two probably belonged to other staff members. She'd barely noticed the cars before, but the lot was spacious enough that they hadn't been damaged during the attack.

She shivered as the memories ran through her. The car speeding around the corner, the squeal of the tires, the roar of the engine. The vehicle had come out of nowhere and disappeared just as quickly. Everything looked normal now, but was it? *Was someone out there waiting to get another shot at Megan?*

Griffin came back into the room and joined her at the window. "See anything?"

"No, it's quiet and dark."

"We need more lights, more security," he muttered.

She turned to face him. "What did Vinnie say?"

"The marshal is on his way to pick up Megan. He should be here shortly. He'll get her to a safe place."

"I hope so. I feel like he never should have let her out of his sight. Isn't it his job to stay with her?"

"There are different levels of protection depending on the level of the danger, the individual involved. It's not uncommon for people in the program to be on their own, with a local contact. And he's actually not that far away."

"I didn't know that."

"How would you? Anyway, Paul had been with Megan for a while, but she was losing her mind being isolated from the world. That's why he brought her here. I've done it before and it's been a successful experience. He doesn't have to lie to me, and I can watch out for the person. Although, in this case, I didn't do a very good job."

She could see the guilt in his eyes and she didn't know how to address it or if she even should address it, because frankly she still had a lot of unanswered questions. But she was too worked up to ask them now. "I'd like to say good-bye to Megan."

He nodded. "I'm sure she'd appreciate that."

"Did Vinnie see anything on the security camera?"

"Nothing beyond what you saw."

"And the police?"

"Paul is going to talk to them. He'll fill them in on Megan's situation. They'll get a copy of our security footage. And if they need to speak to you, I'm sure they will be in touch."

"So that's it?"

"That's it."

"Okay, I guess this doesn't really have much to do with me."

"Wrong place, wrong time."

"That seems to be happening a lot lately. I thought San Clemente was going to be a sleepy little beach town, a good place to hang out and relax, but I was almost attacked by sharks and now almost run down by a mysterious maniac."

"The key being *almost*," he reminded her. "They were close calls, but you survived."

"And here I thought you were more of a glass half-empty kind of guy," she said lightly.

The tension in his expression eased. "I usually am, but it's been a different kind of few days for me, too."

As they gazed into each other's eyes, desire ran through her again. She could still taste his mouth on her lips, and she wanted to see if another kiss would be as good as the previous one. *How crazy was that?*

Her breath grew shallow and her palms began to sweat as she fought against the strong current pulling her toward

Griffin.

He seemed to be fighting, too, his eyes darkening, his jaw tightening, his hands moving into his pockets, as if those pockets would keep him away from her.

He'd taken the kiss he wanted. Why shouldn't she take the kiss she wanted? She licked her suddenly dry lips, feeling as if she was about to step off a cliff.

Then three sharp raps came on the door.

And her opportunity was lost.

She blew out a breath as Griffin went to answer the door. She had a feeling she'd just had another close call...

Eight

"This is Paul Daniels," Griffin told her, introducing the man she'd seen in the bar on Saturday night. "Annie Callaway."

"Miss Callaway," Paul said with a short nod, his expression somber. Then he turned to Griffin. "We need to talk—in private."

"You can have this room," she said. "I'm going to check on Megan."

She walked over to the bedroom door, gave a knock, and said, "Megan, I'm coming in." She didn't wait for a reply, stepping into the room and closing the door behind her.

Megan was in the middle of a queen-sized bed, lying on her side facing the door, her eyes red and swollen, but there were no tears now. She looked defeated, completely lost, and Annie's heart went out to her.

She sat down on the edge of the mattress and gave her a tentative smile. "How are you feeling?"

Megan's thin shoulders gave a shrug, but even that small gesture seemed to exhaust her.

"Griffin told me a bit about your situation," she said. "I

don't know much, but I do know that you're in trouble because you're trying to do the right thing. I'm so sorry for what you're going through. I want to help."

"There's nothing you can do," Megan muttered. "There's nothing anyone can do. I just want this to be over."

"Griffin said that's going to be happening soon."

"If they don't kill me in the next couple of weeks."

She didn't know what to say to that. "I can't imagine how you're handling all this."

"You really can't." Megan sat up and moved back against the headboard. "And I would never want you to experience life as a fugitive. I did nothing wrong, but I'm the one who's running. It seems upside down."

"It certainly doesn't sound fair."

"Paul brought me here because I was really depressed. I felt so isolated and lonely. I didn't want to do it anymore. What I thought would be days turned into weeks and then months, almost a year. I tried running away. I thought maybe I could just reinvent myself and skip the trial. But Paul found me and convinced me to give him another chance. He said he knew a place where I could go and be around people. I didn't think it would work out, and Griffin kind of scared me when I first met him. But then I met you and the other employees. You were all really nice to me. You all treated me like I was a normal person. It had been so long. I started to think maybe I could do it for another few weeks. Now it's over. They'll take me somewhere else. I heard Paul's voice. He's already here."

"Yes, he's talking to Griffin."

Megan nodded. "Thanks for pushing me out of the way, Annie. I froze when I saw the car. I didn't understand what was happening."

"I know that feeling. Luckily today, I found a way to act. I wish I could do more for you."

"I wish you could, too. But no one can. I have to testify. Otherwise, all of this will have been for nothing, and I will never ever be free." She paused. "I'd tell you more, Annie, but I don't want to bring you into this. You almost got killed because of me."

"I understand your need to keep your secrets, but you still have my number, right?"

"Yes."

"You can always call me. I'm happy to listen to you rant or to talk your ear off just to distract you. Maybe after you testify, you can come back here. Although, I'm sure you probably want to go home…wherever that is." It was so difficult to hold back the questions running through her head, but she didn't think Megan was up to a grilling, and maybe she didn't need to get any more involved in a dangerous situation.

"I do miss home. It's hard to believe I'll ever feel safe there again, but maybe I will."

"All you can do is take it one step at a time."

Megan gave her a sad smile. "That's what Paul always tells me, only he says one day at a time."

A knock came at the door, followed by the sound of Griffin's voice. "Annie, Megan? Can we come in?"

"Yes," Megan answered.

Annie stood up as Griffin and Paul walked into the small bedroom together.

Paul gave Megan a supportive smile. "We need to move, Megan."

"I figured. I already packed my bag," Megan said as she got to her feet. She turned back to Annie. "Thanks for being a friend."

"You're more than welcome," she said, giving Megan a hug. "Be safe."

"I'm going to try." Megan gave Griffin a sad, tired smile. "Thanks for letting me stay here and work at the bar."

"That reminds me," he said, digging into his pocket and pulling out a wad of bills. "Here's your pay for the week."

"It wasn't a week; it was just a few days, and I told you that you didn't have to pay me."

"Take it. It's always nice to have cash in your pocket. Just don't use it to run away from Paul." Griffin paused. "He's your best ally in getting through this, Megan. Don't ever forget that."

She nodded and grabbed her bag off the chair. "I'm ready."

They filed out of the bedroom.

When they reached the living room, Griffin put a hand on her arm, holding her back as Paul and Megan left the apartment.

As the door closed behind them, she was suddenly very aware that she was alone with Griffin, and it was only a short time ago that she'd been fighting a very strong desire to kiss him. She turned to face him, feeling unsettled and uncertain. She was both relieved and disappointed when he let go of her arm.

"What—what's next?" she asked, wrapping her arms around herself, feeling suddenly cold. "Should I go home? Should I talk to the police? Should we at least get out of this room?"

He stared back at her and she could see the same indecision in his eyes. Then he nodded and said, "Let's go downstairs. Let me buy you dinner. See if we can get this day back on an even keel."

"It would have to be some dinner to do that. I feel very off my game at the moment."

"Vinnie can work magic," he said lightly. "And just so you know—how you've handled everything has been fairly amazing."

She liked that he thought she was amazing even though she wasn't sure she was handling anything very well. "I don't think it's all set in."

"No, probably not. But you have other things to think about."

"Like…"

"Like the designs you owe me."

"Right—work. Work is good. Art is good. And dinner is good."

"You do like to work through your emotions out loud,

don't you?"

"Bad habit," she admitted, as she followed him to the door. "Everyone always knows what I'm thinking, whereas most other people, especially you, don't give away a thing."

He didn't answer, and she wasn't surprised. He might have told her a little about Megan and his arrangement with the witness protection program, but she had a feeling there was a whole lot he hadn't told her. Maybe she'd find out more over dinner.

———⋙⋘———

Annie might think he was giving away nothing, but Griffin felt like she was slowly but surely tugging away at all his hidden secrets, and if he wasn't careful, he was going to end up spilling his guts to her, and that would be bad—very bad. But for now, he was going to buy her dinner, get her mind off Megan and everything that had happened and hopefully set things right again.

He still had an itchy feeling at the back of his neck about the attack on Megan and Annie. They thought they'd been lucky to get out of the way, but had it been luck? Had the attack been orchestrated to hurt or kill someone, or had it been a warning?

If it was a warning, would there be another one? Would anyone know that Megan was gone? She'd left, but had the danger gone with her?

He needed to be careful, and he needed to keep an eye on Annie. She'd looked straight at the driver of the car and while she couldn't identify the person, the driver might not know that.

"It's packed," Annie said, as they walked into the bar.

"It's dinner time." The weekday nights had been getting busier since the local businesses had discovered Vinnie's food and their happy hour priced drinks to be a good after-work watering hole. "There's a table," he added, heading toward a small table for two next to the stage. As Annie sat down, he said, "Do you want a menu or do you trust Vinnie to send out something good?"

"So far Vinnie has not disappointed me. I'll take whatever he cooks."

"I'll let him know. What about a drink?"

"A Chardonnay would be great."

"I'll be right back. Don't go anywhere."

"Don't worry. I'm very happy to sit and catch my breath."

He made his way into the kitchen, which was also busy, with Vinnie working at the grill, his assistant, Jose, making salads, and his other assistant, Paula, plating the orders.

Vinnie looked up and motioned for Jose to take over at the grill. Then they left the kitchen and walked down the hall to the office.

"I saw Paul leave with Megan," Vinnie said, a grim note in his voice.

"Yeah. They're gone." He moved around the desk to look at the security feed. Vinnie came up behind him as they ran the feed several times, looking for any small clue, but there was nothing. "No license plate, no visual ID. The car comes very close to Megan and Annie. Another few feet, and the outcome would have been different."

Vinnie's lips drew into a hard line. "I never should have told Megan to take out the trash."

"You had no idea."

"I put her in danger."

"Maybe it's a good thing. You flushed out the danger. Megan is safer now."

Vinnie didn't appear entirely convinced. "He must have been watching the bar, waiting for an opportunity."

"I think so. Paul obviously underestimated what kind of danger she was in. He was very surprised. He said he'd had no inkling that her name or whereabouts had been discovered."

"If we're going to keep doing this, we need to make some changes. We talked about it before, but we didn't do it."

"I agree. We need more security, better cameras." He paused. "Or we could stop. I know you were interested in doing that before Megan showed up. We had agreed to take a break. I'm the one who said yes to Megan."

"Well, Paul didn't give you much of a choice. Honestly, I'm torn. We've had two problems now, which is two problems too many. But...Megan blossomed in the few days she was here. We did that. We gave her a sense of security, a place to belong, and we've done that for other people. We just need to make sure we can keep them safe and that we can keep everyone here safe."

"I agree. We'll take a break for a few weeks and figure things out."

"That's a good plan. What are you going to do about your other problem?" Vinnie asked.

"My other problem?"

"You know—the very pretty redhead with the curious green eyes, the big, wide smile, and the chatty personality."

"Hell if I know," he muttered. "But I owe her at least dinner for everything she went through today. What's your special tonight?"

"Spaghetti and meatballs. My mother's recipe. It's incredible."

"Sounds good. We'll take two."

"And after that?"

He shrugged. "What do you want me to say?"

"You need to think about what you're doing with her, Griffin."

"I know. But Justin bailed on the art for the flyers and shirts, and Annie has stepped in. I need to get that order in by Thursday. If she's still willing to do the designs, I need her to do them."

A gleam entered Vinnie's eyes. "Are you sure you don't need her for something else? She's a looker."

"Who asks a lot of questions."

"So, don't talk. I'm sure you can think of other things to do with her."

"Too many," he admitted. "And they're probably all bad ideas. But at the moment I'm more concerned about her safety. She was with Megan when that car came into the lot. She's a witness and that bothers me. I need to make sure Annie is safe before I cut her loose."

"I doubt she's in danger. They probably didn't even get a good look at her."

"I'd like to believe that, but I need to make sure," he said, as they left the office and headed down the hall.

As Vinnie returned to the kitchen, he moved into the bar. Danielle gave him a distracted nod as she filled orders. Not wanting to bother her, he grabbed an open bottle of white wine and two glasses and took them over to the table.

Annie was scribbling on a notepad, and she was so engrossed in what she was doing that she didn't even look up at him. It wasn't until he set the bottle and glasses down that she jerked her head up.

"Sorry. Didn't mean to startle you."

"Still a little jumpy."

He sat down across from her. "Vinnie is making us spaghetti and meatballs. He claims it's his mother's recipe and out of this world."

"I love spaghetti and meatballs."

He had a feeling Annie loved a lot of things. She was certainly open to life—probably too open.

He poured the wine and pushed her glass across the table. "Are you working on a design?"

"Yes." She covered the drawing with her hand. "But it's too early to show you."

"Not even a peek?"

She picked the notebook up and put it in her purse. "Nope. I don't like to show my work until it's ready. Right now, it's just a stream of consciousness, and the first ideas that come out of my brain can be downright ugly."

He smiled at her candor. "You're very honest."

"I try to be ruthless with my art, keep my standards high, but it's not always easy. Sometimes I really like the ugly ideas and I keep trying to make them pretty for far longer than I should."

"Because you don't like to give up. I've seen your determination show itself quite a bit the past few days."

"Persistence is a Callaway trait," she said lightly.

"You're quite proud of your family, aren't you?"

"I am. They frustrate me at times, but they're great. They're some of the best people you could ever meet."

He couldn't imagine what it would be like to grow up in a family as large as hers or as tight-knit. "You're lucky."

"I did draw a good card at birth," she admitted. "Not like some of the kids we saw at Hamilton House. They didn't ask to be born into such difficult situations. I'm glad you're going to let me help you with the art. I've been a little…blocked, kind of drifting for a few weeks, and it's nice to work on something positive, something that can help someone."

"Why have you been blocked?"

"I think it was the result of a number of things. It started about six months ago. I was working for a production company and we had some movie ideas we were working on, and the competition is fierce in Hollywood. I made the mistake of showing one of my friends, one of my coworkers, a design, and she took it for her own."

"And you let her?"

"I didn't *let* her. I went after her, but we'd been working as a collaborative team, and it was difficult for anyone besides the two of us to know who had done what. Unfortunately, she had better relationships with our bosses than I did. We were put on different teams, and I don't know…after that, I kind of lost my mojo. It wasn't just that she stole my design; it was that I trusted her, and I lost a friend that day. I still remember walking into the conference room and seeing her pitch my character idea. I wasn't supposed to be in until later that day; she'd gone behind my back to set up the meeting while I was out."

Something clicked with her words, and he remembered what she'd said earlier. "That was the time you walked in on someone."

She nodded. "Yep. And I didn't say anything until later. I

just sat down in shock and watched her do it." Shaking her head, she added, "Not my proudest moment."

"What happened after that? Did you quit? Is that why you're unemployed now?"

"No, I stuck it out. But there were actually a lot more problems at the company than the theft of my design. We weren't doing well. Our pitches were getting shot down, and eventually the owners of the company decided to dissolve their partnership, and I was laid off. Since then I've been trying to find a new job."

"What about the teaching job?"

"That's temporary. I'm just filling in for the teacher who had to go on maternity leave early. It's been nice to have that to do, but I still have too many empty hours. I come from a blue-collar family, raised with a sense of responsibility. I have been feeling way too idle and lax, and it hasn't helped that I haven't been able to use the free time to come up with something brilliant. But I feel like I'm on the edge of a breakthrough."

"I hope it comes by Thursday morning."

"Don't worry. I'll come up with something. I already have some ideas. And working on them is keeping my mind off other things. Although, I have a feeling I'll be seeing that car racing at me in my dreams tonight."

"I hope that won't happen…"

"But it probably will." She cleared her throat. "Let's not talk about it right now."

"Fine with me."

"Let's talk about you."

He groaned. "You know that's my least favorite subject."

She smiled. "Easy questions, I promise."

"We'll see."

"Have you always worked in a bar? Did you grow up with a dream to open your own bar?"

He cleared his throat, thinking he should have anticipated that question and had a good answer ready to go, but when he was with Annie, the blood that usually fueled his brain headed to other parts of his body.

Thankfully, Vinnie interrupted them with two large bowls of spaghetti and meatballs.

"Oh, wow, this is huge," Annie said. "It smells delicious. Thanks, Vinnie."

"You're welcome, Annie. I hope you enjoy it."

"I'm sure I will. You're a fantastic cook. I was just asking Griffin how he got into the bar business, and I'm kind of curious about you, too."

"Well, you can start with Griffin. I have to get back to the kitchen." Vinnie shot him an amused look and then walked away.

Despite Annie's proclaimed interest in his life, she now seemed a bit more captivated by the food in front of her, twirling the strands of pasta around her fork with great enthusiasm. She certainly brought energy to everything she did.

He liked that—it made him wonder what she'd be like in bed—probably very creative, very enthusiastic, very hot... *Damn!* He needed to send his brain down another direction, but the kiss they'd shared in the apartment had whetted his appetite for her, and he wanted more.

It had definitely been a mistake to kiss her. He didn't know what had come over him. He usually had absolute and total control over his emotions and more importantly his actions, but Annie continually put him off-balance.

He dragged his gaze away from her and concentrated on his own food. He had a feeling the respite from questions would be brief, and after dinner he was going to have to figure out what to do with her.

Could he really let her go home alone? What if Megan's danger followed her?

But if he went home with her, that could create another set of problems.

He'd known she was going to be trouble the first night she'd walked into the bar; he'd been right.

Nine

She'd told Griffin after dinner that he didn't have to follow her home, but he'd insisted, and as Annie glanced into her rearview mirror, she had to admit she was happy to have him behind her. Maybe she'd feel better tomorrow, when the sun was up, when there weren't any scary, dark shadows, when the memories of what had happened earlier got pushed to the back of her mind. But now, she was still spooked, still nervous, and still not sure what she'd gotten herself involved in. She also wasn't sure about Griffin.

He seemed to be a good guy, a hero, a protector…but then why all the secrets? Why couldn't he talk about his past? Why did he change the subject whenever she asked him a personal question? She still didn't know how or when he'd decided to become a bar owner, although, that was partly her fault. Vinnie's spaghetti and meatballs had completely derailed her from the conversation. She'd enjoyed the comfort food far too much and the wine and the meal had taken away some of her drive to get to the bottom of Griffin Hale.

But there might be time now…if she invited him into her apartment.

She really shouldn't do that—should she?

They hadn't talked about the smoking-hot make-out session they'd had back at the apartment, but she didn't think either of them had forgotten. She knew she hadn't.

She looked in her rearview mirror one last time, and then pulled into the garage under her building. There was no space for Griffin's car in the garage, so hopefully he could find street parking. Or maybe he'd just double-park until she got inside.

As she moved out of the garage, a gate came down behind her, and she walked out to the street. The lights of Griffin's car went out as he found a spot down the block. She waited as he got out of his car and made his way back to her.

"You didn't have to park," she said.

"It's been a crazy day. I'm going to walk you inside, make sure everything is good here."

"I can't imagine that it wouldn't be." Actually, her fertile imagination had already come up with some terrifying scenarios related to Megan, but the logical part of her brain told her she was taking things too far. Megan was in trouble. She was the one in danger, not her.

After inserting her key in the building lock, they walked up the stairs to her apartment.

Once inside, she quickly scanned the room, happy to see nothing was out of order.

She was also glad she'd taken all of her sketches into the bedroom the night before instead of leaving them spread out on the dining room table. She didn't want Griffin to see her depiction of him as a superhero when he was already so uncomfortable with the idea that she saw him as any hero at all.

"This is a nice place," Griffin said, wandering over to the windows. "Great view."

"I know. I'm feeling very spoiled, but it's a sublet. A friend of mine is on location for a TV series for the several months. He wanted a house-sitter, and I wanted cheap rent."

"Sweet deal."

"I agree. I love sitting out on the deck in the daytime, watching the beachgoers, the surfers…"

He shot her a quick, questioning look. "That's right. You said you'd seen me before."

"From a distance. You stood out, because you were always alone. You were never with the other surfers. There might be some nearby, but you were on your own. It made me wonder about you."

"You wonder about everything."

"I'm a curious person."

"It's easier to catch a wave when you don't have competition."

"Is that the reason, or do you just dislike being close to people?"

"That's the reason. I run a bar; I'm around people all day. Surfing is my time for myself."

That made sense, but even though Griffin ran a bar filled with customers, there was always a little barrier between him and everyone else, except maybe Vinnie. He was the exception. He'd been let into Griffin's inner circle.

She'd like to be the exception, too.

That fleeting thought made her catch her breath, as she was once again caught up in her incredibly strong attraction to Griffin. He was such a handsome man with his thick, dark hair, perfect for running her fingers through, she was dying to taste his sexy mouth again. She knew that the body under the jeans and knit shirt was to die for. She'd seen him in a wetsuit. She'd also felt that powerful body over hers when he'd paddled her to shore on his surfboard.

Clearing her throat, she said, "Do you want a drink or do you need to get going?"

He hesitated, then said, "I'll take a water."

She was both relieved and disappointed by his answer. She wanted him to stay, but she also thought getting him out of her apartment fast would be a better idea.

Retrieving two bottled waters from the fridge, she tossed one to him and then she made her way over to the couch.

Griffin followed, taking a seat on the sofa as well, but leaving a few feet between them.

He propped his feet up on the coffee table and said, "You can really hear the waves from here."

"They lull me to sleep at night. It reminds me of my childhood. I grew up in a house across the street from Ocean Beach in San Francisco."

"You're a beach girl from way back."

"Yes. But the Northern California beaches have a different feel; they're colder, the sand is rockier, and there's often fog and wind. It's not like down here. It's wilder."

"I'll have to surf up north some time."

"You should. It's definitely a challenge my brothers enjoyed. They grew up surfing."

"Not you or your sisters?"

"Kate used to go out. She was a tomboy. She liked to keep up with the boys, but Mia and I were more sunbathers. Actually, after a bad experience when I was ten, I didn't spend much time on the beach at all."

"What happened?"

"A friend of mine got swept out to sea by a rogue wave. She was rescued by my brothers, but for those few minutes when they were racing out to get her, and she was screaming and disappearing in and out of the waves, I was terrified. I didn't know how it had happened. One minute I was standing in the sand only a short distance from her, and then the ocean grabbed her and carried her away." She took a sip of water at the end of her story. "It was awful."

"It sounds awful, but I'm glad she was all right."

"I didn't go back into the water for eighteen years, not until…"

His jaw dropped. "Seriously? The first time you went back in the ocean was last Friday?"

She nodded. "I've spent the past few weeks watching all the fun everyone is having in the ocean and on the beach, and I decided it was time to put my fears behind me. I told you I was feeling at loose ends and kind of down on myself for my lack of a job. I needed a win. I thought beating back an old fear was a good way to get that win. I was actually enjoying myself for a minute. And then I heard you shouting. I felt something bump my leg right before you pulled me onto your board. I'm sure it was a shark." She shuddered. "I feel sick every time I think about what could have happened."

"Just think about the outcome. You made it to shore."

"Because of you." She gave him a thoughtful look. "I know you don't like to be thought of as a hero, but you were that day. It's not my opinion; it's a fact."

He shrugged and swigged a long gulp of water. "I was on my way in to shore."

"I know. You don't think it was a big deal, but I do. Anyway, I have no plans to ever go back in the water. I think the universe has made it clear to me that the ocean and I cannot be friends."

"It's at least a million to one that it would ever happen again."

"But there's that one…"

"I can't imagine not going back into the water. The sea is rejuvenating. It's invigorating. It releases you from the world. It makes you feel alive."

"Too alive for me. And wouldn't you be slightly worried about running into another shark? It's not like you had a surfboard made of steel."

"Sharks are the least of my worries. I'll go out again as soon as they lift the restrictions. I like the challenge of the waves and the current. It's me against Mother Nature, a battle worth fighting."

"Mother Nature could crush you," she said.

A gleam entered his eyes. "That's why it's a worthy fight. Who wants to go up against someone weak? What's the fun in that?"

"I don't see the fun in any of it."

"Come on, you just said you were enjoying yourself until the sharks came around."

"But that was just for a minute. And as usual, my luck

turned bad."

"As usual?"

"You were right when you said you thought I was trouble…it does seem to follow me around. Look what happened today."

"That wasn't because of you. That was my fault. I've been thinking about putting in some security fencing in that parking lot for weeks. I also could have made sure Megan stayed inside."

"Have you ever had any other problems with the people who have stayed there?" she asked, curious to know more about his side operation.

"Everything was fine for a long time. We haven't always had people stay in the apartment; sometimes they live nearby and just come to work at the bar. But about two months ago, a woman's ex caught up with her. We were able to protect her, and the guy went to jail, but it made Vinnie and I realize we were putting our staff and customers in danger. I told Paul we were going to take a break. I knew I needed to rethink our security before we continued. But then he showed up with Megan, and he wouldn't take no for an answer."

It all suddenly made more sense. "That's why you were so angry when I met you. I thought it was just me you were pissed at, but it was Paul, too, wasn't it?"

"It was. You were just another complication."

"Will you do it again after what happened today? Will you take someone else in?"

"I don't know. Vinnie and I are going to think about it."

She wondered why his answer wasn't an unequivocal *no*. He'd already admitted that he'd put his staff and customers in jeopardy. "What do you have to think about?"

"Whether the potential good outweighs the potential risk."

"Does anyone else at the bar besides Vinnie know what goes on in the apartment upstairs? Justin mentioned to me that you help a lot of people who seemed to come and go."

"Only Vinnie knows who they are."

"Are you protecting someone else right now?" she asked, wondering if any of the other staffers were like Megan, but not staying at the Depot, as had been the case with some of the other witnesses he'd protected.

"That I can't tell you."

"Really? Why not?"

"Because I can't."

"Is Shari a witness to something? She has a haunted look about her. Although, maybe that's too obvious. Wait, is it Justin? He's such a California beach boy, no one would ever think he's on the run."

"Whoa, put the brakes on, Annie."

"Sorry. It's the curse of my imagination. I'm a storyteller at heart. It's what drives my art." She paused. "Maybe it's Vinnie. He looks like he could have had a hard past with all those tattoos. Do they have a particular meaning?"

"You'd have to ask him."

"Danielle seems totally out there—bold, brassy, full of sarcasm and sass. But maybe that's just a cover."

"Are you going to go through the entire staff, Annie?"

"I might. I like mysteries."

"Do you?" He finished off his water and set the empty bottle on the table. "Why?"

"Because it engages my mind. I like to figure things out."

"Does that include figuring me out? Do you think you can do that?"

She felt like there was something deep behind his question, but she didn't know what. "I'm not sure if I could ever crack your hard shell. You're good at keeping people out. Why is that, Griffin? What makes you so secretive?"

"Maybe I just like my privacy. Unlike you, I don't feel like sharing every thought the instant it comes into my head."

She made a face at him. "I know I speak before I think sometimes and that can get me into trouble, but I just can't analyze every word that wants to come out of my mouth. That would be exhausting. Doesn't it make you tired?"

He frowned at her words, and she had a feeling she'd

given him something to think about.

"For a man who likes the freedom of the ocean, you might want to consider how freeing it is just to say what's on your mind," she added.

"You want me to say what's on my mind?"

A nervous shiver ran down her spine at the challenging look in his eyes. "Sure, if you want to."

"I'm thinking about whether I should go home or if I should kiss you again."

She wet her lips with her tongue. "Okay…"

"Now what are you thinking?" he asked, his gaze shimmering with all kinds of interesting possibilities.

"I'm thinking that…you should go home."

"Really?" he asked in a voice laced with disappointment.

"I might be fearless when it comes to talking, but action is a little different. I'm not just scared of being swept away by the ocean… I think you could do the same thing, and I don't know if I'm ready. There was a lot of current when we kissed."

"Then ride the wave, don't fight it."

"Or I could just stay out of the water."

"You're back to playing it safe?"

She swallowed back the desire to say to hell with being safe, she wanted the ride… But she couldn't quite get herself there. "I think we should get to know each other better."

"I thought you liked mystery."

"I do, but I also like knowing who I'm riding the wave with."

"I saved your life. Doesn't that earn your trust?"

"Now you want credit for that?" she said, teasing him a little.

He tipped his head, a small smile playing across his lips. "I took a shot."

"I like it when you let down your guard, even if it's just to smile."

"Why don't you show me how much you like it? I'll go whenever you want me to go, but in the meantime…"

In the meantime suggested all kinds of delightful possibilities. "Can you keep the walls down for another second?"

"I could do that."

"Then..." She scooted next to him, put one hand on his thigh, and the other on his chest as she leaned forward to kiss him.

The same electric tingle she'd felt earlier touched off a fierce firestorm of feeling.

She leaned into the kiss, tracing his mouth with her tongue, delighting when he parted his lips and invited her inside.

His arms came around her as he took the kiss deeper, as the heat enveloped them, as she felt that oh so dangerous current tugging at her body. She could easily get lost in this man. They were only kissing, and she wanted so much more.

Griffin seemed to feel the same way, his hands creeping under her top, his fingers setting off more heat as he stroked her bare back, as his fingers slipped under the strap of her bra.

Things were moving too fast and too slow—at the same time. Her body was going all in on the idea of getting to know Griffin in a very physical way, but her brain was screaming caution.

She didn't know this man at all. And while she could probably trust him with her life, what about her heart?

This might not be about heart for him, but for her, it always ended up in an emotional place. It was that reminder that finally made her pull away.

Her breath came fast; so did his.

She liked that he'd been as caught up in her as she was in him.

"Damn," he murmured. "Your mouth is definitely good for more than just talking."

"That sounds like an insult and a compliment at the same time."

"Definitely a compliment," he assured her.

"I want to say the same about you, but you actually kiss

better than you talk."

He smiled. "I'd probably agree with that."

"You should go, Griffin."

"I know. I don't want to. But I will."

They got up, and she walked him to the door, already regretting that she'd called a halt to the most fun she'd had in a while. "I'll work on the designs tomorrow."

"I'm looking forward to seeing what you come up with." He paused. "Keep your doors locked, and if you see anything or hear anything out of the ordinary, I want you to call me." He took his phone out of his pocket. "Let's exchange numbers." After they did that, he said, "I'll check in with you tomorrow."

"Okay. You don't really think I'm in any danger, do you?"

"No, but I still want you to be careful."

"I usually do play it safe, but I guess you figured that out."

He leaned over and stole a surprising kiss. "Good-night, Annie."

"Good-night."

After he left, she flipped the lock and then leaned back against the door, her heart still beating a little too fast. She had no idea where things might go with Griffin, but she sure wanted to find out.

Ten

───⟫⟪───

Griffin hit the beach Wednesday morning as the sun was coming up, choosing to surf on the southern side of the pier instead of the northern end that faced Annie's apartment.

He didn't like this side very much. It was closer to the surf school, so there were a lot of beginners out on the waves. He was also finding that his rescue the week before had gotten around the surfing circles, and more than a few guys paddled over to him to ask him what had happened, what he'd seen, what it had felt like to be that close to the sharks.

He tried to answer their questions and be friendly, but he was really missing his alone time on the waves.

Annie had asked him last night if he just didn't like people. He'd dismissed that idea out of hand. He worked at a bar. He volunteered at Hamilton House. He was around people all day and all night. On the other hand, most of those people were customers or employees, or kids needing someone to care about them. They were not real friends. The only person in San Clemente who knew anything about him was Vinnie, and even their relationship had boundaries that both of them respected.

He'd dated a few women over the past couple of years, but none of those relationships had gone deep. It had just been about sex and fun—for both parties. He didn't mess around with women who wanted deep conversations.

Which brought him back to Annie...

Kissing her had been like walking into a fire. That red hair. Those green eyes. That sexy, sweet mouth that seemed compelled to not only question him but tell him everything she was feeling. He didn't know how to handle all that honesty. He also didn't know how to handle how he felt when he was with her.

He'd tried to use anger and rudeness to get rid of her, but that hadn't worked. Now she was designing flyers for him, and she knew about Megan and Paul. What was going to happen next? What layer of his life was she going to peel away and how was he going to stop her?

He didn't particularly want to be a man of mystery, but it had become a necessity, as had his isolation. Hearing her talk about her family with such affection and joy had made him feel wistful for a life he'd left a long time ago.

He couldn't afford nostalgia. That could make him vulnerable. He had to find a way to get Annie out of his life. It would be better for him. It would be better for her.

But he couldn't do it today. Once she was done with the art for the party, then he'd say goodbye.

Riding one last wave into the beach, he hit the sand, then headed for home.

When he entered the employee lot at the Depot, he was taken back to the day before, only there were no cars in the lot today other than his, and no sign of the Ford without any license plates.

He went up to his apartment, showered, changed and then headed downstairs to see what he could grab to eat. With the bar kitchen so close, he didn't bother to keep much in his apartment.

He had just pulled out a carton of eggs when his phone rang. It was an unidentified number, which always made him edgy. "Hello?"

"It's Paul."

"New number?"

"Keeping things moving," Paul replied.

"How's Megan?"

"Better this morning. We just got some good news. The trial was moved up, and Megan will testify on Friday. We're getting on a plane in an hour. This is going to be over soon."

"That's great. I know she's ready to be done."

"Any problems around the bar after we left?"

"No, it has been very quiet."

"Good. I want you to know I didn't think I was putting you in danger when I brought Megan there."

"I know."

"I wouldn't jeopardize your safety or the people you work with. At any rate, Megan told me she feels better just having been around normal people for a few days. She has bounced back from yesterday's attack, and she looks stronger to me, both physically and emotionally. She has a new determination that was lacking before I brought her to you."

"I'm glad we could help. And I hope she will be free to return to her life. Tell her if she ever wants to come back and work here for real, she's welcome."

"I'll tell her, but she actually has some skills that would be wasted in a bar."

Paul's words made him curious, but unlike Annie, he kept his questions to himself. He might want to know something, but that didn't mean he needed to know.

"By the way," Paul continued. "How's Annie doing?"

"She's fine. She's very resilient."

"Beautiful, too. You got something going on there?"

"Trying not to," he muttered.

"Interesting. Good luck with that."

"Thanks."

He set the phone down on the counter, happy that Megan's case was heading to a finish. He broke some eggs into a bowl and whipped them with a little water. Then he pulled out a frying pan and set it on the stove. As he turned the knob to light the burner, it clicked, but no flame appeared. He tried the next burner, but the same thing happened.

"Morning," Vinnie said, as he came into the kitchen, shrugging off his jacket and hanging it on a hook by the door. "Hey, these burners aren't working."

"I know. The stove has been acting up. I've had someone out to look at it, but they couldn't fix it. We might need to spring for a new one."

"Hopefully, not until after Christmas."

"Use a match to light it," Vinnie said, opening a drawer and tossing him a matchbook. "I didn't see you come back last night."

"It was late. I went straight upstairs."

Vinnie gave him a speculative look. "Anything you want to share?"

He opened the matchbook, then paused. It wasn't one of their cream-colored books with the Depot logo on it. This matchbook was bright red with gold coins falling into a pile of money, the words Gold Mine written across the front. His heart skipped a beat, and his body tightened. "Where did this come from?"

"What?" Vinnie gave him a confused look.

He held up the matchbook. "It's from a bar in Chicago called the Gold Mine."

Vinnie's gaze met his. "You been there?"

"More than once. But I never brought back a matchbook. How did it get into our drawer?"

"A customer must have left it behind."

His gut tightened. Was it just a coincidence? It didn't feel like it."

"Griffin?"

"It's fine." He pulled out a match, turned on the gas, and lit the stove. Then he put the matchbook into his pocket.

"You sure?"

"Forget about it."

"If you say so. I'm going to start prepping for lunch."

He nodded, tossing his egg mixture into the pan. As he cooked his breakfast, his thoughts went back in time to an old bar in downtown Chicago. It was the kind of bar where the locals went, not the tourists. It was a hole in the wall. The drinks were cheap. The food was greasy. But the music was great, and on the weekends the place was packed.

He told himself it was just a coincidence that the matchbook had shown up in his bar. Only problem was—he had never believed in coincidences.

Annie spent Wednesday working on the design for the Depot's holiday fundraiser. By late afternoon, she thought she had it just right, and she was eager to show Griffin, but first she had a class to teach.

On her way to the community college, she gave Griffin a call. She'd probably spent as much time thinking about him as she had about her design. But today she was only going to talk about art. Everything else was just too complicated.

"Hello?" Griffin said.

And just like that, his husky voice sent shivers down her spine. "Hi, it's Annie."

"Everything all right?"

"Yes. I think I have a design you'll like. Actually, I have two, and you can choose which one you prefer. Hopefully, one of them will work."

"When can I see them?"

"I'm on my way to teach my class right now, but I was thinking I could drop by the bar afterward, or if you want to come by my apartment later, that would work, too."

He hesitated for a minute. "What time does your class end?"

"Six."

"Why don't I take you out for dinner? There's a great Mexican place down the street from the college."

She was surprised by his words but also excited by the

invitation. "If you're talking about Juan Delgado's, I'm in. I've only been there once, and I've been dying to go back. But there's one problem; I don't have the designs with me."

"No problem. We'll eat and then go back to your apartment."

"Okay," she said, her mind already racing ahead to what might happen at her apartment once they were alone again.

"I'll see you at the restaurant."

"See you then." She ended her call and turned into the faculty parking lot, feeling a little more excited than she should. Griffin was just taking her to dinner to thank her for working on the designs for free. But even if it was nothing more than that, she was really looking forward to seeing him again. She knew she needed to be careful. Griffin had the potential to break her heart. She shouldn't let him get close enough to do that.

—➤➤◄◄—

Two hours later, Annie walked into the Mexican restaurant a little past six. Griffin was already there. He was talking to the hostess, an attractive young blonde, who was gazing at Griffin like he was a god, reminding Annie that the man probably had more than his fair share of women.

"I'm here," she said.

He turned and gave her a smile that surprised her with its warmth. She was never quite sure what kind of welcome she was going to get from Griffin, but tonight was starting on a good note.

"Follow me," the hostess said, looking disappointed by Annie's appearance.

As they sat down, a busboy dropped off chips and salsa, immediately followed by a smiling blonde waitress, who asked them what they'd like to drink.

"I'd love a margarita," Annie said. "Blended, no salt."

"Same," Griffin added.

"I'll get your drinks and give you a minute to look at the

menu," the waitress said.

"So, what's good?" Griffin asked, as the waitress left.

"Last time I was here, I had a chicken enchilada. It comes in a bowl with rice and beans underneath, and it's basically out of this world. Oh, and did I mention the guacamole that comes with it? To die for."

He smiled again. "Sold. Maybe you should be in sales instead of art. You're very persuasive."

"I might be able to talk you into an enchilada, but I'm not sure about anything else."

"How was your class?"

"It was fine. Tonight's class was the last one of this semester. The students have all next week to work on their final project, and I think they were eager to get on with it."

"And Justin is in this class?"

"Yes, but he wasn't there. I was surprised. He hasn't missed a class until now, and we did go over tips for the final. Is he working?"

"He's supposed to be. I left before he would have checked in for his shift, though."

She dipped a chip into some salsa and popped it into her mouth. The heat ran through her like a freight train, and she reached quickly for her water glass. "That's hot," she said a moment later. "But really good."

He tried the salsa. "Not bad. And not that hot."

"Always the tough guy. So, have you heard from Megan or Paul?"

"Yes. Paul told me the trial got moved up, so hopefully Megan will be able to testify and move on with her life by next week."

"Oh, that would be great. She was in such despair when I spoke to her. It was hard to see her like that."

"It's almost over."

She sat back as the waitress came over. After ordering, she said, "What did you do today?"

"I caught up on some paperwork, dealt with vendors, inventory, the usual."

"I asked you last night if you'd always worked in a bar, but you didn't answer. In fact, I think you changed the subject."

"Did I? I don't remember."

"Well, tell me now."

"I helped out in my grandfather's bar when I was in my late teens, not that I could serve alcohol, but I bussed tables and served food, and I always liked hanging out there."

She was surprised he'd actually told her something personal. "You followed in his footsteps."

"In a way. It took me a long time to do it."

"What other jobs have you had?"

"Random stuff."

"Like?"

"Sales."

"Selling…" she pressed, feeling like she was always playing twenty questions with Griffin.

"Surfboards, bicycles, electronics—whatever."

She gave a sigh of exasperation. "You're so damn vague, Griffin."

"My life isn't that exciting, Annie. I met Vinnie a couple years back and we talked about how he always wanted to be a chef, and I'd thought about running a bar, and eventually our talking turned into action. We had the opportunity to rent the Depot for a good price. The owners didn't care what we did with it, as long as we improved the property, which we did, and customers started to come pretty quickly. We got some regulars and they told their friends."

"I'm starting to feel like a regular," she said with a laugh.

"You have been there a lot this week."

"In my defense, I don't know a lot of people in this town, and the bar makes me feel like I'm part of something, too, which I'm sure is what you were going for, so you should be happy I keep coming back."

"You're starting to grow on me."

"Hopefully, not like a bad mole."

He grinned. "Much prettier than that."

She smiled back at him as the waitress brought their food. So far, dinner was going pretty well.

An hour later, she was feeling even better about the evening. Not only had the enchiladas been as good as she remembered, but conversation had been as easy as it had ever been. Griffin dropped a few nuggets here and there about his interests in running and biking. It wasn't surprising that those activities were also fairly isolating. It didn't seem in his nature to be part of a team, although he seemed like he would be a good team player if he wanted to be. His staff at the Depot seemed to respect him and like him.

She wondered about the women in his life. He was too handsome and sexy not to have had a girlfriend, but she hadn't broached the topic, because part of her didn't want to hear about any other women. She also didn't want to make things awkward by digging too deep into his life. *Baby steps*, she kept telling herself, wondering if there would come a time when Griffin would really trust her.

After dinner, they made their way out to the street, and once again Griffin followed her back to her apartment so he could see the designs she'd come up with. She was happy to keep the evening going and a little nervous and excited about being alone with him.

When they got to her building, she pulled into the garage, while Griffin searched for a spot on the street. Luckily, he managed to find one not too far away. She waited for him on the sidewalk and then they headed toward the front door.

They were almost there when a man came through the side gate.

His sudden appearance was startling. The light from the man's phone flashed in her eyes, blinding her for a second.

Griffin pushed her aside, grabbed the guy by both arms and shoved him up against the side of the building with lightning-fast moves.

"What the—" the man swore.

"Who are you? What do you want?" Griffin demanded.

"Get your hands off me," the man yelled, kicking out at

Griffin.

Suddenly, their fists were flying. She didn't know what to do, how to help. And there was something about the man, his voice, that was very familiar…

Eleven

As the moonlight captured the man's features, Annie shouted, "Stop!" When neither one listened to her, she yelled louder. "Stop!" She grabbed Griffin's arm before he could land another punch. "I know him."

Griffin stared at her in surprise. "You know him?"

"Yes, I do. This is my brother Hunter." She looked back at her brother. "What are you doing here?"

"I came to check up on you," Hunter said, adjusting his jacket, his eyes burning with anger. "Who's this guy, Annie?"

"Griffin Hale—Hunter Callaway," she said, introducing the two men.

"Why did you come at me like that?" Hunter demanded.

"I thought you were going after Annie," Griffin replied. "You came out of the shadows."

"I went around back to check out the view while I was waiting for her to come home," Hunter said, rubbing the side of his jaw where Griffin's fist had connected. "And why would anyone be going after my sister?"

That was a loaded question and one she didn't really want Griffin to answer. She had three older brothers, all very protective, and while Hunter might be the most free-spirited of the bunch, he didn't shirk his brotherly responsibilities.

"It's dark. You surprised us," she said before Griffin could answer. "Let's go upstairs."

She opened the door and led the way up to her apartment, happy that the scuffle hadn't brought out any of her neighbors. When she ushered them into the living room, she got a better look at both men, and she could see bruising on both of their faces.

"I'll get ice," she said practically.

"I'm fine," they choroused together.

She sighed. "Two tough guys—got it. I'm sorry you got hurt, Hunter. I had no idea you were coming here. Why didn't you text me?"

"I wanted to surprise you." Hunter brushed a strand of brown hair away from his face. He had a three-day growth of beard on his face, and she thought he looked tired. "Who is this guy?" He glared again at Griffin. "Is he your boyfriend?"

"No. He's a friend. He was just protecting me, Hunter. I'm sorry you got hurt."

"And neither of you has told me why you need protection," he said.

"I was acting on instinct," Griffin said, thankfully picking up on her desire not to tell her brother about Megan or almost being run down the previous day. "I'm going to take off, Annie. I'll let you catch up with your brother."

"What about the designs?"

"Can you bring them by the bar tomorrow?"

"Of course." She walked him to the door and followed him into the hallway, pulling the door closed behind her so that her brother couldn't hear them. "Griffin, wait. I'm sorry you got hurt."

"It's not a big deal."

"I appreciate the way you protected me. And it was a fun evening…until the last few minutes. I wish things hadn't ended up the way they did," she said, giving him a wistful smile.

"It was fun," he agreed. "You should get back to your brother."

"Thanks for not saying anything about Megan and...you know. I don't want my family to worry."

"I figured. I'll see you tomorrow."

"What time is good?"

"I'm going to be out in the morning. Maybe around noon. Would that work?"

"Sure." There were things she wanted to say, but Griffin seemed uninterested in more conversation right now. She could hardly blame him. "I'll see you then."

Griffin turned and walked down the hall. She watched him until he was out of sight and then went back into her apartment. Hunter had grabbed a soda out of the fridge and was working his way through a bag of pretzels while he leaned against the kitchen counter.

"So, what are you doing here?" she asked. "I thought you were still on your road trip."

"I am. I've been in Mexico the last two weeks, and decided I'd stop in to see you on my way up the coast."

"It is good to see you, but I think your face is swelling up. Are you sure you don't want some ice?"

"Not the first fist I've taken this trip," he muttered.

Her gaze narrowed. "I don't think I like the sound of that."

"That guy knows how to fight. Who is he? What's his deal?"

"He's a friend. He saved me from a shark attack last week."

Hunter raised an eyebrow. "Wait? What?"

"I guess you have been out of touch. I was in the ocean when some sharks got really close. Griffin was surfing. He rescued me."

"And he's still rescuing you," Hunter said speculatively. "That guy got the jump on me really fast. It didn't feel like it was the first time he'd done that."

It hadn't felt like that to her, either. "I don't know what to say. He runs a bar. I guess he's used to dealing with potential trouble in a fast way."

"Something else is going on," Hunter said. "Are you really going to make me grill you, Annie?"

She sighed. "If I tell you, will it stay between us? Because it's bad enough that the family is still reeling from my shark attack. I don't want them to start worrying again."

"What would they be worrying about?"

"First you have to promise."

"Fine, I promise."

"Yesterday, I was talking to a woman outside Griffin's bar when a car came out of nowhere and almost ran us both down. This woman has a troubled past," she said vaguely. "I didn't know that at the time, but apparently someone tracked her down who wanted to hurt her. I was in the wrong place at the wrong time."

"You seem to be making a habit of that. Did the woman get hurt?"

"No. I was the one with lightning-fast reflexes yesterday. I shoved her out of the way. The woman is being protected and is no longer in this city. It's all good now. I'm not in danger, but I think both Griffin and I were a little on edge after what happened yesterday. That's why he jumped on you so fast."

"Are you sure you're not in danger?"

"I was never the target, just an unlucky bystander."

"Damn, Annie, trouble follows you around, doesn't it?"

"Enough about me. What is going on with you? Are you still filled with wanderlust? Or are you ready to go home now?"

"I'll be home for Christmas, but I'm not planning to put down roots any time soon."

"Where will you go next?"

"I'm thinking about heading east, taking the southern route to avoid the winter snow and stopping wherever looks interesting."

While she loved to travel, she'd never been inspired to

just drop out of life and head off on her own for months on
end. The family had been speculating for months that
Hunter's wanderlust was fueled by something he wasn't
talking about, but so far no one had come up with any solid
motivation beyond his desire to just do something different
for a while. Hunter had been a firefighter since his early
twenties, and he was thirty now.

"Is this about your thirtieth birthday?" she asked. "Are
you having some sort of early mid-life crisis?"

"No crisis. I just feel like seeing the world while I'm
young enough to enjoy it."

"You'll be young enough to enjoy it for a few more
decades, Hunter. You know, we have bets on why you really
took a leave of absence from the department."

"Really? What are the bets?"

"Dylan thinks you got spooked on that fire last year when
the woman you tried to rescue didn't make it."

"That's not it."

"Ian said you probably ran up some gambling debts and
had to leave town to avoid getting your legs broken."

"Nice vote of confidence from my brother."

"Kate suggested you slept with a married woman whose
husband threatened to kill you if you didn't leave town."

"Another nod to my brilliance."

"And Mia thinks you're lonely because everyone else is
getting married and you don't have a girlfriend."

"That's pathetic. What do you think?"

She considered his question. "I think you're either
looking for something or running away from something. I'm
not sure which. Want to clear it up for me?"

"I just like to travel."

"Liar."

"What about you? Last I heard you were jobless,
homeless, and had no-one to spend your birthday with."

"Thanks for making me sound pathetic. Look, I might not
have a job, but I have a sweet deal on this place, and I have
friends who just aren't particularly close to me at this point,

but it's fine. I don't need a birthday party. And I'm okay with my life. I'm interviewing for a new job on Friday and I'm teaching, freelancing on some art projects. It's all good."

"And the bar guy? You're into him, aren't you?" Hunter gave her a knowing look.

"Maybe. But it's new, so we'll see. It probably didn't help that you gave him a black eye."

"He came at me first. I was just defending myself."

"Next time, call and give me a heads-up."

"I will. Can I crash here tonight? I'm tired."

"You look like you haven't slept in a week. What exactly were you doing in Mexico?"

"Drinking a lot of tequila."

She didn't believe him for a second. Not that Hunter couldn't party with the best of them, but there was something off, and she just didn't know what it was. "I'm really tired of men who don't want to share. What is it with you guys? Why does everything have to be a secret?"

"We're not talking about me anymore, are we? There's something about that guy that's bugging you."

"He just doesn't like to talk about himself, but then neither do you."

"All I can say is trust your instincts. If you think something is off, don't dismiss it. Figure it out before you get in any deeper."

"That's surprisingly good advice."

He laughed. "Do you have any food besides these pretzels?"

"I can scramble you some eggs."

"You're now my favorite sister."

"Yeah, yeah. Maybe you should take a shower while I'm cooking. You smell kind of ripe."

"Good idea."

As Hunter went into the bedroom, she frowned, feeling more than a little concerned about him. She hoped that it was just fatigue and too much tequila that had put him in this state, but she didn't really think that was it.

—▶◀—

Hunter was gone when Annie got up on Thursday morning, leaving her a scrawled *thanks for everything* on the back of a take-out menu. She didn't know why he'd taken off so early, but it was just as well. She wanted to take her designs over to the Depot and then she needed to spend the rest of the day working on her pitch for her job interview tomorrow.

After a quick breakfast on the deck, where she spent too much time looking for Griffin out on the waves, she took another look at the two designs for the holiday party and did a bit more tweaking. After finishing that, she still had an hour before she needed to leave for the Depot, and Hunter's words from the night before kept going around in her head: *Trust your instincts. If you think something is off, don't dismiss it. Figure it out before you get in any deeper.*

She didn't normally stalk guys, preferring to make her own judgment after she met them, but maybe she should find out what the Internet knew about Griffin Hale.

Grabbing her computer, she entered his name into the search engine.

The first few results were for a professional golfer named Griffin Hale, who was at least ten years older than her Griffin and thirty pounds heavier. She dug a little deeper, checking out various social media sites, but there was no sign of Griffin. When she put in the Depot, the owner of the business came up as Barrel Enterprises. She searched on the company but couldn't find any names. Maybe Griffin and Vinnie were Barrel Enterprises, but if they were, they'd done a good job of hiding their personal stake in the company.

Frowning, her uneasiness growing, she spent another thirty minutes putting in search terms, but the only photos she could find were of the Depot and its customers. Although, there was the photo of her and Griffin after the shark attack, but his name had not been mentioned in the caption.

She probably shouldn't be surprised she couldn't find

anything about him on the Internet. He definitely guarded his privacy. And she doubted he ever spent time on social media. But as she closed her computer, she couldn't shake the gut feeling that something was off.

Her heart told her that Griffin was a good guy. She'd seen his protective side. She'd watched him with Megan and with Vinnie. People liked him. She liked him. But he was hiding something, and until she knew what it was, she needed to be careful.

Despite that promise to herself, she couldn't help the excited feeling that ran through her when she got to the bar just before noon. Lunch was in full swing, almost every table taken. She was surprised to see Justin there. She thought he generally worked nights.

"Hey, what happened to you in class yesterday?" she asked, as he came over, a sheepish smile on his face.

"I had problems with my car, and then I missed the bus. Sorry. I got the notes from a friend. I'll be working on my final project starting this weekend."

"That's good. Is Griffin around? I have my initial design drafts for him to look at."

"He's in his apartment. Why don't you go on up?"

She hesitated, not sure she should invade his personal space. On the other hand, she wouldn't mind seeing where he actually lived, and it wasn't like he didn't know she was coming by.

As she climbed the stairs and passed by Megan's closed door, she was reminded of the last time she'd been upstairs. Hopefully, there would not be as much drama this time around.

She knocked on Griffin's door, taking a deep breath as she heard footsteps. She felt nervous, excited, and wary all at the same time.

Griffin opened the door and her smile faded when she saw the dark-purple bruise around his left eye. "Oh, my God, your face. It's so much worse than I thought."

He put a few fingers to his eye. "It doesn't feel as bad as

it looks. Your brother packs a good punch."

"Hunter was the youngest of my three brothers; he had a lot of practice fighting with them. I feel awful about this."

"I told you last night it wasn't your fault. Your brother came out of nowhere. I reacted a little more extremely than I should have."

"But after what happened with Megan—"

"I was on edge."

"So was I," she admitted. "I have the designs. Can I come in?"

He hesitated. "We can do it downstairs."

"It's really crowded down there. Why don't you show me your apartment?" *How was she ever going to get into Griffin's life if he wouldn't even let her into his home?*

"All right, but there's not much to see." He stepped back and waved her inside.

Griffin was right. His apartment was very basic, not even as nice as the one Megan had stayed in, which had also been pretty sparse.

In the living room was a black couch, glass coffee table, and a brown chair with an ottoman. A newspaper was spread out on the table along with a half-filled coffee mug. Two barstools faced the small kitchen island where there was a bag of apples and another bag of oranges.

She searched for something personal, but she didn't see a single photograph anywhere in the living room and the only pictures on the wall were watercolors of surfers that looked like they'd probably been picked up at one of the local art fairs.

"What's the verdict?" Griffin asked.

"It definitely looks like a guy's apartment."

"You could have said something worse, so I'll go with that." He waved her toward the couch. "Let's see your designs."

"Okay." She took a seat and then pulled a folder out of her bag. She opened it and placed the two designs side by side on the coffee table. "This first one, as you can see, plays

off the theme of trains, which I know kids love, and it fits
with the Depot."

Griffin picked up the sketch, taking a long look at the trio
of train cars winding their way up a mountain of dreams, the
first car showing a female driving the train—the woman had
been modeled off Deb Johnson, the manager of Hamilton
House. The second car was filled with hopeful kids, and the
third car filled with presents. Swirling around the
mountaintop were clouds filled with inspiring words: love,
peace, joy, share, and family.

"This is great," he said. "There's so much detail."

"Take a look at the other one, too," she said, handing him
the second sketch.

She'd gone a more traditional holiday direction—a tall
Christmas tree set in the Depot. Kids' names were etched on
the colored ornament balls, and there were piles of presents
under the tree. Santa sat in a royal chair and a nearby
doorway showed three kids running into the room, excited to
see what Santa had brought.

"This is good, too," he murmured. "You're really
talented, Annie. These kids look so real."

"I like drawing characters. So, which one?"

"Which one do you like?" he returned.

She shook her head. "No way. You're the client. You
pick."

"Well, I can't lose because they're both better than I could
have imagined. I think I like the train the best. The mountain
imagery feels inspiring."

She grinned. "That was my favorite. We're finally on the
same page. That's printer-ready, by the way."

"Perfect." As he handed her the discarded sketch, he said,
"This drawing did remind me of something else I have to do
today."

"What's that?"

"Get a Christmas tree."

"That's fun. Are you going to cut one down?"

"I was thinking about going to a shopping center and just

bringing one back."

"That's no fun. You should drive down the coast to one of the Christmas tree farms. The tree will be really fresh, and it will last longer. That's really the only way to go. Not that you asked for my opinion."

He laughed. "I never ask for your opinion, and yet I always get it."

The teasing light in his eyes lessened the harshness of that remark. "Lucky you, because I have very good opinions."

"Okay. Then you're coming with me."

"What?" she asked, surprised by his words. "You want me to come with you? Most days you try to get rid of me."

"Well, that hasn't worked, and I'm not cutting down this tree alone. Plus, left to my own devices, who knows how bad a tree I would pick?"

"Good point. Judging by this apartment, you don't put a lot of thought into how things look."

"We can drop off the sketch at the printer on the way," he said, getting to his feet. "I'm going to grab a jacket."

As Griffin went into the bedroom, she got up from the couch and meandered around the living room. There was nothing of personal significance in the room. She knew he wasn't close to his family, but it seemed odd for there to be nothing. It wasn't like he was subletting the place from someone else, and he hadn't just moved in; he'd been there for two years, he'd said. On the other hand, he was a guy, and she'd seen enough of her brothers' apartments over the years to know that men did not think the same way about their living space as women did.

"Ready to go?" Griffin asked, returning to the room with a black leather jacket over his dark-gray sweater and black jeans.

He looked so handsome, her mouth watered. Going with him was probably another bad idea but there was no way she was bailing now. As they left the apartment, she said, "What kind of tree are you looking for?"

"Something big and green."

"Well, that narrows it down. I think you need me, Griffin."

His blue eyes darkened as he looked at her. "I think I do, too."

And suddenly, she didn't think they were talking about Christmas trees anymore.

Twelve

— ►►◄◄ ◄ —

Griffin regretted his impulsive comment the minute it left his mouth. Fortunately, Annie had let it go, which was unusual, since she rarely seemed to let anything go. But she was unusually quiet on their way to the printer, and he found himself needing to break the silence on their way to the Christmas tree farm.

"Do you cut down a tree every year?" he asked.

"No, I haven't done it in years."

He shot her a surprised look. "After the lecture you gave me earlier?"

She smiled. "The last few years I've barely had room in my apartment for a couch, much less tree. But when I was a kid, we used to go down to Half Moon Bay—it's on the coast south of San Francisco. They didn't just have trees to cut down; there were also pony rides, sleigh rides, hot apple cider and hot chocolate with marshmallows. I have a lot of great memories. It would always take us a long time to pick a tree, too. My parents insisted we had to agree, and with six kids, that wasn't easy."

"I bet you were the last to give in."

"I could be stubborn. So could Dylan; he's the oldest, and he always liked being in charge. In fact, he still does."

"I can't imagine being one of six kids. How did you even fit in one car?"

"We didn't. When we went somewhere all together, we had to be in two cars."

"You said your dad is a retired firefighter?"

"Yes, but he's not really retired. He helps his brother, my Uncle Kevin, with his construction business."

"What does your mom do?"

"She's a nurse in the neonatal intensive care. She takes care of the really sick babies, and she is great at it. When I was in high school, I used to volunteer to go in and hold a baby after school. They need that human contact, and sometimes their mom isn't well enough to do it, and there are only so many nurses. I liked it, but sometimes it made me sad when things didn't end happily. I like good to win out."

He flung her a thoughtful glance, seeing the seriousness in her expression. Annie had a big heart, that was for sure, and she was definitely looking for a happily-ever-after—a reminder that he probably wasn't the person to give her that. He looked back at the road. "Did you have a big Christmas every year?"

"Absolutely. Our family is very Catholic, so the religious part of the holiday was important. Going to midnight Mass was part of our tradition, even when we were little. Sometimes I think they kept us up late on Christmas Eve so we'd have to sleep in on Christmas Day. But once we got up, it was mayhem, big family breakfast, presents in our PJs and then we'd play with our toys and get dressed for an extended family dinner at someone's house, which could be forty or more people. It was a lot, but it was always fun."

He felt an odd wave of envy. The Christmases in his life had always been small, and even when they'd gotten bigger, it was only because there were more strangers around, not family, not people who he really felt connected to. He cleared his throat, not wanting to think about his past, when Annie's was much more interesting. "Are you going home for the holiday this year?"

"Yes. I missed Thanksgiving. I was caught up with moving, and I just didn't feel like making the trip up north. But if I don't go home for Christmas, I have a feeling I'll have more siblings showing up down here."

"Maybe they can give you a heads-up first, or at least not come out of the shadows when I'm around."

"Hunter was impressed with your attack skills. He said you had lightning-fast moves. Where did you get those?"

"I grew up in a rough neighborhood."

"What neighborhood was that? Care to pinpoint an area less broad than the Midwest?"

He really didn't want to tell her outright lies. He didn't know why. He'd had no problem lying to a lot of other people.

"Griffin? Why the mystery? What aren't you telling me?"

"I don't like to talk about the past or where I grew up, because it's not happy. It doesn't make me feel good, and it certainly wouldn't make you feel good. I like to live in the present."

"I looked you up on the Internet."

His gut tightened at her words. "Oh, yeah, what did you find out?"

"That the Internet doesn't know anything more about you than I do."

He was relieved to hear that. He'd checked online—more than once—but not in the past few weeks.

"Your name isn't even mentioned in connection to the bar. It says it's owned by Barrel Enterprises, which I assume must be you and Vinnie."

"What exactly are you trying to find out, Annie?"

"I'd like to know if you're a good guy."

"If you didn't think I was, would you really be sitting in my car right now? It's your brother, isn't it? He got into your head last night."

"Hunter might have said a few things," she admitted.

"But nothing I wasn't already considering. I just don't know why you're so secretive when I'm clearly an open book. Do you think I'll judge you?"

She was probably the least judgmental person he'd ever met. "No."

"Then tell me something about your past."

"I grew up outside of Chicago, but I have moved around a lot since I became an adult. I've lived in New York, New Jersey, Boston, New Orleans, Houston and eventually made it all the way to the west coast.

"You and my Hunter have more in common than the ability to throw a quick punch. He likes to wander, too. So, you were born in Chicago, huh?"

"Outside of Chicago, in the suburbs," he corrected.

"You grew up with cold, white Christmases. You don't miss them?"

"There are some things I miss about Chicago, but winter isn't one of them."

She turned sideways in her seat and had a feeling the information he'd given her still wasn't enough. "What about women? Girlfriends? Have you had any?"

"A few."

"Anyone serious? Anyone you wanted to marry?"

His gut clenched at that question. "Yes. There was one serious relationship, but it didn't work out."

"Why not? What happened?"

"We didn't love each other enough," he said simply, realizing that was probably the truest thing he'd told her.

"I'm sorry it didn't work out."

"I'm not. I'm glad we figured that out before we made things permanent. How about you, Annie? Ever made it close to the altar?"

"No. I've had a couple of boyfriends. One lasted about two years in my early twenties. Nothing dramatic broke us up. We just realized we weren't that awesome together. We were more likely to bring out the worst in each other than the best."

He was continually taken aback by how candid Annie was. He wished he could be as honest with her.

"Hey, there's a sign for the Christmas tree farm," she said. "It's the next left."

He turned off the main highway and took a side road to the farm. They parked in a dirt lot and then got out of the car.

The sun was shining more brightly now, bringing a warmth to the sea air. They picked up a saw at the counter and then Annie suggested they go toward the back where the bigger trees were. He wasn't that picky about trees and would have been happy to chop down the first one that seemed fairly symmetrical, but Annie clearly had other ideas.

"It doesn't have to be perfect," he told her.

"Not perfect but perfectly right," she said with a smile. "Let's keep looking."

They spent several more minutes roaming through lines of trees. Annie might not be judgmental about people, but when it came to Christmas trees, she had a lot of opinions. One was too short, another too thin, one was lopsided, another had sagging branches. He didn't think he'd ever spent so much time studying trees. But he wasn't going to complain, because it felt good to be out of the bar, and more importantly to be with her.

Finally, she paused in front of a nine-foot tree. "What about this one?"

"Looks good to me, but then so have the last dozen."

She walked around the tree, viewing it from a few different directions. "I like it. I think we found our tree, Griffin."

He wished he didn't like the way she'd said *our* so much. It made him think of spending Christmas with Annie. Images of the two of them decorating a tree in front of a roaring fire with Christmas music on in the background shot through his head, and he was truly stunned that his brain had gone there. He'd never had that kind of idyllic Christmas. Why he would even consider he could have it with her was beyond him.

He really needed to get Annie out of his life fast. She was

making him want things he'd never had and things he never could have.

He hadn't had this problem before. He'd always been able to compartmentalize his life, but Annie's bright light was spilling into every dark corner of his life, and while he knew what to do about it, he just didn't know if he could. It had been a long time since he'd felt connected to anyone. Surprisingly, it felt pretty good. Almost normal. *Almost…*

"Griffin," Annie said, waving her hand in a questioning motion. "What are you waiting for? This tree isn't going to chop itself down."

"Right." He put his mind on the task at hand. He'd get rid of Annie later—much later.

After cutting down the tree, an attendant helped them wrap it and tie it to the rack on top of his SUV.

As he drove out of the lot and north on Highway 1, he knew he wasn't ready to take her home because when he did, he would have to say goodbye and mean it. "Are you hungry?" he asked.

"I am. Do you want to stop? Can we do that with the tree?"

"I don't think anyone will steal it. There's a café down the road a few miles from here. But I don't want to keep you from prepping for your interview tomorrow."

"I can do that tonight. I'd love to have lunch."

"Okay, good." A moment later, he turned in to the parking lot in front of the Fantastic Fish Shack.

"They're not shy about their food proclamations," Annie said with a laugh as they got out of the car. "Is the fish *fantastic*?"

"I've had fish tacos, fish and chips, a filet of cod sandwich, and a crab omelet, and they've all been good."

"You come out here often." She gave him a questioning look.

"I do. It's a great surfing spot." He opened the door for her. "After you."

He followed Annie into the open, airy restaurant whose

wall of windows overlooked the beach. A large aquarium ran the length of another wall and the décor was definitely ocean related.

"Patio or inside?" the hostess asked.

He tipped his head to Annie. "Your call. Will you be cold outside?"

"No, I think it will be perfect."

"We'll take the patio."

The hostess picked up some menus and led them outside. It was almost three, late for lunch, so there was only one other couple outside enjoying their meal.

"Wow, another spectacular view," Annie said, taking a seat by the rail, while he sat down across from her. She glanced back at him. "Everywhere I look these days, I see the ocean."

"It never gets old."

"It doesn't. I can see why you like this beach. It's very isolated," she added with a teasing smile.

He couldn't help but smile back at her. As much as he tried to keep a solid line between them, Annie kept crossing over it. He wanted to lean across the table and kiss the smile right off her lips, but then what?

He knew the answer, but he also knew he couldn't go there. So, maybe it was a good thing there was a table between them.

Annie's cheeks heated up with pink, and he didn't think it was completely due to the sun.

"You're staring," she told him.

"How can I not? You're beautiful, Annie."

Her lips parted as her gaze widened. "Well…I wasn't expecting you to say that." She tucked a strand of hair behind her ear, then looked down at the menu, clearly uncomfortable with his words.

He liked that she was flustered by his comment, that she didn't even know how pretty she was. He couldn't remember going out with a woman who was such a mix of sexy and sweet. He wanted to help her off with her clothes and wrap her up in his arms.

With his body hardening uncomfortably, he also directed his attention to the menu, the words blurring in front of his eyes.

The waitress set down two glasses of ice water, and he drained half of his in one gulp.

"I'm going to have the crab salad," Annie said.

"I'll do the same," he added, as they handed their menus to the waitress.

"I feel like we're playing hooky," Annie said. "Hanging at the beach in the middle of the day on a Thursday afternoon."

"You should enjoy your free time while you can."

"I know. As stressful as it is not to have a job, I have enjoyed having some time to myself. The last ten years have been really busy: school, work, more school, more work."

"Everyone needs to regroup now and then."

"Which you obviously did when you went into the bar business. How did you come up with the name Barrel Enterprises? Is it for a wine barrel?"

"No," he said with a small laugh. "Barrel is also a surfing term. It's the space inside a breaking wave. When you're in the barrel, you can be completely hidden from view. It's a difficult but thrilling ride."

"That makes more sense. Is Vinnie a surfer, too? I can't quite picture him on the waves. He's so—solid."

"He mostly likes to paddle out, hang out on his board, and then when he's over it, he paddles back in. So, he does have a board, and he does go out, but I rarely see him catch a wave."

"Isn't that the most fun of all?"

"It's definitely fun, and I love it. But there is also something peaceful about just being out on the water, away from the shore, from reality. Vinnie seems to enjoy that the most. But he doesn't spend a lot of time out there. He's good for twenty or thirty minutes, and then he's bored. I could stay out there for hours."

She nodded. "You definitely like solitude."

He shrugged. "I can't deny that."

"You told me earlier that you met Vinnie through friends? He's a bit older than you, isn't he?"

"He's forty-five, so eleven years older than me."

"Wait, you just told me your age—thirty-four. Another detail slips past your defenses."

He smiled at the triumphant gleam in her eyes. "My age has never been a secret."

"Unlike every other part of your life."

"You're just nosy, Annie."

"Well, I can't deny that," she said, repeating his words. "But I prefer to use words like curious, interested, attentive."

Her smile warmed him all the way through. He loved how willing she was to admit to her faults, even if she did want to cover them up with prettier words. "I'll bet you do."

She rested her arms on the table as she gave him a thoughtful look. "I think this is the most relaxed I've ever seen you."

"I'm tired from cutting down the tree."

She rolled her eyes. "That was super easy."

"Hey, I was the one doing the work; you were just directing."

"Well, we make a good team." She gave him a mischievous grin. "I'm the brains; you're the brawn."

"I'm good with that," he said, feeling as relaxed as she'd just mentioned. It felt like centuries since he'd embarked on some light-hearted flirting with a beautiful woman—a woman he felt like he could be himself with. Although, that was part of the problem. Annie reminded him of who he used to be, and he couldn't be that person again.

"Oh, you're good with it," Annie said with a gleam in her eyes. "Or we can make it good with another little kiss."

"That would definitely work," he agreed.

"But..." She tipped her head toward the approaching waitress, who was bringing their food. "I think it will have to wait."

"We will wait," he agreed. "But when it happens—it won't be a *little* kiss."

Heat ran through her gaze and warmed her cheeks, but she remained silent as she sat back in her seat and the waitress set their food on the table. He'd probably just made a promise he *shouldn't* keep. But he knew he would.

"This looks perfect," Annie said, changing the subject as she picked up her fork.

"Hopefully fantastic."

"I'm counting on that."

He dug into thick pieces of crab, avocado and tomato with hungry delight. It had been hours since his very skimpy breakfast of oatmeal and an orange.

"I hope Megan's trial goes well tomorrow," Annie said, several minutes later. "I keep thinking about her. Do you ever hear what happens to people after they leave?"

"I don't ask."

"You're not curious about them? Because I'm dying to know what's going to happen to Megan after she does whatever she has to do. I really want her to be safe. I want her to have a life."

"Hopefully, she will, but you can't give that life to her."

"Maybe I could help. I genuinely liked her."

"She liked you, too. But you have to let her go. This was just a stopover in her life. She's not coming back."

"Couldn't she come back if she wanted to—once she's safe?"

"Of course. I always tell people that, but when they're at the Depot, they're not themselves. They're just pretending. And they usually are happy to be done with the pretense, to be back in their old life."

"Megan isn't her name, is it?"

"No. And before you ask—I don't know her real name. I'm not keeping it from you."

"That I believe." She paused. "By the way, this fish is as *fantastic* as the sign proclaimed."

"I'm so glad the restaurant didn't let you down."

"It was definitely not false advertising." She wiped her mouth with a napkin. "Are you going to decorate the tree when we get back?"

"I'll do that tomorrow morning when we're closed."

"You're going to need a lot of ornaments."

"I have some, but I'm probably going to have to get more," he agreed.

"Maybe I could contribute. I have a big box of ornaments that I'm not going to use this year, and most of them are handmade. They would add a nice, warm touch to the tree, unless you're going for something more sophisticated."

"You should use them yourself, Annie. Put up your own tree."

"Not this year. I'd rather let you borrow them."

"What if they break or someone takes one? I wouldn't feel right about it."

"Most of them are not breakable, they're just fun." She paused. "My mom used to give each of us kids an ornament every Christmas. It was often about what we were doing at the time, a sport, or playing a musical instrument or dancing, something that would fit us personally. She took a lot of care in doing it. When we turned eighteen, she gave us each our eighteen ornaments and said they'd be our starter set for our trees as adults."

Annie's childhood sounded wonderful and nothing like his own. "You definitely don't want to put those ornaments on my bar tree."

"I wasn't going to give you those. They're...special."

He saw a glittering light of moisture in her eyes. "Something about Christmas makes you a little sad. What is it?"

"Hey, you have your secrets; I have mine."

"I guess I can't argue with that." But he found himself wanting to know what had brought the surprising tears to her eyes. Unfortunately, for the first time in forever, Annie didn't seem inclined to share.

She sat back as the waitress asked them if they wanted

anything else.

As Annie gave a negative shake of her head, he said, "We'll take the check."

"Here you go." The waitress handed him the check and then cleared their plates.

He put down some cash and then looked at Annie, who was gazing out at the ocean, lost in thought. "Annie?"

She turned back to him. "I guess I feel a little sad this year because I'm rootless. I'm living in an apartment that isn't mine. I don't have a job. Putting up a tree just doesn't feel right. I'm kind of a loser at the moment."

"That's not true."

"My siblings are so on top of their games, living their lives, doing important things, and I'm stuck." She let out a breath. "And obviously I am not good at keeping my thoughts to myself. It's just that I don't have a lot of people to talk to right now. I'm sure I'm really attractive with my pathetic loser talk right now."

"You're not a loser. You're just gearing up for the next step. And I wish you could be unattractive, because that would make things a lot simpler."

"You always want things to be simple, but hardly anything is."

"That's true."

Her gaze met his. "What are we doing, Griffin?"

He drew in a breath at her blunt question. "I don't know."

"You run hot and cold with me. I never know which Griffin I'm going to get."

"I'm sorry about that. Here's the thing, Annie—I'm not looking for a relationship. I don't want to be responsible for someone else's happiness. I don't want to worry about them or have them worry about me. I don't want to lead you on."

She swallowed hard, looking a bit hurt at his words, but she gave a nod.

"I get it, Griffin. I'm not looking for a relationship, either. I don't even know where I'm going to be next week or six months from now. And for the record, I never asked you for anything. Men like to assume women all want the same thing, but that's not necessarily true. Sometimes, it's just about having a little fun. You're not against fun, are you?" she challenged, new fire in her green eyes.

"I'm definitely not against fun," he said dryly. "As long as it doesn't come with strings. And you are the kind of woman who usually comes with strings."

She lifted her arms in the air. "No strings here. How about we walk on the beach before we go back to the bar? I see some stairs over there. Or is that too much of a commitment for you?"

"I'm going to regret putting my cards on the table, aren't I?"

"I guess we'll find out."

Thirteen

They walked on the beach for almost thirty minutes, not talking much, and if they did talk, it wasn't about anything too important. That was fine with Annie. Things had gotten a little too serious at the restaurant. Although, she appreciated Griffin putting his cards on the table and at least admitting there was something brewing between them, she hadn't cared for his immediate dismissal about any possible relationship. But she didn't want to make herself a liar for saying she didn't care about the long-term potential, so she was going to keep things cool, see what happened.

There were a lot of variables in her life right now, and until she knew where she was going to work and live, thinking about a serious relationship was not a good idea anyway.

But fun was a different story, and she was enjoying her day with Griffin. He had relaxed, opened up a little, smiled more than once, flirted and teased. And while he didn't talk as much as she would like, he was a good listener. He was supportive and interested, and even though he still kept a wall of privacy around himself, she was starting to feel like there was a friendship building, along with all the sparks.

When they reached an outcropping of rocks, barring them from going any farther, they turned back around. But she wasn't quite ready to return to the car. She dropped her shoes on the ground, having preferred to walk barefoot on the beach rather than ruin her ankle boots. "Let's sit for a minute."

Griffin joined her on the sand, stretching out his legs in front of him.

She looked up and down the expanse of beach. "There's absolutely no one around. It feels a little odd."

"I like it."

"Big surprise," she said dryly.

He tipped his head. "We're very different, Annie. You love being around people. I like being alone."

"It probably has something to do with the way we grew up. I shared a bedroom with my twin sisters until I was thirteen."

"What changed then?"

"My oldest brother Dylan went to college. He was not thrilled when I took down all his sports posters and put up my art, but he had to deal."

"You must have driven your brothers crazy."

"Oh, and my sisters, too," she said with a laugh. "I think that's the middle child's job, right?"

"I wouldn't know. It must have been really loud growing up in your house."

"Super loud," she agreed. "But now it feels like that time went by in a flash. Ian was the quietest of the bunch. He only got into trouble when he started conducting experiments in the garage and almost blew up the house. Did I tell you he's a genius?"

"You said something about that. What kind of science does he do?"

"No idea. I know he was working on a clean water filtration system for third world countries until last year. Now he's doing something else; I'm not sure what. When he talks, I usually zone out, because it's way over my head. But he fell in love with an elementary school teacher last Christmas, and Grace has brought him down to earth. They're a great couple. They really balance each other out. Ian and Dylan are actually having a double wedding in February."

"That sounds fun. Are you in the wedding?"

"No. Because it's a double wedding, they decided to just have a best man and a maid of honor for each of them. Grace picked my cousin Emma. They've gotten close because they have an Ireland connection—long story. Tori picked a friend of hers from high school. Hunter is going to be Ian's best man, and my cousin Burke, who works with Dylan at the firehouse, is going to stand up for Dylan." She paused. "You should really tell me when you're completely bored with the conversation, because I do tend to run on."

"Your rambling conversations are growing on me," he said lightly.

"Probably because when I talk you don't have to."

"That's a fair point."

"Tell me something about your family, Griffin. How old were you when your mom died?"

"I was ten."

"That's really young. I'm sorry."

"It was a big loss for me."

"Was it an illness or something else?"

"She had an autoimmune disease. She'd had it for a long time, but it just went off the rails, and they couldn't save her."

"Off the rails sounds like a train analogy." She cocked her head to one side. "What's the deal with you and trains? Did you have a train set when you were a kid?"

"Actually, I did. It was my mom's train when she was a child, and then it was mine. She loved that train, and so did I." His gaze grew distant. "We'd spend hours playing with it. After she passed away, it was probably the only thing I did for a long time. It made me feel closer to her." He cleared his throat. "I'd forgotten about that."

"Do you still have the train?"

"I don't know where it ended up. I moved in with my grandparents when I was a teenager, and it did not go with me."

"Maybe your father has it."

"I doubt it. It doesn't matter."

She thought it mattered more than he was saying. In fact, the story about the train felt like the first thing he'd told her that was really true, really personal. Not that she thought he was lying about other stuff, but it always felt like he was choosing his words very carefully. With the train, he hadn't done that.

"We should go," he said, getting to his feet.

She wasn't surprised by the abrupt move. Whenever she got closer to him, Griffin tended to bail. But the day was moving on, and she still needed to work on the sketches for her interview.

As they walked back to the car, she couldn't help but try to get a bit more information before she lost him completely. "It sounds like you and your mom were close."

"That's the way I remember it. Are you close to your mom?"

"I am. She worked really hard to make sure each of us kids got our own time with her and also with my dad. It wasn't easy. There were a lot of us. Even though I am in the middle, I never felt neglected. I just sometimes didn't feel like I really impressed anyone. I wasn't following in the family business. I wasn't changing the world. It's hard to be an average achiever in a family of high achievers."

"You've said that before. I think you're being too hard on yourself, Annie. Frankly, most people don't change the world. You're lucky if you can change yourself or some small situation in a positive way."

"I suppose, but shouldn't I be striving to get to the high bar?"

"I'm not saying you shouldn't reach for the moon, but don't be surprised if you come up with a handful of air. That's reality."

"And that's why I prefer to create my own reality in my art. When my characters reach for the moon, they get there. They conquer demons. They save people. They make the world better. That's what makes them superheroes. And, yes, I know superheroes aren't real, but it's fun to think that they could be."

"As long as you know the difference between fantasy and reality."

"I do, but don't people ever surprise you by doing something good? Because you surprised me when I found out you were a bar owner helping people in trouble."

"That's hardly the work of a superhero. And practically speaking, I get cheap labor for the time that they're with me."

"Don't try to knock it down," she said as they climbed the stairs leading back to the restaurant parking lot. "Just let it be something good. Accept the compliment. And next time someone tries to thank you for saving her life, you might just say you're welcome, instead of how did you find me and what are you doing here."

"Point taken. But I'm beginning to think you could have held your own with those sharks. Maybe talked them into fleeing," he joked. "Conversation is your superhero power."

"Very funny," she said, as they got into the car.

She wasn't offended by his remark. In fact, she actually felt more connected to him when he was teasing her. And she did talk too much. But today she'd gotten Griffin to open up, too, and she was going to consider that her superhero power.

When they returned to the bar, Annie helped Griffin get the tree off the top of the car. They carried it into the back hallway and leaned it up against the wall as Vinnie came out of the kitchen.

"Glad you're back," he said, a serious note in his voice. "Can I talk to you a minute, Griffin?"

"Sure. Is there a problem?"

"Maybe. Maybe not."

She saw Vinnie give her a look and realized he wasn't going to explain his issue in front of her. Griffin came to the same conclusion.

"Are you taking off, Annie?" he asked her.

"Yes. I'm just going to use the restroom first."

"Good luck with your interview tomorrow."

"Thanks. Maybe I'll drop those ornaments off in the morning, unless you're going to decorate tonight."

"That will be tomorrow's job."

"Then I'll see you later."

As she entered the restroom, she heard Vinnie say, "I'm telling you some shit is going down with our bank account."

Curiosity made her leave the door slightly open, and while it appeared the men had moved down the hall to the office, their conversation was fairly loud.

"I'm sure it's just a glitch," Griffin said.

"You better hope so. Or we're not going to make it through the Christmas season."

She frowned at Vinnie's words. The bar was always crowded. How could they be short on money?

"And Shari was late again today," Vinnie continued. "Not only that, when I took the trash out, some dude in a van was yelling at her. It looked heated. He took off when he saw me."

"Did you ask her about it?"

"She said the guy followed her into the lot, saying she cut him off in traffic, that he was a crazy road rage driver. She told me not to worry. But after what happened the other day, I don't like it. And now with all this other banking shit—"

"Yeah, I get it," Griffin said. "We need to look into it— all of it."

As the office door closed on their discussion, she shut the restroom door and stared at herself in the mirror, questions swirling around in her head. *Had some jerk really followed Shari into the parking lot because he was annoyed she'd cut him off? Could he have possibly been the same man who had tried to run her and Megan down?* Vinnie had said the driver was in a van, not a sedan. That was different, but still…it seemed like a big coincidence.

Was Shari one of Griffin's protected people? Was that why they sounded so worried? There didn't seem to be a lot of love lost between Vinnie and Shari, so why did they keep her around if she was coming in late all the time?

As usual, she had more questions than answers about things that were really none of her business. It was time to head home and focus on her own life.

Fourteen

Annie stayed up late Thursday night and into the early hours of Friday morning, working on her sketches. She'd completed drawings of Griffin, Vinnie, Justin, and Shari, and somewhere in the mix she'd added herself, or a faint version of herself—a female journalist who came to the bar to work on stories on her lunch hour and discovers that the bar is a front for an underground railroad for superheroes in training.

It was probably a crazy idea, but she hoped there was something there that the production company would like.

After grabbing a few hours of sleep, she got up at eight, had breakfast, and dressed for her interview in black jeans, black boots, a silky top and a cream-colored jacket. She left her hair long and flowing about her shoulders, put on the dangly earrings she'd gotten from Kate last Christmas and added a bit more gloss to her lips.

Ready to go, she checked her watch, realizing she still had time to spare before her interview at eleven thirty, but she was going to drive herself crazy pacing around her apartment, so she grabbed the box of ornaments she'd pulled out of the closet and took them down to her car.

Griffin had said he was going to put up the tree this morning, and she wanted him to have them. Plus, she needed a distraction. She didn't want to sit around her apartment, getting more nervous by the minute.

When she reached the Depot, she pulled into the customer parking lot out front, which was currently empty, took the box of ornaments out of the back of her car and walked up to the front door. The closed sign was on the door, and it was locked, so she knocked.

A moment later, Griffin opened the door. Her heart skipped a beat as she looked into his beautiful and somewhat surprised blue eyes. He looked deliciously sexy in dark-gray jeans and a long-sleeved white knit shirt. A bit of sexy scruff on his jaw sent her blood on another racing rush through her body. *She really shouldn't have come here. Every time she saw him, she liked him more, wanted him more...*

"Annie. I thought you'd be on your way to your interview," he said.

"It's not until eleven thirty. I brought you ornaments for the tree."

"Come in." He took the box out of her hands as she entered the bar. "This is heavy."

"I didn't go through it, so there might be some you don't want to use. These aren't my special ornaments, by the way, just ones I've bought over the years. They're not expensive, so if something happens to them, no big deal, but hopefully they'll add some color and fun."

Her gaze moved to the tree in the corner. It wasn't decorated yet, but Griffin had unwrapped the netting and the branches were falling and settling into their proper place. There was also a definite scent of pine in the air.

"It's starting to smell like Christmas," she added with a sniff. "And the tree looks good. It's the perfect height."

"I think so, too."

"I wish I could help you decorate it. It looks like a blank canvas to me, and I'm itching to do something with it."

"Why don't you come by after your interview? I doubt I'll

be done by then. I keep getting interrupted with business problems."

His words reminded her of what she'd overheard yesterday. "Is everything all right? When I left yesterday, Vinnie seemed upset about something."

His lips drew into a hard line as his gaze filled with uneasiness. "Someone hacked into our bank account, which is also tied to our business credit card. We lost some money, but hopefully the bank will be able to get it back and figure out what happened."

"That's terrible." She was not only surprised by his words but also that he'd actually told her something personal. Maybe they were starting to be friends.

"It's not good." He ran a hand through his hair. "But we'll figure it out."

"I'm sure you will. I wish I could help."

"I think only the bank can help at the moment."

"Probably. I better go."

He put a hand on her arm as she turned to leave. She gave him a questioning look.

"For luck," he murmured, surprising her with a warm kiss.

She stared back at him as he lifted his head, trying not to show how much his simple kiss affected her. "Thanks," she said. Then she headed out to the parking lot.

She was still in a light-headed, happy daze from Griffin's kiss when she approached her car, so it took a moment for her to realize that something was wrong. Her gaze narrowed. *What the hell...*

Her back tire was flat. So was her front tire. *Had she run over something?* Both tires were flattened. She walked around the car and realized the other side looked exactly the same.

Lifting her head, her gaze swept the area. The Depot was across the street from a dry-cleaner, an electronics store, an office building, and a car dealership. It wasn't the kind of area where there was a lot of foot traffic. There was no one else around now, and no other cars in the lot besides hers.

But someone had deliberately flattened her tires. She took a closer look, seeing a slash on the front tire that made her feel a little sick at the thought of someone pulling out a knife. She straightened, uneasiness sending goose bumps down her arms.

She backed away from the car and then bolted for the door of the bar. She pounded on the frame, realizing that Griffin had locked it after she left.

When he opened it, she practically fell into his embrace.

He wrapped his arms around her to steady her. "What's wrong, Annie?"

She lifted her head to meet his gaze. "My car...the tires...they're flat...all of them." She stuttered out the words.

"What?"

"Someone slashed my tires."

"Stay here."

He strode out of the bar, and she moved into the doorway, wrapping her arms around herself, feeling cold and a little numb. Griffin made the same circle around her car that she'd taken, then gazed up and down the street.

When he returned to the bar, he pulled her inside and locked the door. "It's going to be okay," he assured her.

"Who would do that to my car?"

"I don't know, but we do have security cameras out front."

As he finished speaking, Vinnie walked into the room, giving them a questioning look.

"Annie, hello. Is something wrong?"

"Someone slashed my tires," she replied. "I was only inside a few minutes. How did it happen that fast?"

"We need to check the cameras," Griffin said, striding across the room.

They followed him into the small back office. As Griffin moved behind the desk, she and Vinnie crowded in behind him. Within minutes, he pulled up three screens, each showing different angles of the customer lot.

"I'll go back in time," Griffin muttered, moving through the camera clips until she saw herself driving into the lot.

They watched silently for the next few minutes. She watched herself get out of the car, grab the box from the backseat, walk to the front door. Then she disappeared inside.

Her pulse sped up as she waited to see what would come next.

It seemed to take forever. Finally, a hooded figure came into the frame. He wore black pants, a big overcoat with a hoodie coming up over his head, and dark glasses over his eyes.

She strained to see some identifying feature, but the man kept his face away from the camera as he squatted down next to the car. He pulled out a knife, the sunlight glinting off the blade, and her heart jumped into her throat.

He slashed the front tire, then moved to the back, keeping low to the ground as he moved around to the other side of the vehicle. It took only a few seconds for him to finish and then he walked out to the street, disappearing into an alley behind the dry cleaners.

"He never looked at the camera," Vinnie said in frustration.

"No, he doesn't," Griffin agreed. "He was very good at keeping his face out of view. That can't be an accident."

"I'll call the police." Vinnie pulled his phone out of his pocket and walked into the hall to make the call.

"I'm sorry, Annie," Griffin said, getting to his feet, a mix of anger and compassion in his eyes. "I'll have your car towed to the local shop and pay for new tires."

She suddenly realized that she had a bigger problem than flat tires. Checking her watch, she saw she only had twenty-five minutes to get to her interview, and it was at least twenty minutes away. "Oh, no, I have to go. I have to call for a car. I'm going to be late. I can't believe this. I've waited two weeks for this interview, and if I show up late..." She pulled out her phone, pushing the app for a car service. "I hope there's a car nearby." There wasn't. The nearest one was nine minutes away. "Damn. Maybe a taxi would be faster."

"I'll take you," Griffin said.

"But what about the police, my car?"

"Vinnie can handle everything until I get back. Do you need anything out of your car?"

She had her large tote bag over her shoulder with her sketches and resume inside. "I have everything I need."

They hurried down the hall. She heard Vinnie in the kitchen on the phone and felt a little bad for leaving him with everything to handle, but her interview was too important. "At least your car is fine," she said, as they went through the back door to the employee lot. She was happy to see the tires on his vehicle were intact.

"Yeah," he said somberly, keeping a hand on her arm as they walked to the car.

His protective stance made her feel both better and worse. The fact that he was being so cautious made her uneasy, and she was happy to have him by her side.

She gave Griffin directions to the interview and then settled back in her seat, trying to breathe deeply and calm her nerves. What had happened was upsetting, but she couldn't think about it. She had to pull herself together for her interview. She could not blow this meeting because she wasn't thinking clearly.

As the minutes passed, her pulse began to slow down, and she tried to focus on her pitch, going over in her head the points she wanted to make and the story she wanted to tell.

She should use the tire slashing in her pitch. It could happen to her character—the journalist. It could be part of some villainous plot, a way to get to the disguised superheroes, perhaps to make them drop their masks and show their true selves.

"Are you all right, Annie?" Griffin asked, interrupting her thoughts. "You haven't said a word in the last fifteen minutes, and that's not like you."

"I'm okay," she said, meeting his concerned gaze. "I'm just trying to get ready for the interview."

"Don't let what happened put you off your game. You're a great artist. You'd be an asset to this company or any company. Just remember that."

"I will. Thanks for the pep talk."

"You're welcome." A few moments later, he drove into the parking lot and pulled into an open space.

"I'll take a cab back. I don't know how long this will take," she said, putting her bag over her shoulder as she reached for the door handle.

"It doesn't matter. I'll wait for you. I'll give you a ride back."

"It could be an hour or more, Griffin. I have no idea how many people I'll meet with."

"It's fine. I'll get some coffee. I have some calls to make. I'll catch up on those while I'm waiting."

"It's really generous of you."

"You know how much I hate the word thanks," he said lightly.

"Okay. I won't say it again." She checked her watch, then licked her lips. "I hope I don't blow this."

"You won't."

"You know that kiss you gave me for luck earlier? I think I might need another one."

He leaned over and pressed his mouth against hers in a generous, caring kiss that warmed her up from the inside out and took away the last bit of chill from the disturbing incident at the bar. As they broke apart, their gazes clung together. And for a second, she almost forgot what they were doing, because her world was all about him.

Then Griffin moved back behind the wheel. "You don't need luck, Annie. Just be yourself. They won't be able to resist you."

She gave him a grateful smile, biting back the word *thanks*. She got out of the car, squared her shoulders, lifted her chin and channeled the superhero version of herself. She could do this. This was her world, and she was a good artist. She just had to show them how much they needed her.

And maybe later...she'd show Griffin how much she needed him.

She smiled at that thought and the smile stayed with her as she entered her first meeting.

Fifteen

Griffin drove to a coffeehouse a few miles away from Annie's interview, his mouth tingling from their kiss and his thoughts in turmoil. Every time he touched her, he wanted to do it again—immediately—and for a long time after that. He was playing with fire, and he knew it. But he couldn't seem to put down the matches.

The matches...

That thought reminded him of the Chicago matchbook Vinnie had pulled out of the drawer. It had been a reminder of his past, and now he was starting to wonder if his past was colliding with his present. Too many odd things were happening.

Were they all random? Or was there a bigger plan in motion?

In the last few days, there had been the attack on Megan and Annie, his company's bank account had been hacked, money transferred, the credit card maxed out. He'd been on the phone with several people yesterday and had even gone into his local branch to find out what the hell had happened, and no one knew. He was now working with the fraud division to get the money back and the card charges reversed. But it was going to take time and effort to correct that.

Annie's tires had been slashed by a vandal who had clearly known how to avoid the security cameras.

And what about the incident with Shari? Vinnie had said a number of times that Shari's behavior had changed, and the recent alleged road rage incident lent credence to that fact. But he didn't think Shari had the computer skills necessary to get into his computer and steal his passwords.

If not Shari, who? Someone else on his staff? He couldn't imagine that. He hated having to second-guess everyone in his life. He'd thought he'd moved beyond that.

He pulled into a parking space in a strip mall and went into the coffeehouse. Once he got his drink, he walked back outside and sat down at a table as his phone began to vibrate. It was Vinnie. "Sorry I ran out on you," he said. "I had to get Annie to her job interview."

"I figured. I spoke to Paul first. He gave me the name of the officer he talked to after Megan's incident and suggested I follow up with him, which I did. He took a report, but in light of our security footage, which I sent over to him, he isn't confident they can find the slasher. He suggested that someone might have something against the bar. Since Megan is gone now, I'm thinking he's right. Maybe we were wrong to assume she was the target."

"I was thinking the same thing, especially considering what happened at the bank. This is personal, Vinnie." He hated to say it, but he couldn't deny it. "I think this is about my past."

"That did cross my mind." Vinnie paused. "How is Annie doing?"

"Better than I expected. She was definitely compartmentalizing on the way over here. It's good she has this interview; it distracted her."

"Have you told her about your life before San Clemente?"

"No."

"Are you going to? Because if the answer is no, you need to find a way to say good-bye, Griffin. She's getting too involved in your life, and with everything that's going on, that's a big risk."

"I'm trying to walk away, but Annie doesn't take hints, and she doesn't go easily."

"And you don't really want her to go. I'm not judging. She's a beautiful woman, and she seems like a sweetheart, but you're going to have to make a choice."

"I know."

"On another note, I put in a call to Howard. He's sending a tow truck over. They should be able to put new tires on the car later this afternoon, possibly tomorrow morning."

"Thanks for taking care of everything."

"I'll see you when you get back."

He ended the call, then took his coffee and got into the car. He drove back to the office park, wanting to be close by when Annie finished her interview.

After he parked, he sipped his coffee and tried to think about next steps, but his mind kept going back to Annie. He'd told her yesterday he wasn't interested in a relationship, that he didn't do commitment, that he didn't want someone to worry about. But here he was worrying about her, and he had the feeling they were already in a relationship.

They'd seen each other almost every day this past week. Talking to her was starting to feel like an important part of his day, and kissing her was becoming even more addictive.

He could lie to himself and say she was helping him out or he was helping her out, but that didn't explain why he couldn't stop thinking about her, why her face haunted his dreams, why every time he thought about pushing her away, he chose to bring her closer.

His phone flashed with a text from Annie that she was done. He texted her back that he was out front and tried to ignore the fact that he felt excited just to see her again.

How the hell was he going to say good-bye to her and mean it?

Annie breezed through the door of the office building, feeling excited. The past hour had been a whirlwind of questions and answers, and the producers she'd met with had seemed to enjoy her pitch. Hopefully, that meant a second interview was coming.

At some point, she was going to have to tell Griffin about her story idea, since she had based so much of it on him and his crew, but she was going to wait until it looked like it might actually go somewhere. She had enough experience to know that nothing was a done deal until contracts were signed.

She opened the car door with a smile and slid into the passenger seat. "I hope that wasn't too long."

"It was fine. You're smiling. Is that good?"

"I think so. We had a really easy conversation. We all seemed to click. They liked my sketches. But they didn't commit to anything; they just said they'd be in touch. I do have a positive feeling about it, but I don't want to get ahead of myself."

"It sounds like you did great."

"I hope so. I liked the people I met with. They seem to have the right mix of creative and business skills that I'm looking for, but we'll see. It's a super competitive business and I'd be coming from a stronger position if I wasn't unemployed. But it is what it is. I can't change that. I just have to go forward." She finally stopped to take a breath and saw the look of amusement on Griffin's face. "I really didn't talk this much in the interview."

"I'm starting to like your stream-of-consciousness conversation. It's a challenge to keep up with, but it's never boring."

"I'm going to take that as a compliment. You're lucky you can work for yourself. You don't have to go through these nerve-racking interviews, or if you do, you're on the hiring side of the desk."

"Being the boss has its pros and cons. But it's better than answering to someone else. By the way, I spoke to Vinnie. Your car is being towed to a local mechanic. He's going to put on new tires, and hopefully you'll have it back by the end of the day."

"That's great, and it was nice of Vinnie to take care of it." She paused, feeling like Griffin had more to say. "Is there something else?"

A shadow darkened his gaze. "Yes. There is something we need to talk about it."

"I'm not going to like it."

"It's for your own safety, Annie. You need to put some distance between yourself and the bar. We should stop seeing each other."

"Griffin," she breathed in disappointment. "Don't say that."

"I have to."

"You don't have to," she argued.

His lips tightened and a gleam of anger entered his eyes, but she had the feeling he was more upset with himself than with her. "We're getting too close, Annie. Too much is happening. I need you to be safe and to be somewhere else."

"No," she said with a shake of her head. "You're not getting rid of me that easily."

"Annie—"

"Your bar is filled with people every day and every night, lots and lots of people, who are perfectly safe being there. And if I want to be there, too, you're not going to stop me. Plus, you have my Christmas ornaments. And I want to help you decorate the tree and get ready for the fundraiser next week. Don't shut me out just because of a few random events."

"It's not just that," he muttered.

"I know. I make you nervous. You make me nervous, too, but isn't that a good thing? Doesn't that make it feel like whatever is happening between us could be kind of great?"

"You are so damn hard to argue with," he said with a

frown. "Do you really need me to say I'm not interested in you? Do I have to be that blunt?"

"You can't say that, because it's not true," she returned. "I can feel the sparks between us, and so can you. When we kiss, it's like a fire starts, and it's not a slow simmer—it's an explosion. Do you know how rare it is to feel like that?"

"I do." Conflict tightened his jaw. "But you have no idea who I am."

"That's not true. I may not know every detail of your past, but I know you're a good friend, a great boss. You care about people. You're always trying to help someone. And you risked your life to save mine when I was a complete stranger."

"Yes, apparently, no good deed goes unpunished," he muttered.

She smiled, happier that his determination to get rid of her seemed to be weakening in the face of her fight. "Let's see what happens, Griffin. We don't have to force anything. Just don't push me away. I don't know that many people in town, and I like the Depot. I like you. I like *us*."

He shook his head in bewilderment. "I don't know why you want to be there after all the trouble you've run into."

"Well, I'm not a big fan of either of your parking lots now, but the inside of the bar is good. And if you're going to kick me out because it isn't safe, you should kick everyone out."

"Believe me, that has crossed my mind."

Now she was the one to frown. "I understand that there's something going on I don't understand, and it doesn't look like you understand it, either. But there's strength in numbers, right? You don't have to do this alone or just with Vinnie. I can help."

He gazed back at her with what now looked like admiration. "You are very persuasive, Annie."

"Callaways don't quit."

"I can see that. I hope you won't be sorry."

"I'd rather try and fail than not try at all."

"Okay," he said with what appeared to be an almost fatalistic shrug.

"That's it?" she challenged.

"I've run out of arguments—for now." He started the car and pulled out of the lot.

—➤◄—

Annie might have convinced Griffin to allow her to help with the tree and hang out at the bar, but that apparently hadn't included him spending time with her. When they'd returned to the Depot, Griffin had disappeared into his office, telling her to do what she wanted with the tree and he'd see her after he caught up on some work. That had been four hours ago.

After lunch, she'd spent the day working on the tree. After she finished stringing the lights and hanging the ornaments, she scattered some decorations around the rest of the bar. Various members of Griffin's staff, including Vinnie, stopped by at different points to tell her how much they liked everything. Hopefully, Griffin would, too—if he ever emerged from his office.

Just before five, Vinnie came into the room with an unhappy look in his eyes. "I have some bad news, Annie. Your car won't be ready until tomorrow. They had a problem with one of the new tires and had to order another one, but they can't get it until morning. Sorry about that."

"That's all right. I don't have anywhere to be tonight, and I can always take a cab home."

Vinnie looked past her, his eyes suddenly widening as he took in the tree. "Wow, the tree looks great. It's done. Amazing job, Annie."

"I thought it came out well. Hopefully, Griffin likes it. He didn't really tell me what he wanted."

"I think he trusts you."

"Do you? I can't really tell. He's not the most talkative guy."

"No, he's not, but he seems to talk more when you're around. He smiles more, too."

She flushed at the gleam in Vinnie's eyes. "I kind of like him."

"I kind of figured," he said with a laugh.

"Figured what?" Griffin interrupted, as he joined them.

"That Annie might be hungry after all her hard work," Vinnie answered. "What do you think of the tree?"

Griffin's look of amazement said more than any words, and a little thrill ran down her spine.

"It's not too much, is it?" she asked.

"It's perfect. It's colorful and friendly—it's you."

She sucked in a breath as his eyes met hers. "But I want it to be you, Griffin. This is your bar."

"This is exactly what the bar needs."

She wished he would tell her that she was exactly what he needed.

Vinnie cleared his throat. "I'm going to make you two some dinner. Sound good?"

"Uh…" she hesitated, knowing she'd already pushed Griffin pretty far with their conversation in the car earlier in the day.

"It sounds good to me," Griffin said, surprising her with his words.

"Then I better get back in the kitchen," Vinnie said. "I'll have your food ready around six thirty. We have music later. You should stay and hear the band, Annie."

"It's been a while since I've heard any live music." She looked at Griffin. "Is that okay with you?"

"It's fine." He glanced at his watch. "I am meeting with a security guy in a few minutes, so I'll look for you in a bit."

"Would you mind if I put my bag in your office or your apartment? I have my computer in there, and while I tucked it behind the tree while I was working, once the band gets here, there's going to be a lot of action around the stage."

"You can put it in my apartment." Griffin pulled out a key and handed it to her.

"Thanks." After Griffin returned to his office, she headed upstairs to his apartment, feeling a little weird about letting herself into his place, but he'd given her the key, so he obviously didn't care. He probably wasn't worried about her learning anything about him from his very sparse furnishings.

She put her bag on the kitchen table, then walked over to the window. Griffin's apartment overlooked the old railroad tracks, reminding her of the history of the Depot and also Griffin's story about his mom and their shared love for trains. There was a lot of sadness in his voice and in his eyes when he spoke about his past, but for that moment, there had been a hint of happiness.

Knowing more about his family helped her understand why he was so isolated. He'd grown up without a mom, and it seemed like his dad had disappeared after his mom's death, even if it was just emotionally. Maybe that's why he couldn't bring himself to trust people, to rely on anyone but himself. Although, he did have a strong friendship with Vinnie. She wondered if Vinnie knew more about Griffin's past than she did. Probably. She'd caught them exchanging looks on a few occasions, looks only they understood.

Turning away from the window, she wandered around Griffin's apartment for a minute and then couldn't help but take a sneaky peek into his bedroom.

Two things surprised her—the guitar in one corner and the floor-to-ceiling bookshelves filled with books. She moved farther into the room, running her finger over the paperback titles. They were mostly mysteries, thrillers, with some science fiction mixed in.

Griffin was a reader. She didn't know why she was surprised. When he wasn't being a bar owner, he seemed to have a more introverted side to his personality, but it was still interesting to peel back another layer of Griffin Hale.

Moving over to the guitar, she saw a music book on the table next to the armchair where the guitar rested. It looked like the book had been opened more than a few times. She could picture Griffin sitting in the chair, playing the guitar.

She wondered if he sang. She had a feeling his deep, husky, sexy voice could create a perfect love song.

Her body tightened at that image. She had it bad for the man.

Was she crazy to be fighting so hard for a man who could probably end up hurting her?

That answer was *probably*, too.

But she wasn't ready to walk away. And if she got hurt, then she got hurt. But maybe, just maybe, something wonderful could happen.

Sixteen

Griffin was getting used to seeing Annie's face across the table, feeling the warmth of her enticing smile, watching her emotions spill out whether she was talking or laughing or trying to be serious. She was the most open person he'd ever met. And he was just the opposite. She put everything out into the world, and he put nothing.

But he liked being with her. She made him feel normal again. He realized that was what Megan had said to him, too. When he was with Annie, he felt like himself again.

He couldn't tell her that. She wouldn't understand it, and he couldn't explain it.

There were so many things he wanted to tell her, but so many things he couldn't share.

He wasn't being fair to her. She thought he was resisting her because he didn't want commitment or entanglement, but his issues went far deeper than that.

He would be doing her a favor if he could find the strength to push her away, but that strength seemed to be weakening. There was a voice inside his head suggesting that maybe he should give himself a break, let down the steel walls he had barricaded himself behind. Even if it was only for a short time, wouldn't that be better than nothing?

Or would it be worse?

At this point, he really had no idea.

"Griffin," Annie said, her voice taking on a louder note.

He blinked, realizing he'd gotten lost in his head. They'd finished dinner and were nursing glasses of wine while the band got ready to play. "Sorry, what did you say?"

"I asked you how your meeting with the security company went, what you're planning to do."

"Right. We'll add a fence and a gate at the entrance to the employee lot. We're also going to put in additional security cameras in front and in back and beef up our alarm system, all things we should have done a while ago, but other items took precedence. And we're considering hiring a security guard on Friday and Saturday nights when we have the most problems with drunks, but beyond that we can't turn this place into a prison or no one will want to come."

"I'm sure you'll find the right balance." She paused as Shari came to take their plates.

He hadn't had a chance to speak to Shari about her run-in the other day, and now wasn't the time, but seeing the dark shadows under her eyes, the exhaustion in her expression, he thought he better make time soon.

"Do you want anything else?" Shari asked.

He glanced at Annie, who shook her head. "We're good, thanks."

"So, has this band played here before?" Annie asked, tipping her head to the four guys setting up on the stage.

"A few times. They're very popular."

"Have you ever wanted to be in a band, play on a stage?"

He saw the guilty curiosity in her eyes. "You went snooping in my apartment, didn't you?"

"I walked by the bedroom door, and I might have seen a guitar in there. Are you good?"

"Average. I don't perform; I just play for myself."

"Since you were a kid?"

"No. I didn't get into it until a couple of years ago. I just fool around."

"I don't know if I believe you. I'm beginning to realize you downplay your accomplishments and abilities. You're very modest, Griffin."

"I'm not being humble. I am a mediocre guitar picker at best."

"I also couldn't help noticing that you like books—mysteries, especially."

"I do like to read," he admitted. "I spent a lot of time with books when I was younger, especially after my mom got sick. It was an escape from the not-so-fun real world. What about you?"

"I always escaped into my art. If I had free time, I was drawing, and if I was reading anything, it was probably an art book." She paused, tilting her head to one side, as she gazed at him.

"What are you thinking, Annie? That you have me figured out? You found some clues in a guitar and a bookcase?" he asked with a smile.

"Hardly. But I'm getting a little closer. I know one thing—you like solitude—things you can do by yourself like surfing, reading, guitar playing. But you also like people, or you wouldn't have opened a bar. You're a study in contrasts. You want the noise, but you don't always want to be a part of it."

A chill ran through him as he realized just how close she was getting to understanding him. "I definitely don't always want to be a part of it," he admitted. "And you've made me sound quite boring."

"Not boring, but maybe a little...lonely?" she asked, a bit hesitant with the last word, as if she didn't want to offend him.

He wasn't offended, but he was reminded of just how isolated he really was. He could be in a crowd of people, but he always felt alone. Except tonight. Tonight, he felt connected to someone, and that someone was Annie.

"I've annoyed you again, haven't I?" she asked with a sigh. "I always take it one step too far."

"You're not annoying me at all. I actually wish you were."

A spark lit up her beautiful green eyes. "Because then it would be easier to get rid of me?"

"A lot easier."

"So…" She licked her lips and gave him a nervous look. "What's next? Do we listen to music? Do I call a cab and go home?"

Both of those ideas sounded a lot safer than what he wanted to do. "Do you want to go home?" he countered.

"Not really."

"Do you want to listen to the music?"

She put a hand to her necklace, pulling a pink stone pendant back and forth along its chain. "Do I have a third choice?" she asked.

Her question sent all kinds of ideas into his head. "I could come up with a third choice," he said with a nod.

"What is it?"

He gazed back at her, seeing the mixed emotions in her eyes, the same emotions he was feeling. There was a push-pull between them that neither of them seemed able to ignore. He should be able to ignore it. He'd had years of practice in locking away parts of his life. Did he really want to unlock them now? To Annie? To the one person he really didn't want to send away but probably should?

As his eyes moved from her expectant gaze to her soft, full lips, logic went out the window. He didn't want to think anymore. He didn't want to be on guard. He didn't want to hold on so tight to safety that his fingers went numb. He wanted to fly, and he wanted to do it with her.

"Griffin?" she asked, an edge to her voice.

He looked back into her eyes. "Do you want to jump off a cliff?"

She drew in a quick breath at his words. "Are you going to jump with me?"

At her question, the air sizzled between them. He knew he should end this crazy, seductive conversation right now, but his brain had lost out to the desire rushing through his body. "I would jump with you, but you could still get hurt. I can't promise you won't."

"There's always that risk. I just don't want to take the risk alone. If we do this, we both have to want it."

"Oh, I want it," he murmured. "I want you, Annie." He got to his feet and held out his hand, making a decision he hoped neither of them would regret.

She jumped up, her fingers tightening around his as their gazes locked together. "I want you, too."

That was really all that mattered.

They practically ran up the stairs to Griffin's apartment, and Annie did feel a bit like she was running headfirst toward the edge of a cliff, but she was excited and eager and too caught up in Griffin to think about turning around.

Whatever happened later…would happen later. She wanted now. This moment was everything.

Griffin fumbled a bit with the key as he unlocked his door, and she liked the sign of nerves. He always seemed so controlled, so disciplined, but he wasn't acting that way now, and she liked being the one to knock him off his game.

When they got into the apartment, he kicked the door shut, whirled her around and pushed her back up against it, taking possession of her mouth in a long, deep, wet kiss that sent waves of heat through her body.

The man could definitely kiss!

He angled his head one way, then the other, the demands of his lips making her pulse pound and her heart beat faster.

She ran her hands up under his shirt, feeling the hard plane of his abs, the sculpted muscles, the heat of his skin. She wanted to touch him all over. She wanted to go fast, but she also wanted to go slow. With Griffin, she always felt as if their time together could end at any second, and it was that sense of urgency that fueled her desire.

If things were going to end, they were going to end the way she wanted them to. She parted her lips, sucking his tongue into her mouth, loving the way he tasted, the scent of his aftershave clinging to his cheeks—sexy, musky, manly. His hard angles, her soft curves—they seemed made for each other, and she wanted to get closer, so much closer.

Griffin dragged his mouth away from hers, giving her a second to breathe. He tilted her chin up with one hand, gazing into her eyes. "Last chance."

"I'm not changing my mind. Are you?"

He shook his head, but she could see a struggle in his eyes as well as a hunger. He was battling for a control she didn't think had anything to do with her.

"Are you sure?" she asked, drawing his gaze to hers.

"I don't want to hurt you, Annie. I know I could."

"I'm not worried about that."

"Maybe you should be. You don't know—"

She cut him off by putting her fingers against his mouth. "Don't say whatever you're going to say. I'm exactly where I want to be. I'm not asking you for anything. Well, that's not completely true. I do want to ask you to do a few things."

"Like what?" he asked huskily.

"Kiss me all over. Touch me all over. Let yourself go and then take me with you. It's really pretty simple. It doesn't have to be complicated."

A slow smile curved his lips and the tension in his face eased. "Simple—I can manage." He slid his mouth down the side of her neck, sending tingles to every nerve ending. "How's that?"

"It's a good start." She had to bite back a small moan as his tongue swirled around her earlobe. "You're going to make me crazy, aren't you?"

"I sure as hell hope so, because you're already doing that to me."

His hands crept under her top, and she leaned back

against the door, happy to have something solid behind her as his hands teased her breasts and his mouth set off little fires everywhere it landed. Then Griffin pulled her into his arms, stealing another hot kiss before taking her into the bedroom.

He let go of her hand for one second, saying "hang on," which almost gave her too much time to think about what she was doing.

But when Griffin came back out of the bathroom, gave her a wicked smile and tossed a couple of condoms on the bed, her mouth went dry. "Really?" she asked, raising an eyebrow. "That many? I thought you were a pessimist."

He laughed. "Not now I'm not."

She liked the smile that lit up his eyes. The moody, sometimes grumpy, scowling man of mystery had vanished. He looked happy, younger, carefree, and hot as hell...

And then he bridged the gap between them, sliding his arms around her waist with a hungry, determined look in his eyes. "I need you, Annie."

She took a deep breath. "I need you, too, Griffin. I have to admit I'm a little nervous. If I start rambling in the middle of something, just ignore me, okay? You know I talk too much."

"I would never ignore you. I like the way you talk. I like the way you use this mouth." He ended his statement with a kiss. "We can go as fast or as slow as you want."

"Let's go fast...the first time," she said, already feeling breathless and Griffin had barely touched her.

Which reminded her...She pulled her top up and over her head. She felt momentarily self-conscious in her lacy black bra, but the passion that sparked in Griffin's eyes drove the shyness away. She unhooked her bra and slipped it off her shoulders, feeling brave, daring, reckless.

"We're definitely going to go fast the first time," Griffin said, his voice thick, as his hands cupped her breasts and he sought another kiss.

Desire raced through her as her nipples tightened and when he dropped his head to kiss her breasts, she ran her hands through his hair, holding his head in place as his tongue drew wet circles, setting off all kinds of impatient feelings.

And then Griffin dropped to his knees, kissing her breasts, her abdomen, his fingers playing with the snaps on her jeans.

He helped her off with her jeans, her panties coming off at the same time, his mouth and hands touching her where she most needed it.

But it wasn't enough. And Griffin had far too many clothes on.

"Your turn," she said, helping him off with his jeans and shirt.

His body was everything she'd imagined and more: muscled, lean, tan, just the right smattering of dark hair on his chest. She would have taken more time to look, but he was reaching for her, and now wasn't the time to go slow and savor. That would come later.

They tumbled down on the bed together, seeking each other with greedy hands, impatient mouths, reckless, passionate desire. She'd never felt so consumed by her need, so overwhelmed with sensation. She was breathing him in with every breath that she took. It was a little terrifying to feel so swept away—a bit like going into the ocean, feeling the current pulling her under.

But when Griffin's arms were around her, she wasn't afraid. He would catch her if she fell…so she let go.

And he was there, just as she'd known he would be.

—➤➤◄◄—

Annie woke up Saturday morning, feeling deliciously exhausted and superbly happy. Unfortunately, when she rolled over in bed and did not see Griffin's gorgeous face or his hot body next to hers, a wave of doubt ran through her.

She glanced at the clock on the bedside table. It was almost eight, and the sun was streaming through the windows. It was time to get up, but she really wished she wasn't getting up alone.

The apartment sounded quiet. Griffin wasn't in the bathroom. *Had he left? Gone surfing? Gone downstairs to work? Was it over already?*

He'd told her he couldn't make promises, but she'd thought she might at least get him to have breakfast with her.

Sitting up in bed, she pulled the sheet around her naked body as she considered her options. She didn't have her car, but she could call a car service and go home.

She pushed her hair out of her face. It didn't make sense that Griffin would just leave her without a word. Not in his bed. Not in his apartment. Maybe he'd just gone downstairs to get coffee or something.

She looked around for her phone but didn't see it anywhere. She'd probably left it in her bag, which was on Griffin's kitchen table. The sound of a door closing made her heart jump. Griffin was back from wherever he'd gone. She waited for him to come into the bedroom, but he didn't. Maybe he thought she was still asleep.

Climbing out of bed, she wrapped the sheet around her and went into the living room.

Griffin was standing by the table where she'd left her tote bag. There was a plate of pastries and two mugs of coffee next to her phone.

She let out a sigh of relief, but that feeling quickly passed as he met her gaze with a frown.

"I can't believe you didn't tell me," he said, an accusing note in his voice.

Her gaze moved to the bag. She could see the folder with her sketches of Griffin as a superhero tucked just inside. *He must have seen the drawings.* She really should have told him before now. "I—I was going to tell you."

"Were you?"

"Yes. I just didn't know how to bring it up."

"After last night, you feel shy to bring things up?"

She blushed at the memories. "That was different." Frowning, she couldn't quite gauge his mood. He seemed a

little pissed off, but not in a really angry way. "Do you want
to talk about it?"

"No, I want to do something about it. But first you need
to answer some of these texts."

"What?"

He picked up her phone and handed it to her. "I wasn't
spying, Annie. I set the coffee down, and your phone was
blowing up with Happy Birthday confetti and balloon texts."

"Oh," she said, licking her lips, realizing he hadn't seen
the sketches at all.

She should probably just tell him, now that she'd almost
been outed. But Griffin was putting his arms around her,
kissing her good-morning, wishing her a happy birthday, and
she felt happier than she had in a very long time. She just
could not bring herself to mention the sketches, knowing they
would definitely change the mood.

It was her birthday. She deserved a good day. The rest
could wait.

"What are you doing today?" he asked. "Are you going
out with friends? Do you have a party planned?"

"No, I'm just going to laze around, catch up on my
laundry, whatever. It's not a big deal."

"Catch up on your laundry on your birthday? No way.
That's not going to work for me," he said with a firm shake of
his head.

"Oh, yeah?"

"If you don't have any birthday plans, then we're making
some."

"Don't you have to work?"

"I'm the boss. I can take a day off."

"Really? You would do that for me?"

"I'd do just about anything for you," he said lightly, but
there was enough of a serious note in his voice that her heart
squeezed with happiness. "What do you want to do for your
birthday?"

"I honestly have no idea. I didn't make plans."

"You had nothing in mind?"

"Well, I had thought about maybe going up to Laguna Beach. There's an art festival today, but that would probably be boring for you."

"A drive up the coast sounds perfect, and I can look at some art, as long as I get to look at you at the same time," he said with a sexy smile.

"Wow. I did not know you could be this charming."

He laughed. "I'm glad I can still surprise you. Do you want to get dressed? I grabbed some pastries from downstairs, but we can get a big breakfast along the way."

"Sounds like an excellent plan." She framed his face with her hands. "But I wouldn't mind a little company in the shower." She stepped back and dropped her sheet to the ground, giving him a good look.

He licked his lips. "Now you're talking."

She turned and let him catch a nice view of her ass as she headed into the bathroom, laughing when he caught up with her at the door, having stripped off his clothes in record time.

"That was fast," she joked as he pulled her into the shower.

"You haven't seen anything yet."

Seventeen

—⟫⟪—

It was a day to remember, a day unlike any other: ordinary, normal, carefree. As Griffin watched Annie cruise down a beach path on a rented bicycle, the beautiful red highlights in her hair catching fire in the afternoon sunlight, he felt as if his world had taken on color again. It was no longer black-and-white, no longer filled with shadows and pain. It was bigger, bolder, brighter…but it wouldn't last.

Nothing lasted.

He tried to shake the depressing thought out of his head. He could think that way tomorrow…or the next day, but not today.

It was Annie's birthday and, so far, it had been great. After a late breakfast at a café along the water in Dana Point, they'd made their way farther up the coast, and had spent a couple of hours walking through Laguna Beach's art festival, looking at the work of local artists, listening to music, and sipping wine from a local California winery.

After that, he'd suggested renting bikes and riding along the coastal path, which Annie had happily jumped on.

Now, they were almost out of path. He could see the end

in front of them, about a half-mile away, and it reminded him that his relationship with Annie would have an ending, too.

But he wouldn't have regrets. And nothing was ending today. It was Annie's birthday.

Annie stopped as she came to the end of the path and as she put her feet on the ground, she gave him a wide smile that sent warm feelings all over his body. He was going to make sure she had a happy day and not think about tomorrow until he had to.

He caught up to her and hopped off his bike. "Looks like we have to turn around."

"Not yet. Let's take the bikes over there." She pointed to the wide, flat bluff about thirty feet away.

"All right."

They lifted their bikes over a short fence and then walked across thick grass before putting down the kickstands.

Annie sat on the ground and waved her hand at the cascading colors of pink and orange lighting up the sky as the sun slipped toward the edge of the horizon. "Another great view," she said, smiling as he sat down next to her. "We keep finding them together."

He nodded, thinking that the view he liked most was the one of her sparkling green eyes and beautiful soft mouth. He cupped the back of her head and pulled her toward him, giving her a tender kiss.

"This has been a wonderful day," she said as they broke apart. "The best birthday."

"It's not over yet."

"Oh, yeah, what else do you have in mind?"

"I don't know, but I do know we're not done. There are some great restaurants around here. We should get dinner before we head back to San Clemente."

"I have worked up an appetite. I'm glad you suggested the bike ride. I think the last time I rode a bike for fun, I was about twelve. Since then it's been mostly bikes in the gym."

"You go to the gym?"

She gave him a playful punch in the arm. "You can't tell

how fit I am?"

"You look great. I just didn't know you worked out."

"Well, I wouldn't say I'm a gym rat, but I try to get there a few times a week or I take a class somewhere. I'm still trying to get into a groove since I moved here. Hopefully, once I figure out my job situation, I can get into a steadier routine." She stopped as her phone buzzed. Pulling it out of her bag, she said, "Dylan wants to video chat."

"Go ahead."

"Are you sure?"

"Absolutely. But leave me out of the shot."

"Of course. I know how much you love being in the middle of something," she said dryly. She punched the button on her phone, her eyes on the screen. "Hi, Dylan."

"Happy birthday, Annie," Dylan said. "I have some people here who want to say hello."

Griffin saw a smile spread across Annie's face.

"Who all is there?" she asked. "Wait, I see Tori."

"Hi Annie," a woman said. "Ian and Grace are here, too."

Another chorus of voices wished Annie a happy birthday.

"And here's Mom and Dad. We're going to sing, so I hope you're not in the middle of a crowd, because this isn't going to be pretty," her brother said.

"I'm outside, but you can still sing."

Griffin heard a raucous, off-key rendition of "Happy Birthday" followed by a lot of laughter.

"What are you doing today?" a woman asked. "I hope you're not alone. I wish you were here."

"I'm having a great day, Mom," Annie answered. "A friend of mine took me to breakfast, the Laguna Beach Art Festival and on a bike ride. It has been great."

"Who's this friend?" her mother asked suspiciously.

Annie glanced over at him, then back at the screen. "He's the guy who saved me from the shark."

"I didn't realize you were still in touch."

"That guy?" a voice interrupted. "The one who gave me a black eye. Don't you have any family loyalty, Annie?"

Hunter, Griffin thought.

"Hey, you startled us, Hunter. Next time, don't hide in the shadows."

"Next time tell your friend to ask questions before he puts his fist in someone's face."

"If it makes you feel any better, his eye is bruised, too."

"It better be, or I am losing my touch."

"I should go," she said.

"Have fun, honey," a woman said. "We love you. And you better come home for Christmas."

"I will, Mom. I love all of you, too." Annie disconnected the call and then blinked away what looked like tears.

"What's this?" he asked, leaning over to wipe away the moisture under her eyes.

"Happy tears."

"You miss your family."

"I do miss them. It was nice of them to get together to call me."

"And sing really badly."

She gave him a watery smile. "Callaways are known for a lot of things, but singing isn't one of them. Well, except for my cousin, Sean. Somehow, he got all the musical talent. He's a fantastic singer and musician. He has a studio in San Francisco."

"I thought everyone in the family was supposed to do something to serve or protect someone."

"Sean was the black sheep of his family. In my family, it's me and Mia."

"I actually prefer black sheep; they stand out from the flock."

"I like that," she said with a nod. "I tried to tell my teacher that when I was in the sixth grade and I didn't want to draw the same picture everyone else was drawing. She didn't agree that different was good. She thought different was worthy of a D instead of an A."

"She had no vision."

"I thought the same thing."

"I hope you didn't tell her that." He laughed when he saw the guilt in her eyes. "No way."

"You know I talk too much. It didn't just start yesterday. It's been going on my whole life."

"What happened?"

"I had to write a report about the importance of following directions and learning the basics."

"I'm sure that didn't change anything for you."

"No. I thought she was wrong, but I wrote it, because my mom wouldn't let me go to art camp if I didn't. But I got Miss Owens back."

"What did you do?"

"I turned her into a nasty villain character in a graphic novel that I designed and wrote in my early twenties."

"Wait, you do graphic novels?"

"I play around a little. It's just for fun."

"I want to see them."

"I have some at the apartment. I can show you sometime. Anyway, I tormented her in my story. She got what was coming—finally."

He laughed. "I didn't know you had it in you to be that mean or so thirsty for revenge years after the fact."

"She was mean first, and you know what they say about revenge being best served cold." She paused, giving him a thoughtful look. "My family would like you, Griffin. You could have been in the shot with me."

"I didn't want to interrupt, and you already have one brother who doesn't like me. And my bruise is barely noticeable now. His punch was not that great."

"I had to give him something for his male pride." She scooted a little closer to him and brushed a strand of hair off his forehead, giving him a warm smile. "And I know that once they meet you, my entire family will like you, because I like you."

His gut clenched at her words, at the feel of her sweet breath against his face, the loving look in her eyes. Once her family met him? That wasn't going to happen.

How had he let things go so far?

He should have known better. He *had* known better. But still he'd let her into his life—and not just his life but also his heart.

This was going to hurt; this was really going to hurt.

"Griffin," she said softly, giving him a questioning look. "It feels like you're here but not really here. What's going on?"

"Nothing. We should get going. The sun is almost down, and it will be dark soon."

"What are you afraid of?"

"Crashing our bikes in the dark."

"You know that's not what I meant."

"I'm not afraid of anything," he lied. "I saved you from a shark, didn't I? What other proof do you need?"

"I'm not talking about the way you protect people. I know you're good at that. But I'm more interested in why you protect yourself with thick walls of steel. Someone hurt you. That woman you were involved with. Is she why you can't trust me?"

He swallowed a knot in his throat. "No, that's not it."

"I think it might be part of it. Who was she? You don't have to tell me her name. But tell me something about her, something about your relationship. Can't you open up a little?"

He found himself wanting to open up a lot, to tell her everything, but he couldn't—not just to protect himself but also to protect her.

"There came a time in our relationship when she couldn't support me in what I wanted to do, and I couldn't support her in what she wanted to do. We were going in different directions, and neither one of us was willing to change paths."

"Then it wasn't right. If it was meant to be, someone would have compromised."

"Exactly. As I said before, we didn't love each other enough to work through it. But it wasn't just about us. There were other people involved. We ended up on different sides of something, and I'm not going to say any more about it," he warned.

"She let you down. She hurt you."

"I let her down, too. And I'm sure I also hurt her. I'm not good at relationships, Annie. You should consider this a cautionary tale."

"Well, I don't. Because I'm not her, whoever she is. Our relationship is ours—whatever it turns out to be."

"We're not having a relationship," he reminded her. "This is just about fun. Or have you forgotten?"

"I haven't forgotten, and I am having fun. Thanks for sharing, Griffin."

She leaned in and pressed her mouth against his in a sweet, sexy kiss that made his entire body ache. They'd made love three times already, and he still couldn't wait to get her back to bed.

She pulled away and gave him a smile. "Now we can go."

He blew out a breath, torn between wanting to return to the life he'd built and wanting to take Annie somewhere far, far away, where it could be just the two of them and no one else—no past, no future, just the beautiful present.

But reality was calling…

———————

After dinner in a lovely seafood restaurant, they got back into Griffin's car and headed home a little after eight. Annie sat back in her seat, watching the moonlight play off the ocean as they drove down the coast.

This birthday might have been one of the best she'd ever had. Griffin had not just been fun and charming, he'd shared a little more of his past, and he'd talked, not a lot about himself, but about what he liked, what he didn't like.

The moody man she'd first met had evolved into a fascinating, interesting, generous man who was also one of the hottest guys she'd ever been with. And she wanted to be with him again. She couldn't wait until they got back to his apartment—or hers. She didn't know where they were going, and she didn't really care; she just wanted to spend more time with him.

But as the minutes ticked by, and Griffin remained quiet, the silence in the car began to feel tense. Griffin was pulling away from her again; she could feel it. And she didn't like it.

It was her birthday, and she didn't want it to end on anything but a fantastic note.

"Do you want me to take you home?" Griffin asked, making her fears come true, because the way he asked the question didn't sound like he was planning to go home with her.

"Actually, I left my computer at your apartment. I didn't want to bring a heavy bag with me. Maybe we should go back to your place, so I can get it. We could also have a drink in the bar and then..." She glanced over at him. "And then we could see what else we want to do together."

He gave her a quick look. "I know what I want to do."

"Am I a part of it?"

"Do you really need to ask?" he said with some surprise.

She felt better with that response. "Sometimes I don't know what you're thinking, Griffin. But I'm glad my birthday isn't over yet."

"Me, too," he said with a smile. "We'll go to my apartment and figure things out from there."

"Great."

He pressed his foot down harder on the gas.

She laughed as she braced her hand on the console. "Better be careful you don't get a speeding ticket."

"It would be worth it. It has been too long since I kissed you."

"And I think that will be worth the wait," she said confidently.

Twenty minutes later, Griffin pulled into the employee lot behind the Depot. He'd no sooner parked, then his phone buzzed. "Vinnie," he said. "Hey. I just pulled into the lot. I'll be inside in a second."

"I hope there's not more trouble," she murmured.

"We'll find out."

As they got out of the car and walked toward the building, he grabbed her hand, his warm fingers closing around hers, sending a little thrill down her spine. She didn't know if he held her hand just to keep her safe and keep her close, but she liked feeling connected to him.

When they entered the back hall, she could hear the buzz of people working in the kitchen, and live music coming from the bar. There were even a few people lined up for the restrooms. The Depot was hopping on a Saturday night.

Vinnie walked out of the kitchen, a pleased gleam in his eyes. "Perfect timing."

"Perfect timing for what?" Griffin asked.

"You'll see. Meet me in the bar," Vinnie said, disappearing through the kitchen door.

"What's that about?" she asked.

"I honestly have no idea, but Vinnie was smiling, so it doesn't seem bad," he said, as they walked down the hall.

When they entered the room, she could see that the bar was crowded, every table taken, some people dancing to the band, others trying to talk over the music. They waited at the end of the bar, by the door leading into the kitchen. A moment later, Vinnie came out with a small cake lit up with candles. He set it on the end of the bar. "Happy birthday, Annie."

She was incredibly touched by the gesture. "I can't believe you did this."

"You have to have a cake on your birthday," he grumbled.

"Make a wish," Griffin encouraged.

She looked down at the candles and thought about what she wanted. Then she looked up at Griffin and realized she already had what she wanted—*who* she wanted. But the men were waiting for her to blow out the candles. She closed her eyes and wished that Griffin would let her all the way into his heart. Then she blew out the tiny flames.

The crowd around the bar burst into applause.

"Thank you, Vinnie," she said, giving him a hug.

"You have to have a cake on your birthday."

Danielle joined them at the bar with plates, forks, and a knife. "Happy birthday, Annie," she said in her loud, brassy voice.

"Thanks, Danielle." As she looked at the people around her, she was beginning to realize that she'd found a new family at the Depot.

She cut the cake, forcing Danielle and Vinnie to take a slice. As expected, the luscious chocolate cake was rich and delicious. "Chocolate is my favorite," she told Vinnie.

"It's everyone's favorite," Danielle said with a laugh, as they all cleaned their plates in record time. Then Vinnie went back to the kitchen and Danielle returned to serving drinks.

"Do you want something to drink?" Griffin asked.

"Maybe some water."

He stepped around the bar to get them each a glass of ice water. "We can take the rest of the cake upstairs. In case you get hungry...later."

"At this moment, I cannot imagine eating anything else. I might have to dance off a few calories first."

"I know how you can work off some calories and it does not involve dancing."

"I'm starting to like the way you think."

Before Griffin could reply, they were interrupted by an attractive blonde woman, who appeared to be in her early thirties.

"Excuse me," she said, giving Griffin a confused look. "Michael? Is that you?"

Griffin started, his body tightening, his face turning pale. "What?"

"You're Michael Payton," she said. "Right?"

He cleared his throat. "No, you're mistaken. I'm Griffin Hale."

Bewilderment ran through her eyes. "Really? You look

exactly like someone I used to know. His name was Michael."

"And that's not me. Sorry." He looked at Annie. "Ready to go upstairs?"

"You have a twin then," the woman said, apparently not ready to walk away.

"They say everyone does," Griffin replied. He grabbed Annie's hand and pulled her toward the door.

She was surprised by his tight grip. He was crushing her fingers, and she could feel the tension running through his body. When they got upstairs and entered his apartment, he finally let go, and she shook out her hand with relief.

"Sorry," he muttered.

She was more concerned about what had just happened than the pain in her hand. "Griffin, who was that woman?"

He walked around in a small circle, running a hand through his hair, as he contemplated her question. When he stopped in front of her, he said, "I don't know. I've never seen her before."

She saw truth in his eyes, but there was something he was holding back. "You're rattled. I've never seen you like this. Not even when a shark almost got us. Why?"

He shook his head, but he didn't answer.

"Griffin—do you know who Michael Payton is?"

He took a quick breath. "Yes."

Her heart sped up, and she had a feeling they were heading for another cliff, but this one was not going to be nearly as pleasurable. "Who is he?"

He gazed into her eyes with what looked like a plea for understanding. "He's me."

Eighteen

Griffin's answer shocked her. "What do you mean he's you? You just told that woman you weren't Michael Payton. I don't understand."

"I know you don't," he said tersely.

"Then explain."

He put his hands on his hips, his mouth drawing into a hard line. "Griffin is my middle name. I was born Michael Griffin Payton. Hale was my grandmother's maiden name."

"You changed your name to Griffin Hale?"

"Yes."

"Why? Was that to cut out your dad? I know you said he wasn't that great of a father after your mom died."

"It was partly because of that."

He was talking, but she still didn't know what was going on. "Why didn't you tell the woman that you were Michael Payton? Why lie to her? Why lie to me?" She suddenly realized the man she'd spent the night with was living under a different name than the one he'd been born with.

He had secrets, dark secrets, maybe terrifying secrets. Her imagination went into overdrive. Griffin had told her on more than one occasion that she didn't really know him. For the first time, she believed that.

"I lied to her because I didn't know her. I have never seen her before in my life," he said.

"Maybe she knew you through friends."

"I don't think so. And why would she be here in San Clemente? Michael Payton has never lived here. This isn't good. This is not good at all." He walked over to the window and looked out. Then he came back to her. "We need to get out of here."

"Why?"

"It doesn't matter why. It just matters that we go. Get your computer, whatever else you left here, and we'll go to your house."

"Griffin, I'm not going anywhere until you tell me what's going on."

"This isn't the time to talk."

"It's the perfect time to talk," she said stubbornly. "Why would I go anywhere with you? You've been lying to me since I met you."

"I haven't been lying to you. I changed my name to Griffin Hale."

"But you haven't told me why you did that. I need something."

He gave her a hard look, his blue eyes dark and unfathomable. "I was in trouble in Chicago. That's why I left. I'm concerned now that that trouble has followed me here. If you want to know more, then let me take you home. We will have a longer conversation, but it's not going to happen here or now." He paused, looking into her eyes. "You're not in danger from me, Annie, but I can't promise that you're not in danger from someone else. I need to get you to a safer place."

"Fine." She grabbed her computer and stuffed it into her bag, then followed Griffin out of the apartment. He didn't speak on the way to the car, but he was extremely wary as they entered the parking lot, his gaze darting in every direction. Once inside the car, he sped out of the lot.

"You're going the wrong way," she said a few minutes later, feeling incredibly on edge and way out of her depth.

"I'm making sure we're not being followed," he said, weaving in and out of traffic.

Was he telling the truth? Had she made a huge mistake getting into his car? He could be taking her anywhere.

But she knew him. She knew he wasn't a bad guy, she reminded herself. He'd saved her life before. He wasn't going to hurt her now. She looked into the side view mirror, but she couldn't see anything but headlights.

Turning back to him, she said, "Who would be following us?"

He didn't reply, but he made several quick turns, his gaze moving back and forth to the rearview mirror. "I'm not sure. But I'm not going to your building until I know we don't have a tail."

She wrapped her arms around her body as they drove in a random fashion for another twenty minutes. Finally, Griffin seemed convinced they weren't being followed.

When they got to her building, she told him he could park in the garage since her car wasn't there. He got out of the car to punch in her security code, and then drove inside.

Leaving the car, the garage, and heading up to the front door of the building took more long minutes and careful review of each move before they made it. By the time she got into her apartment, her nerves were screaming. She didn't actually let out a breath until Griffin went through her apartment and told her everything was fine.

Then she sank down on the couch. "You should sit, too," she said, as he continued to pace.

"I don't know if I can sit," he said tensely.

She didn't know if he could, either; he was completely amped up. "Then don't sit. Tell me what's going on. What kind of trouble were you in?"

He gave her a long, measuring look. "I don't know if I should tell you, Annie."

"You said you would. You can trust me, Griffin."

"It's not about trusting you; it's about keeping you safe. I don't want to put you in more danger."

"More danger?" she echoed. "What does that mean? And if you're in danger, then I probably am, too. We were together last night. We were together all day. I've been at the bar several times. I've had my tires slashed, and I almost got run over, so if there's something else coming, I'd sure like to know what it might be."

"I didn't mean to bring you into this," he said, shaking his head in self-recrimination. "I told you to go that first day. Remember? But you could not take a hint. You could not stay away. You could not keep out of my life."

She frowned, knowing what he was saying was partly true, but she still didn't like his attitude. "We can't change how we got here. We're here, so let's deal with it."

He walked around the room again, taking another minute to pull his thoughts together. She'd seen Griffin in a lot of different moods, but this one was different. He was angry. He was wary. He was worried.

And she was more than a little nervous.

Had he committed some terrible crime? Had she completely misjudged him? Was he a criminal? A murderer? A thief? Her mind raced with every terrible possibility. She didn't want to think she was a bad judge of character, but maybe she was.

"Griffin? You have to talk to me. I'm going crazy here."

"Okay." He took another minute, then said, "I used to be a cop."

Of all the things he might have told her, that was not one of them. "What?"

"I was a police officer in Chicago."

"That doesn't sound so bad. Does this danger you're worried about have something to do with an old case?"

"Yes."

"What happened? Did you put someone away? Hurt someone? Kill someone?"

"I put someone away, and I hurt him, too. He was a

criminal, but he was also my partner." He drew in a shaky breath and then let it out. "Four years ago, I crossed the blue line, and my life has never been the same."

She was shocked by his words. "You were a cop? Wow. Okay. I wouldn't have guessed that. And you went after your partner?"

"Yes."

"What did he do wrong?"

"Everything. He took bribes, leaked information, protected criminals, hid evidence...whatever he was required to do, because he'd been bought and paid for. He was the greatest guy in the world, but he was also corrupt." Griffin paused. "I probably should have seen it all sooner, but he was someone I looked up to. Tom was eight years older than me, and he was the big brother I never had. I couldn't imagine he was anything but honorable. But too many things were happening that I couldn't explain. I tried to talk to him. At first, he came up with excuses, and then eventually he looked me in the eye and told me to mind my own business, that he knew what he was doing, and that if I didn't stop asking questions, a lot of people were going to get hurt."

"He threatened you."

"And people I cared about."

"I'm guessing you didn't mind your own business."

"I'm ashamed I didn't act as soon as I could have. There was an armed robbery at a convenience store by a gang that my partner was connected to. A little boy got hit in the crossfire. He died. I was with his mother when she found out, and she begged me to find the people who had killed her son and get her child justice." He blew out a breath. "I didn't have to look very far. One of the men responsible was sitting right next to me. He didn't pull the trigger. He wasn't even at the scene, but he was already covering up evidence. He tried to bury the testimony of a witness, and it was the last straw. I went to Internal Affairs. I became part of a sting operation that would take him down, and strip him of everything."

She could see the pain in his eyes and couldn't imagine

how torn he must have been.

"My part in the sting eventually came out," Griffin continued. "There was a lot of pressure on me to back down, change some of what I'd said, refuse to testify. But it was too late. I'd made my choice. I had to live with it."

Words from earlier that day came back into her head. He'd said his girlfriend hadn't been able to support what he wanted to do. "The woman you spoke of—your girlfriend— she didn't take your side?"

"No. Paige's father and brother were both police officers. Her family was true blue. I actually confided in her before I went to IAD. She begged me not to do it. We'd met through my partner. She cared about Tom. She didn't want to see him get hurt. I didn't, either. But Tom wasn't going to come clean until he was forced to." He paused. "After I went to IAD, I had to lie to Paige. I had to pretend that I had decided to protect Tom. Because if I'd told her the truth, she would have warned him. After everything was made public, she and her family made it clear I was not welcome in their lives. That was the end of that." Griffin walked across the room and sat down next to her. He gave her a questioning look. "What do you think?"

"I have no idea. My head is spinning. Why did you decide to tell me all this now?"

"Because of the woman at the bar—because she knew my old name."

"But you said you didn't know her."

"I didn't. I don't. I think she's a message."

"What do you mean?"

"I left Chicago and changed my name because there were threats against my family and my friends. My grandfather was attacked outside his bar one night. He was beaten up, and his bar was vandalized, thousands of dollars in damage. His entire life had been about that bar. After my grandmother died, it was his home away from home. Not only would it have cost a tremendous amount of money to rebuild it, his customer base was not going to come back. They were mostly cops, and I was a traitor."

Having grown up in a firefighting family, she knew a lot about loyalty in both the fire department and the police department, but it seemed that Griffin had done the right thing. "Not everyone could have been against you."

"There were probably a few who weren't, but they were too afraid to speak up. It was easier to cast me aside. After my grandfather got out of the hospital, I encouraged him and my dad to get out of town. We'd been talking about it for a while, but they hadn't really believed they were in danger until then. They left a week later. And I disappeared soon after that."

"Wait. Were you in witness protection? Is that how you met Paul?"

"I met Paul when I was a police officer. We became friends. I wasn't under his protection, but Paul helped me to disappear, to change my name, to move money, and to start over."

"You told me earlier that after people testify, they're not usually in danger. Why would someone come after you now?"

"I'm guessing revenge. My case was different. No one wanted to shut me up; they wanted to take me down, hurt me, make me pay. The entire police department suffered when Tom's corruption was made public. A lot of people looked bad. Some of them lost their jobs."

"And now you think one of those people has found you?"

He nodded, his eyes dark. "It's been four years, Annie. I didn't really think anyone was still looking for me. I believed the car that tried to run you and Megan down was about Megan."

"But now you think it was about you."

"Yes. My financials were hacked this week. Your tires were slashed. I found a matchbook from a Chicago bar in the Depot, a bar I used to go to with Tom. And tonight—the woman who asked if I was Michael Payton—she was sent there to shake me up. Someone is coming for me, and I need to get you out of harm's way." He drew in a quick breath. "I never should have gotten involved with you, Annie. I've avoided relationships because I didn't want anyone else to get hurt. But I couldn't stay away from you. I'm sorry."

She didn't know what to say. She was flattered that he'd found her irresistible, but was that even true? He'd lied to her about the most basic thing of all—*his name*. How could she believe anything else he said?

"Annie?" he pressed. "You're not talking and that's not like you. I'd rather you scream and yell at me than just sit there silent."

"I don't know what to say. I don't know what the truth is."

"Let me clear one thing up. You may not know Michael Payton, but you do know Griffin Hale. I run a bar. I surf in my spare time. I play guitar. I read books. And I help people who are on the run. That's who I am, Annie."

"But what about who you *were*? What about your family? Was any of what you told me true?"

"It was all true. My mom died. My father had drinking problems and trouble keeping jobs. I lived with my grandparents in high school. My grandfather ran a bar in Wrigleyville, near the ballpark. It was his place that I modeled the Depot after. I wanted it to feel like a local hangout, a place you wanted to go to every weekend. I wanted it to feel like home, a home I could never see again."

"Where is your family now?"

"They're safe. That's all you need to know."

"Still keeping secrets?"

"I promised I would never give away their location."

"Do they know where you are?"

"No," he said, shaking his head. "I haven't spoken to them since the day they left town. It was too risky. I've had Paul check on them a couple of times. He assures me that they're fine."

She wanted to know more about his family, but she had more pressing concerns. "Do you know who is after you now? I thought your ex-partner went to jail."

"Tom is in jail, but he could have someone working for him on the outside."

"Like who?"

"That's what I need to figure out. In the meantime, it might be good for you to go home for a while."

"I am home."

"I mean your parents' place in San Francisco."

"No. I can't do that. I'm probably going to have another job interview next week. I can't just leave. And the last thing I want to do is run to my parents and tell them I'm in the middle of this mess."

"You don't have to tell them. It doesn't have to be for long."

"I'm not leaving."

"I can't guarantee you'll be safe if you stay."

"I'm not asking for a guarantee. What about Vinnie? What does he know?"

"He knows what I did in Chicago. I told him before we went into partnership together."

"You must have come to trust him really fast." She was disappointed to realize that Griffin had only told her because that woman had shown up in the bar. If she hadn't, who knew how long he would have waited, or if he would have told her at all?

"I told you Vinnie and I met through a friend. That friend was Paul. Paul and Vinnie served together in the Marines. When I got to San Clemente, Paul hooked us up. Vinnie had been through hard times himself. He'd been injured, he'd suffered from PTSD and he had trouble finding his life outside the military. I got him to go out on the water with me. I told you he didn't like to ride the waves much, but he did like to talk, and when we were out there, we talked a lot."

"Go on…"

"We were both looking to start a new chapter. Vinnie had always wanted to cook. I had fond memories of my grandfather's bar. It felt like something we should try. We spent months coming up with a plan. Vinnie had some money from his grandfather. I had a little cash from when my grandmother had died. She'd told me to save it for when I bought a house. A house didn't seem like it was in my future, so I put the money into the bar. When we found the Depot was available to lease, everything clicked into place."

"It reminded you of your mom and your train," she said, as another piece of the puzzle fell into place.

"That was part of it."

"Well, you've built a great business together."

"Yes. But it could all end very soon. I'll talk to Vinnie tomorrow to see what he wants to do, if he feels we should shut down for a while. So far, the threats, the warnings, whatever you want to call them, have been minor, but they could escalate at any point."

She felt a little sick at that thought. "I need a drink." She got up from the couch and went into the kitchen.

Griffin followed her, watching as she opened a bottle of red wine and poured them each a glass.

"Thanks," he said. "I'm a little surprised you haven't kicked me out yet."

She was a little surprised, too. She was also worried she wasn't seeing things clearly through her hazy, lusty gaze for Griffin. *Was she letting him off the hook in some way? Was she believing in his latest story too easily? Was it all just another lie?*

"I still might kick you out." She took a sip of her wine, then added, "I feel a little hurt, Griffin."

His gaze darkened. "The last thing I wanted to do was hurt you. I did try to warn you that you didn't know me."

"People say that all the time. They mean you don't know I'm a slob or that I eat cookies in bed or that I binge watch reality TV. They don't usually mean I've changed my name and someone might be trying to kill me."

A faint smile entered his eyes.

"It's not funny," she told him.

"I know. Sorry. I thought you were trying to lighten the

mood."

Maybe she had been trying to do that, because the darker part of this story was a little more difficult to absorb. "We need to keep talking."

"As much as you want, but it doesn't have to be tonight. I'm sorry I messed up your birthday."

"It was really perfect until about an hour ago."

"I want you to know, Annie, that everything that has happened between us is completely real. It's honest. I have not lied to you about how I feel about you. If you can believe anything, I hope you can believe that."

She wanted to believe that. "You haven't actually said how you feel about me."

"I thought I'd showed you."

"You did, but sometimes words are good, too."

"I care about you, Annie, probably more than you would believe. And I trust you. I really hope you can find a way to trust me, but I understand if you can't."

"I need to think. We should continue this tomorrow."

"That's fine, but I'm not leaving, Annie."

"You have to go, Griffin. I can't—"

"I know you can't," he said, cutting her off. "I'm going to sleep on the couch. I won't bother you, but I wouldn't feel right leaving you here alone tonight."

She drank the rest of her wine and put down her empty glass. "Fine." She walked over to the hall closet, pulled out a pillow and a blanket and tossed them onto the couch. "Goodnight, Griffin."

And then she walked into her bedroom and closed the door firmly behind her, deciding there was at least one mistake she didn't need to make again. But as she got undressed and crawled into bed alone, she couldn't help wishing that nothing he'd told her was true, that he could just be Griffin Hale, no dark past, no secrets, no danger threatening to destroy them both.

Nineteen

---><><---

Had he lost Annie?

Probably.

Griffin stretched out on the couch in Annie's living room and stared at the ceiling. Maybe that was for the best. But imagining a life without Annie put him in the same dark place he'd been in four years ago. He couldn't go back to that darkness, and he wasn't going to run again. He'd made a new life for himself, and he wasn't going to lose it without a fight. He would find out who was messing with him and then he would put an end to it. He hadn't been a cop in four years, but he needed to start thinking like one again.

Questions ran through his head: *Why now? Had his whereabouts suddenly been discovered? And if so, why not a more direct attack on him?*

It felt as if someone was playing with him. And what didn't make sense was why or how Tom could orchestrate an elaborate plan of slow torture from a prison cell. If he'd just hired a hit man to go after him, he'd be dead by now, and that would have made more sense. But this cat-and-mouse game of revenge—was that really Tom?

If it was Tom, he had to have help, someone in San Clemente, and that person had been in the bar. *Was it the woman who had come up to him? Was it the guy arguing with Shari in the parking lot? Was it the person who had slashed Annie's tires?*

Or was it someone closer to home? Someone on his staff? He trusted Vinnie implicitly. And Justin didn't seem like the type to be that manipulative or crafty. Shari had been secretive lately, but she wasn't tied to his Chicago past. Still, he needed to talk to her, find out what had happened with the guy in the van. He'd do that tomorrow.

He also needed to check in with his dad and his grandfather as well—but it was too late to call them tonight. Maybe he shouldn't be the one to call them. Perhaps Paul could do it. He'd used him as an intermediary before; Paul might be able to help again, keep the distance between himself and his family.

Rolling onto his side, he could hear the waves hitting the shore, but they didn't sound soothing tonight. They matched the pounding beat of his heart, the uncertainty in his head.

He was restless. He wanted to do something. He wanted to take back control. He thought he'd done that by building a new life, but he was right back where he'd been.

Maybe not all the way back.

Things were different now. He had Annie—maybe. She was conflicted, torn, and he couldn't blame her. He just didn't want to lose her.

On the other hand, what did he have to offer her? *What if he had to go on the run again?* He couldn't take her with him. He couldn't disrupt her life. She had family, a life.

Flopping onto his back, he closed his eyes and just tried to let go. If he slept, time would go faster.

Only he couldn't sleep—he was too worked up. He'd thought he could live without a relationship. He'd thought fun, no-strings sex, could work for a long time. But now he wanted more than that. He wanted Annie in his life—with all her chatter and curiosity and imagination. He wanted to share his meals with her, his bed, his bar, his life…

But again, he came back to—what did he have to offer her? *Nothing.*

He sighed again. Then his heart jumped as he heard Annie's door click open, followed by the sound of soft footsteps. She came over to the couch, wearing a loose T-shirt and PJ shorts. She stared down at him.

"You're awake," she said, an uncertain note in her voice.

"Can't sleep."

"Me, either." She perched on the edge of the coffee table. "I keep thinking about everything."

He turned onto his side to face her. "Come to any conclusions?"

"You said I was the one who was going to complicate your life, but it turned out to be the other way around."

"I guess it did."

"I want to believe you're the person I think you are. The connection we have between us is not easy to find. I don't want to let it go, but I can't help wondering if the connection is as false as your name."

"You know it's not," he said quietly.

"I like to think I'm a good judge of character. I notice details about people. It comes with being an artist. I look at things more closely than others do. But I looked at you, and I didn't see the pretense."

"Didn't you? Isn't that why you always had so many questions?"

"Maybe," she conceded. "I knew you had secrets; I just didn't know that they were this big."

"Now you do."

"When you said you used to be a cop, I was shocked, but the more I think about it, the more I realize how much sense that makes. You're a natural born protector. You watch out for people. That's why Paul trusted you with his witnesses."

"He knew I would do everything I could to take care of them. He also knew that I understood what it was like to live as someone you're not."

She nodded. "I get it. Were you always so isolated? Or was that just because you couldn't let yourself get close?"

"To be honest, I've always been alone. It started when I was young, when I didn't want to bring friends home after school because my dad might show up drunk. But it probably got worse after I left Chicago. I had to be really careful all the time, especially in the beginning."

She drew in a breath and let it out. "It's a lot to process, Griffin."

"I know. And I can say I'm sorry again—as many times as you need to hear it. I knew I should have said good-bye to you days ago, but I couldn't pull the trigger. When I did make a half-hearted attempt at it, you talked me out of it."

"I didn't know what I was talking you out of—I just thought you were afraid of commitment. It's not like you're the first guy I've met who wanted to have no-strings fun."

"I'm not afraid of commitment; I'm just not in a position to commit to anything or anyone." He paused for a moment. "I thought I could live the way I was living and be happy enough, but I have to say that once I met you, everything changed. You made me want to have a better life."

"I did that?" she asked doubtfully.

"You did. While the bar has been going great, my personal life was one boring, dull shade of endless gray until you walked through the door, and then it was filled with bright colors, with optimism, with lots of conversation. I didn't want it to end."

Her breath hitched and she clasped her hands together. "Maybe…"

His heart sped up. "Maybe what?"

"Maybe tonight we could just be the way we were yesterday, before I knew anything."

"Can you really put what you've learned out of your head?" he asked doubtfully.

"It wouldn't be easy," she admitted. "But if I had some help from you…a little distraction, something else to think about, it might work." A smile played around her lips. "Are you up to it?"

"Most definitely," he said, sitting up. "Are you sure?"

"About being with you tonight—yes. Everything else—no idea."

"I'll take it. But we're not making love on this couch. It's really uncomfortable."

"I agree."

He took her hands in his as they got to their feet. "I can't promise that tomorrow isn't going to bring more problems. I don't want to lead you on, Annie."

"I understand. Is there anything else I don't know about your past?"

"I don't think so. Nothing big anyway. I haven't shared all my childhood stories. But you know the important stuff."

"Then we'll let tomorrow take care of itself." She let go of his hands and pulled her top over her head, revealing her beautiful breasts, with the faint dusting of freckles. But he didn't have time to really appreciate them before she turned and ran toward the bedroom.

He pulled off his shirt as he followed her. He found her PJ shorts and panties on the floor next to the bed when he entered the room, and he got rid of his own clothes as he joined her in bed. He thought she might hold back, still unsure about him, but their first kiss was explosively tender, filled with so much longing and desire, it sucked the breath out of his chest.

Annie was the most generous, forgiving, honest person he'd ever met, and he felt like the luckiest man on earth.

He wanted to show her how much he cared about her, how much he wanted to win back her trust. So, despite the furious, driving need running through his body, he went slow, savoring every kiss, every touch, making her as crazy as she was making him.

Annie smelled coffee. Blinking her eyes open, she saw

Griffin set a mug on the nightstand next to her bed.

"Good morning," he said, giving her a kiss, then sitting down next to her.

She was sorry to see his sexy male body covered in clothes. His hair was damp, and he smelled like soap, so he'd obviously gotten up a while ago and grabbed a shower as well as made her coffee.

She scooted up into a sitting position, keeping the sheet in front of her breasts.

A look of amusement ran through Griffin's eyes. "Really? I know you're not shy. Not after last night."

"I'm a little less shy in the middle of the night," she said, reaching for the mug. She took a sip and let the caffeine wake her the rest of the way up. "When did you get up?"

"About an hour ago. I've been thinking about my next move. I want to talk to Shari this morning. I don't know if she's involved, but her behavior has been off, and she has access to the office and the computer. She also knows where I am most of the time. I've always thought of her as a good employee and a friend, but she has changed, and I can't overlook that. Someone could be threatening her, bribing her, who knows? I just know that I need to take action, and she's first on the list."

"Okay. Can I come with you?"

"I was thinking you could hang at the bar with Vinnie."

She made a face at that suggestion. "So he can babysit me?"

"He's an ex-Marine; he can keep you safe."

"Or I could go with you, an ex-cop, and you could keep me safe."

"But I'm the one who's the target. I don't want you to be collateral damage."

"We'll keep an eye on each other. We're just going to Shari's apartment." She could see that Griffin really didn't want to take her with him. Perhaps she would be in more danger if she hung out with him, but on the other hand, she never felt safer than when she was with him. "I want to stick close to you, Griffin. If anything looks really off, I'll stay in the car, or I'll take a cab somewhere else, maybe the nearest police station. Speaking of which, are you going to call the police?"

"That's farther down the list. I want to figure out a few other things first."

"Like what?"

"I called Paul earlier. He's going to see what he can find out about Tom's visitor list at the prison. That might help me pinpoint who he's using on the outside."

"That's a good idea," she said with a nod. "Very smart."

"I was on my way to detective when I quit the department."

"I'm sorry you had to give that up. Would you ever go back if things were different?"

"No, never. I'm done with that life. I like running the bar. It fits me better than I thought it would."

"You have a lot of your grandfather in you."

"I've wanted to tell him about it a dozen times, but I can't call him. It's too risky. I have asked Paul to check on him and my father as well."

As Griffin spoke, she wondered if he would leave San Clemente. She wanted him to stay, but she also wanted him to stay alive.

Seeing the worry and uncertainty in his eyes, she put her hand on his arm and then leaned forward to kiss him, wanting to give him what little comfort and reassurance she could. Then she said, "We're going to figure it out, Griffin. You've got a partner whether you like it or not. And you know how pushy I can be when I want something."

"I do know that."

"I should get dressed."

His gaze dropped to the thin sheet covering her body, and she saw a new gleam of hunger.

"No," she said, bringing his eyes back to hers. "Or we'll never get out of this apartment."

"It's not my fault you're so damned beautiful and

irresistible."

She flushed at his words. "You're pretty irresistible, too."

"So, I distracted you last night?" he teased.

"Yes. And we can consider more distractions later, but right now I'm going to shower and get dressed."

"I'll make you breakfast. I'm not Vinnie, but I can whip up scrambled eggs, and I noticed you had some in the fridge."

"I am not going to turn that offer down. There's turkey bacon, too."

"Coming up. Don't take too long in the shower, or I might have to join you."

She was tempted to test his resolve, but as his phone buzzed, she realized they had more important things to do today. "Who's that?" she asked, as he read a text.

"It's Vinnie. I'm going to call him back."

As Griffin left the room, she headed into the shower, wondering if it was really Vinnie. There had been something off about his response. He'd told her that he'd given her the whole truth last night, but there was still a part of her that wasn't completely sure. She wanted to trust him, because she was falling in love with him.

That thought stopped her in her tracks.

Was she really falling in love with him? A man whose real name she hadn't learned until after she'd slept with him?

That question followed her all the way into the shower, and she still didn't have an answer when she got out.

"Okay, I now know one more thing about you." Annie set down her fork next to her empty plate. "You can cook scrambled eggs. And you can even fancy them up with some cheese and scallions."

He smiled at her from across the table. "I used what I saw in your fridge."

"I'm surprised you found that much. I haven't done a lot of shopping lately." She paused. "Griffin, there's something I want to ask you about—make that *someone*. Paige."

"I told you everything you need to know about Paige."

"Actually, you didn't tell me much at all. Or if you did, it didn't stick. I know you met her through your partner."

"Yes. She was friends with Tom and his younger brother. They brought her to a pizza party one night, and that's how we started dating."

"What was she like?" she asked, curious to know what kind of woman had gotten into Griffin's heart. "What did she do for a living?"

"She was smart. She worked in finance for a fashion company. She loved clothes, loved to shop. She could be a little dramatic, emotional, but she was also fun. I loved her family. Her dad was a great guy. He was the kind of man anyone would want to have for their dad. Her mom used to bake up a storm at the holidays. She'd always send me home with cookies and pies. I probably gained ten pounds while we were dating." He paused. "In retrospect, I'd say that I might have liked Paige's family even more than I liked her. It felt good to be part of Sunday dinner and Christmas Eve. But, of course, that all went away when I betrayed the family."

Her heart went out to him. She doubted Griffin would ever admit to how much he'd been hurt by the people who had turned their backs on him, but clearly it had been painful. And she could understand why. His own family had shattered with his mom's death, his dad's drinking. He'd been looking for a way to replace that loss. She wished her family was nearby. The Callaways would take him in and hug the hell out of him. But for now, she would have to be the one to do that.

"Do you think you would have stayed together if you hadn't turned Tom in?"

"No. We didn't bring out the best in each other. We would have ended, no matter what. Now, can we be done talking about Paige?"

She nodded. "Yes, I was just curious."

"Imagine that," he said dryly.

She made a face at him, then stood up. "I'm going to

finish getting ready and then we'll go see Shari."

"If you insist on going with me, yes." He picked up their dishes and took them to the sink.

"Don't worry about washing them. Just stick them in the dishwasher. I'll run it later."

After putting on her shoes and grabbing a jacket, she and Griffin went downstairs to his car. Once again, Griffin was on high alert, his gaze darting in every direction, but everything was fine. There was no one around, and they got into the car without incident.

As she fastened her seat belt, she said, "Now that I know you were a cop, your skill level at taking my brother down so quickly makes a lot more sense."

"He was fast on the rebound," Griffin said, as he pulled out of the garage.

"Hunter has never backed away from a fight, and as charming as he is, he does seem to get into more than his fair share of trouble. I don't know what's going on with him these days. He took a leave of absence from the fire department to travel. He said he wanted to see the world, and he has certainly been doing that, but I feel like there's more behind his desire to be on the road than just wanderlust, but if there is, I can't get it out of him." She glanced over at Griffin. "Maybe I was so pushy with you because I'm used to stubborn men."

"I'm kind of glad you didn't give up on me."

"Kind of?" she challenged.

"Very glad," he corrected.

"Better. Where does Shari live?"

"A couple of miles from the bar."

"I asked you once if she was part of your sideline witness protection program, but you didn't really answer me."

"She was not brought to the bar by Paul, but Vinnie and I met Shari when she was homeless. She had left an abusive partner behind in Phoenix, and she was down on her luck. She used to sleep behind the bar, under the overhang. Vinnie and I offered her a job and helped her find a place to live."

More evidence of Griffin's generosity. "That was very nice of you."

"It wasn't just me; Vinnie was there, too. We gave her a hand up. The rest was on her. She didn't let us down. She turned her life around. She got a roommate. She worked hard. She seemed to be fine, until a couple of weeks ago. Then she started coming in late, calling in sick, and she had a lot of excuses. But I don't think she could hack into my bank accounts, and I can't imagine how she could be behind the tire slashing or the almost hit-and-run in the parking lot."

"But..." she pressed.

"If she was in trouble or needed money, I don't know. Hopefully, I can clear up any doubts when we speak to her."

"I hope so. You know, I do need to get my car back at some point. We never got it yesterday."

"They're closed on Sundays; we'll do it tomorrow. Sorry again about the inconvenience."

"It hasn't been too bad having you as my chauffeur."

He gave her a smile, then checked the mirror as he changed lanes and turned right at the next corner.

The apartment buildings in this neighborhood were extremely modest and a bit rundown. It was certainly a far cry from the beachfront apartment she was lucky enough to be able to sublet.

Griffin parked on the street. Then they walked down the block to a three-story building. There was no security door, and Griffin led the way up to the second floor. She didn't know why, but she felt a bit nervous, and was happy to keep one hand on Griffin's back. The halls were dark and felt a bit damp, and there was an odd smell in the air, burnt popcorn, or something worse.

Griffin suddenly stopped.

"What's wrong?" she murmured.

He tipped his head toward the door, which was slightly ajar. "Stay here."

She was hesitant to have him move even four feet away from her, but he was already gone.

He knocked on the door and said, "Shari," as he pushed it open. "Oh, God," he said, rushing into the room.

She couldn't stop herself from moving down the hall. When she got to the doorway, she saw Griffin kneeling next to Shari, who was sprawled on the ground, blood dripping down her face, her hands pressed against her side where more blood was dripping through her fingers.

A wave of fear raced through her.

"Call 911," Griffin ordered as he grabbed a kitchen towel and pressed it against Shari's side. Shari appeared to be semiconscious, her eyes opening and closing, her voice mumbling words that didn't make sense.

When the operator came on the line, she reported that a woman had been assaulted, repeating the address Griffin shouted out to her.

Then she moved closer as Shari gasped for breath.

"Hang in there," Griffin told Shari. "Help is coming. You're going to be all right. Stay with me."

As he finished speaking, he looked up at her, and she saw the fear in his eyes. He had no idea if Shari was going to survive, and neither did she.

Twenty

Griffin pressed firmly against the knife wound in Shari's gut. Her head was also bleeding, but that appeared to be from falling and striking her head against the coffee table. He thought the real danger would be coming from whatever damage had been done to her internal organs. He prayed for the ambulance to arrive quickly.

"I'm—I'm sorry," Shari said, stuttering out the words.

"Don't talk. Just breathe."

"I didn't want to hurt you."

His stomach turned over at her words. "What did you do?"

"They said they wanted to mess with you. I—I needed the money. They gave me a lot of money."

"Who's they?"

Her eyes fluttered closed.

"Shari," he said, caught between wanting to take care of her and needing to get the truth before she passed out. "Who wanted to mess with me?"

"They're not done," she whispered. "Don't hate me. I couldn't end up on the street again. They just wanted to get into the bar."

"To do what?"

"Want you to suffer, lose everything," she murmured. "Annie."

"What about me?" Annie asked sharply.

"They know..." Shari's voice drifted off.

"Know what?" Annie asked, an urgent note in her voice.

He understood her desperation. Shari had answers, but while she was still breathing, she was no longer conscious. Thankfully, the paramedics were entering the apartment, followed by two uniformed police officers.

He got to his feet to let the medics do their work, thinking about all the times he'd arrived on a scene like this, a victim fighting for her life, and two people needing to be questioned.

But there were a lot of things he didn't want to talk about. While the San Clemente Police Department was on the other side of the country from Chicago, blue ties could run deep. He couldn't take the chance that this investigation would tip even more people to his whereabouts. He needed to call Paul to run interference, but he wasn't going to be able to do that for now. He would have to stall.

His gaze moved to Annie. She was pale and shaken, her eyes wide with fear and uncertainty. He wanted to talk to her, to tell her it would be all right, to ask her to think about what she would tell the police. But there was no time. The officers would separate them. He would give his story, and she would give hers. And knowing how much Annie loved to talk, he suspected her story would be much longer than his.

As the medics took Shari down to the ambulance, he glanced at his hands, realizing they were covered in blood— Shari's blood. He felt sick at the thought that Shari might die, and it might be because of him. Maybe he shouldn't feel bad, because clearly Shari had sold him out in some way. But he still felt like she was a victim. He still cared about the woman he'd watched pull her life together only to end up like this— because someone had used her to get to him.

Annie surprised him by handing him a clean kitchen towel.

"Thanks," he said, wiping off his hands as best he could.

She put a hand on his arm, drawing his gaze to hers. "You did what you could."

"I hope it's enough."

The female officer interrupted them, asking Annie to step into the hall while the male officer asked him to stay behind.

The officer, a tall, Hispanic man, with the last name of Rodriguez, asked him to explain what had happened.

"I'm Griffin Hale, Shari's boss. I run the Depot, a bar where Shari is employed as a waitress. She's been calling in sick lately, and I was concerned about her, so I came by to check on her. When I got here, I found the door open. Shari was on the floor. I tried to apply pressure to her wounds while Annie called for help." He deliberately kept his narrative short, not wanting to sound like the cop he'd once been.

"Was the victim conscious?"

"Some of the time."

"Did she say who did this?"

"I tried to get a name out of her, but she just kept saying *they*. I assume there was more than one person."

"Did you see anyone leaving the scene when you arrived? Were there any neighbors out?"

He shook his head. "I didn't see anyone in front of the building or in the hallway. I'm surprised none of the neighbors have come over here. Shari must have screamed. It looks like there was a struggle," he said, tipping his head to the overturned chair and the broken lamp.

"We'll talk to the neighbors," the officer said.

"Was your employee having problems with anyone?"

He debated how to answer that question and decided there was one incident he did feel comfortable mentioning. "There was an incident at the bar a couple of days ago. A man in a van followed her into our employee lot. They exchanged words. She said that the man believed she'd cut him off in traffic, and he was yelling at her. He drove off after a minute, and she said she didn't know who he was."

"You saw this happen?"

"No. my partner, Vinnie Price, saw it. He told me about it."

"You didn't talk to her about it personally?"

"No. I didn't have a chance, but, as I said, I was concerned about her. That's why I came here this morning." He drew in a breath. "I hope she makes it, so she can tell us who did this to her."

"Does she have a husband, a boyfriend, a roommate?"

"She had a roommate until a couple of months ago. That woman moved away, out of the city. I don't know about her personal relationships. She doesn't share that information with me. One of her other coworkers might know more. I can give you the names of everyone I know her to be in contact with."

"That would be helpful."

He gave the officer the names of all of his employees. As he finished doing that, Annie came back into the room, followed by the female officer.

"I've got everything I need for now," the female officer said.

Officer Rodriguez nodded, then turned to him. "We may need to question you both further."

"We'll make ourselves available," he said. "Right now, we want to get to the hospital. Shari doesn't have any family. I don't want her to be alone."

"We'll be down there soon," the officer said.

He ushered Annie out of the apartment. They didn't speak until they were in the car with the doors locked.

"That was horrific," Annie said, turning in her seat to face him.

"Yes, it was." Despite his desire to get to the hospital, he didn't start the car. Instead he leaned across the console and put his arms around Annie, giving in to the desperate need to hold her. He didn't know if he was comforting her or if she was comforting him, but they stayed like that for a long minute. Then he gave her a quick kiss and sat back in his seat.

"Do you think Shari will make it?" Annie asked, her eyes filled with fear and worry.

"I don't know. I really hope so."

"There was a lot of blood. I've never seen anyone— anyone hurt like that."

"You held it together. You called for help."

"That was nothing. You put pressure on the wound. You probably saved her life."

"I want to believe that." He drew in a breath then said, "I have to ask—"

"What I told the police?" she finished, meeting his gaze.

"Whatever you said is fine. I just need to know."

"I didn't tell them about your past, Griffin. I thought about it, but the police officer just asked me about Shari and how I knew her and how I knew you. I told her that Shari murmured some words, but I didn't really hear them. I did lie a little about that, because I heard enough to know Shari was involved with whoever is after you. I didn't know what to say beyond that, so I decided to say as little as possible."

"I would never ask you to lie, but I'm glad you were careful."

"Did you volunteer information about your past?"

"No. Like you, I stayed on topic."

"Even though Shari was apologizing to you? You didn't want to share that with the police? How are they going to find out who did this if they don't have all the information?"

"They'll get the whole story," he assured her. "I just want to talk to Paul first. He already has a contact in the San Clemente Police Department that he spoke to when we thought someone was after Megan. That's the person who needs to hear the story first."

"I guess that makes sense." She paused. "I know you probably don't trust the police anymore, but this department could be different."

"They probably are different, but we'll see. I did tell Officer Rodriguez that Shari was going in and out of consciousness and that she did not name her attackers, which is true. As for what she said to me—it sounded like she was paid or blackmailed or threatened to help someone get to me. I just wish she would have been able to tell me who came after her."

"And why," she muttered. "If they were using her to get to you, and she was going along with them, then why did someone stab her?"

It was a question that had been going around in his head. "I can only assume they asked her to do one thing too many."

"She said my name. She said 'they know' and then she said my name. What do you think that meant?"

"That they know we're together." As fear leapt into her eyes, he quickly added, "We already knew that, Annie. That's why I'm staying close to you."

"Knowing it and hearing it from the mouth of someone who had just been stabbed by the same people makes it a lot more real and terrifying."

"I want to get you out of this, Annie. I still think you should go to your parents' house in San Francisco."

"No way. Shari said they know about us. It doesn't matter where I go; someone could find me. They could use me as leverage against you, no matter where I am."

He wanted to argue, but everything she was saying was true.

"Let's go to the hospital," Annie said. "Maybe Shari will be able to give us more answers."

On the way to the hospital, Griffin called Vinnie and filled him in on what had happened. With the speaker on in the car, she could hear the shock in Vinnie's voice, as well as a sense of betrayal. But for the moment, Griffin and Vinnie were more focused on Shari's recovery than on what she'd allowed to be done to them. Vinnie said he would tell the staff and keep things going at the bar but to notify them as soon as there was any news.

Unfortunately, when they got to the hospital, they discovered that Shari was in surgery, and there was no news to be found. They settled into chairs in the fifth-floor waiting room.

Now that the adrenaline rush was wearing off, Annie was starting to really feel the fear of what had happened to Shari and what danger might be lurking in the shadows for her and for Griffin.

Everything that had happened before today had felt more like a warning, but this—this was different. Someone had violently assaulted Shari. They could have killed her. And she didn't want to consider the possibility that Shari could still die.

She knew Griffin was worried. Even now, he was staring at his hands, probably still seeing Shari's blood on his fingers, even though he'd already been to the restroom to wash his hands again. It was a little surprising that Griffin could care so much about a woman who had obviously betrayed him. Maybe he hadn't gotten to that realization yet. Maybe he was still thinking of Shari as a friend and not as the person who had been willing to sell him out for some cash.

Griffin raised his gaze from his hands and turned to face her. "If Shari dies, it's on me."

"No. This is not on you, Griffin. You cannot think that way."

His anguished gaze met hers. "They would have never approached her if she wasn't working for me."

"She could have said no. She could have come to you and told you what they wanted. You saved her when she was homeless and in need of a job. You gave her back her life. She owed you her loyalty." She realized she had gone from trying to make him feel better about Shari's betrayal to nailing down the fact that his employee and friend had sold him out. But she just couldn't stand the thought of him taking responsibility for what had happened to Shari.

"I know you're right. I'm just tired of people getting hurt because of me. Sometimes, I do look back and wonder if it was worth it. My family suffered. My friends suffered, and now it's happening again. All of my employees could be in danger right now. I need to shut down the bar."

"But you have the holiday party for Hamilton House next week."

He frowned. "I know, but I can't put all those kids in danger."

"What about hiring security for it?"

"I have to think about it. And I'll need to talk to Vinnie again." His phone buzzed. "It's Paul. I'm going to take this somewhere else," he said, tipping his head toward an older couple seated on a couch at the other end of the room.

She nodded, watching him go, hoping he would get some information that would help them figure out who was after him.

———

"I can talk now." Griffin opened the door to the rooftop deck and stepped outside, happy to let the crisp air clear the fog from his head. "I'm glad you called. One of my employees was assaulted, stabbed; I'm at the hospital now."

"What the hell?"

"Yeah, and all this is definitely about Chicago, Paul."

"How do you know?"

"Shari, the employee who was stabbed, wasn't making a lot of sense, but she told me someone approached her with cash. They wanted to mess with me, get into the bar, make me suffer. She needed the money, so she helped them. I'm not sure exactly what she did or what the end game is. She's in surgery, so I won't be able to talk to her again for several hours."

"Did you tell all this to the police?" Paul asked.

"No. I wanted to speak to you first."

"Good. Let me run point on this. I already talked to a Detective Baker in regard to Megan's situation. I'll start with him. It will make things easier for you. Otherwise, you're going to waste a lot of time explaining who you are and what you were involved in. I'll be a more objective narrator."

"I agree." He hadn't been looking forward to discussing his past involvement with a sting operation against his fellow police officers. That wouldn't sit well no matter how far he was from Chicago.

"I also wanted to let you know that I checked with my contacts at the prison," Paul said.

"Did you find out who has been visiting Tom?"

"Well, here's the thing. Tom was seriously injured in a prison fight last month. His injuries were extensive. He's been in a coma since then, and he's not expected to recover."

"What?" he asked, shocked to the core by Paul's words. "How did it happen? Who did it?"

"There were several men involved in the attack, but one of them had direct ties to the Lavizzo gang, which, as you know, was the organization that paid Tom off."

"Why would they go after him now? It's been four years."

"Apparently, during the last year, Tom found his conscience. He's been feeding information to the feds. This was payback."

"Tom was finally talking," he murmured, surprised again. Tom had refused to give any information that might have helped him at sentencing saying he'd be safer on the inside if he didn't. Apparently, he'd been right about that.

"Yes, he was talking—a lot. He has also had a stream of visitors since his attack, many of whom worked with you and Tom."

"And probably blame me for what happened to Tom. It's my fault he was in there."

"That would be my guess, especially in light of the nature of the incidents. They're personal. As you said, someone is messing with you. I'm going to do some more digging, see if I can find out if anyone connected to you or Tom bought plane tickets to Southern California or might be in your area."

"Shari referred to her attackers as *they*. We're dealing

with more than one person." He paused. "I appreciate your help, Paul. I know this is way outside of your job."

"You've helped me a lot in the past two years, Griffin, and not just me, but a lot of people."

"Is Megan free now?"

"Yes, she's officially out of the program. She isn't quite ready to be home, but she has been reunited with her sister and they're spending some time out of the country in a very beautiful and sunny location."

"I'm glad. It's nice to hear some good news."

"Watch your back, Griffin. I don't think this is over yet."

"Neither do I."

Twenty-One

$\longrightarrow$ ✦ ❦ ✦ $\longleftarrow$

While Griffin was talking to Paul, Annie pulled out her phone and went on the Internet. After bouncing around on social media for a few minutes, she impulsively typed in Michael Payton, Chicago police officer. She hadn't had much luck when she'd looked for Griffin Hale, but to her surprise, there were several pages of results for Michael Payton.

She quickly discovered that most of the articles were about the trial of Tom Holtzer and the testimony of his partner Michael Payton. There was even a photo of Griffin/Michael at the courthouse. He looked incredibly somber and isolated, as he walked down the steps wearing a black suit. It looked like he was going to a funeral, and it had probably felt that way to him.

Was this all about revenge? Had Tom and his cohorts finally discovered Griffin's location and decided to make him pay?

It certainly seemed the most likely scenario. But since Tom was in prison, someone else was making the threats. And if they were willing to kill Shari, they surely would have no problem going after Griffin or her.

Was she foolish to stay with him? Was she blinded by her mad crush on the man? Would it be smarter to get out of town for a while, let Griffin figure things out?

But would that matter? She and Griffin had been together a lot, and if someone had been watching them, they'd know that she was involved with him. If they wanted to hurt Griffin, destroy everything he had, as Shari had said, then she could still be a target. She'd told him that she didn't think she'd feel safe anywhere without him, and that was still true, but she didn't know if she'd feel safe with him, either.

Where had her normal, boring life gone?

Everything had changed when she'd gone into the ocean, when she'd decided to test herself. And she couldn't feel bad about it, because with all the danger had come the man she was falling in love with.

She clicked away from the photo at the courthouse, looking for more images of Griffin and his past. Several results later, she found another picture of him with an attractive brunette at a charity fundraiser—Paige Marquette. She drew in a quick breath at the image of the woman Griffin had been involved with. She was pretty—tall and slim, wearing a body-hugging black dress and black boots with a heavy gold necklace. She had a smile on her face, but it didn't seem all that friendly.

Clicking through to the next photo, she saw a photo of Paige standing between Griffin and Tom at the same fundraiser, and her heart skipped a beat.

Tom was taller than Griffin by a few inches, lean, lanky, a relaxed, happy, easygoing vibe to his smile. He was handsome, too, with blond hair and a short beard.

This was the man who might be trying to hurt them?

It was hard to connect this image with that thought, but then she didn't know Tom at all. And obviously, he'd been quite good at deception, until Griffin came along.

Griffin looked happy in the photo, too. It must have been taken before he realized what Tom was doing.

He'd said he didn't think he and Paige would have ended

up together even if the problem with Tom hadn't come along, but she wondered if that were true.

Frowning at that thought, she clicked out of the Internet. She didn't want to look at Paige anymore. She didn't want to think about Griffin and another woman.

She straightened in her seat as Griffin came back into the waiting room. He'd been gone awhile, and judging by his worried expression, whatever he'd learned from Paul had not been good.

Fortunately, the other couple who had been in the waiting room had already left, so they could speak freely.

"What did Paul say?" she asked, as Griffin sat next to her.

He met her gaze. "Quite a lot actually. Tom was brutally attacked in prison several weeks ago. He's been in a coma ever since. They don't expect him to recover."

"What?" she asked in surprise. "Tom is not the one doing this or ordering it to be done?"

"Not unless he set the plan in motion before he was injured, but that's doubtful. Apparently, Tom found religion in prison and was trying to change his life around. Some of his former colleagues decided to shut him up before he said too much."

"I'm confused. If it's not Tom, who is it?"

"I suspect that what happened to Tom motivated one of his friends to come after me, possibly someone I used to call a friend as well."

She put a hand on his arm, seeing the pain in his eyes. "I'm sorry, Griffin."

"I never wanted this to happen, Annie. I never wanted Tom to get hurt, to possibly die for his crimes. I just wanted him to take responsibility for what he did. But then I have to ask myself, what did I expect to happen? I put a cop in a prison full of people who hate cops."

"Tom put himself in that prison. His actions made that happen, not yours."

"Maybe I could have done something differently."

"Protecting him, going against your own conscience, would have destroyed you, Griffin."

"Well, it doesn't matter now. Tom is as good as dead from what I hear."

"Then let's start talking about who else was his friend, who would try to find you, come after you, be willing to kill a woman in the process of getting revenge against you."

"I've been thinking about that. Tom had a cousin who was also a cop—Kenny Taylor. He came at me one day after work. We slugged it out while several of our cop friends watched, most of whom cheered him on. Eventually, the captain broke it up."

"That's disgusting, and he sounds like a good suspect."

"But he wasn't the only one who'd told me I'd be sorry. Tom's partner before me also had a lot of anger—Hank Palmer. He gave me a difficult time on more than one occasion as well."

"Then we'll start with them. But do you really think another cop would stab Shari?"

He frowned at her question. "That does seem like an anomaly. There are a lot of people who would like to do that to me, but why her?"

"Obviously, she angered them in some way. What about whoever attacked Tom? You did take down their inside person. Maybe it's not a cop who's after you at all, but someone from that gang."

"It's possible, but this criminal organization would have been more likely to hire a hit man to take me out with one shot. Shari said they want me to suffer. I think Tom's friends are behind this. Maybe they're cops; maybe they're not, but my gut says I probably know at least one of them, if not both of them. Paul is going to send me the log of visitors to Tom's hospital room. He's also going to check on whether any of those people have booked a trip to Southern California in the past week."

"Maybe that will help."

"I just wish I knew how they found me. I've been so

careful to cover my tracks, to stay offline, out of sight."

"Except the day you rescued me from the sharks. Your photo was online."

"I forgot about that. My name wasn't mentioned, so I thought it would be fine, and it was local. But maybe that photo came up in front of the wrong person."

"Nothing is local where social media is concerned. Anyone could have shared that story on one of their sites, and who knows where it went from there? Not that it has to be because of the photo—"

"But it is the one thing that changed. The timing fits," he said with a nod.

"I'm sorry if that's the reason why they found you."

"I can only blame the sharks, certainly not you."

"So, what's next?"

"Shari makes it through surgery and tells us everything we need to know."

"In the meantime…"

"We try to find out who Shari has been talking to in the past few weeks. I'd like to get Shari's phone."

"The police probably have it. Maybe you should share your past with them, Griffin. Give them the whole story, so they're not operating in the dark."

"Paul is doing that as we speak. He can provide a more objective narrative, and I don't have to be the cop telling another cop why I broke the code."

"You know I come from a family of firefighters, and I know that they stand by each other. But I don't believe that anyone in my family would not do exactly what you did. You're a man of honor, Griffin. I am sure there are other police officers who were proud of what you did, even if they were afraid to say so. I know I'm proud."

He stared back at her. "That means a lot to me, Annie."

"Good." She stopped talking as a doctor came into the room. They quickly got to their feet, and she grabbed Griffin's hand, hoping for good news.

"Are you here for Shari Carlan?" the doctor asked.

"Yes, I'm her employer, Griffin Hale. She doesn't have any family," Griffin said. "How is she?"

"She made it through surgery. Her condition is critical, but we're hopeful. The next twenty-four hours will tell us more. If you leave your number at the nurse's station, they can give you a call when she wakes up."

"Thanks," Griffin said.

As the doctor left, she felt some of the tension leave Griffin's body. He gave her a smile, and she smiled back.

"Shari is going to make it," she said.

"I am so glad and not just because I want answers."

"Oh, Griffin, I know that. You care about Shari. You care about everyone who works for you. That's very, very clear."

He slid his arms around her waist and pulled her into a long hug. "Can I just say that while I hate that you're going through this with me, I'm really glad you're here."

She was touched by his words. "Me, too. I want to help you, Griffin."

"You are helping." He stepped back as they let go of each other. "I think we should go back to the bar. There's nothing more we can do here until Shari wakes up."

"I agree." As she moved to grab her bag from the chair, a man in a dark suit came into the room, flashing a badge.

"Mr. Hale? Miss Callaway?" he asked.

"Yes," Griffin said warily.

"I'm Annie Callaway," she added.

"I'm Detective Mark Baker. I just got off the phone with a US marshal by the name of Paul Daniels. He filled me in on your situation, Mr. Hale. I've also spoken to Officer Rodriguez, who said you did not share your personal story with him. Why not?"

"It's a complicated situation. I thought it might be better if an objective party shared it with you first."

"Possibly," Detective Baker said, giving Griffin, a long, measuring look. "How's the stabbing victim?"

"The doctor thinks she'll make it, but she won't be awake to question for several more hours."

"The marshal told me what happened in Chicago and that this stabbing is most likely related to that. Is there anything else you want to tell me?" the detective asked.

"Shari told me she was sorry before she passed out. She didn't say what she'd done, but she'd apparently been helping someone get to me. That is truly all I know. She did not give me names. I wish she had."

"You didn't tell Officer Rodriguez that, either."

"I'd be happy to add to my statement."

As Annie watched Griffin and the detective size each other up, she couldn't tell what the detective was thinking, if he would also consider Griffin a traitor for turning in a fellow cop, or if he would be more objective because he wasn't part of the Chicago police force.

"Let's take a little walk," the detective said to Griffin as a young couple came into the waiting room. "I have a few more questions for you."

"Do you need me, too?" she asked.

"Not at the moment," the detective said.

She sat down after they left, wishing she could hear what they were saying.

As the minutes passed, she grew more restless. She pulled out her phone and texted her sister Kate: *Are you around? I have something to ask you.*

While she was sure the police and Griffin's friend Paul would do everything they could, she wanted to bring Kate in. Kate had FBI resources, and if nothing else she might be able to keep an eye on the investigation and make sure Griffin wasn't going to get shafted by the local cops.

Her phone buzzed a moment later. "Hi, Kate, that was fast. I wasn't sure if you were still in London and I was hitting you in the middle of the night."

"I actually just landed at Dulles," Kate replied. "I'm waiting for my bags. Is everything okay?"

"No. I'm in the middle of a mess."

"Why? What's happened?"

"This guy I've been getting to know—he's in some

trouble, and now I'm in trouble, too."

"This does not sound good. Where are you? Do you need someone to come and get you? Mia is not that far away and Jeremy is a police officer. Did you call them?"

"I don't want to leave Griffin—that's the guy I'm seeing. He's not the problem. He's a good person. But several years ago, he testified against some people in Chicago, and now it looks like someone is trying to get revenge. We've already spoken to the police and Griffin has a friend with the US Marshal's Service who is helping us, but I was hoping you might be able to stick your nose in the investigation and make sure no one is missing anything."

"Of course. I will do whatever I can. But I have to tell you I'm really concerned. I think you should get out of San Clemente. Go to Mia's."

"I can't go to Mia's. She's pregnant. The last thing I need to do is stress her out."

"She told you she was pregnant?"

"Yes. She came down last weekend. I'm so happy for her."

"Me, too. Okay, don't go to Mia's. Go home. Be with the family. You'll be safe there. Tell your guy that's what you want to do."

"That's what he wants me to do, too, but I can't. I don't want to bring danger to anyone in the family, and I don't want to leave him on his own."

"I sometimes forget how stubborn you are," Kate said with a sigh.

"Just like you."

"Why don't you text me all the pertinent information, and I will go straight to the office and see what I can find out?"

"I really appreciate it. I'm sure you'd rather be getting home to Devin."

"He's actually working today, so it's fine."

"Good. Thanks again."

"Be careful, Annie. I wish someone was there to protect you."

"Griffin is an ex-cop. He will protect me."

"Wait, he's an ex-cop who testified against someone?"

"Another cop, actually. Griffin crossed the blue line, Kate."

"Great, so he has pissed off a lot of people." She paused. "The bags are coming out. I'll call you later."

As their call disconnected, she texted her sister the short version of what had happened and all the names Griffin had mentioned when he'd spoken about the case. She had just finished when Griffin came back into the room alone. "What did the detective want to talk to you about?" she asked, getting to her feet.

"He just wanted to hear the story from me."

"Do you think he's going to help us?"

"I believe he's committed to finding out who attacked Shari. Whether or not he really wants to help me…we'll have to see. He's going to put a security guard outside Shari's room."

"You think they'd go after her again?"

"We can't rule anything out."

The grim look in Griffin's eyes was not inspiring. "I talked to my sister, Kate, the one who works for the FBI. I hope you don't mind, but I texted her the information on your past case and what's going on now. I feel like we need someone else we can trust."

"We can trust Paul."

"I hope that's true, but I don't know him, and I do know my sister. I hope you're okay with it. But even if you're not, I'm not sorry I did it."

"I'm fine with it," he said wearily. "You have every right to talk to whoever you want to talk to."

"Thank you. What are we doing now?"

"I need to go back to the Depot and talk to Vinnie and the rest of the staff. We need to shut down for a few days, and I want to make sure that we cover the staff for lost wages, so I need to talk to a few people and make some calls. Then we can go to your place. It shouldn't take too long."

"Of course. Let's go."

As they walked out of the hospital hand-in-hand, she was as aware as Griffin of everyone they passed. She hated feeling like there were unseen eyes on her, and maybe that was just her imagination, but she couldn't be sure. Whoever had almost killed Shari was not done. Shari had never been the target. Griffin was who they wanted, and maybe her, too.

"What do you think their next move is?" she asked Griffin, as they got into the car.

"I wish to hell I knew," he muttered. "I think it's coming soon."

"Well, that's not terrifying at all," she said.

"I will protect you, Annie. With my life."

"I hope it doesn't come to that."

Twenty-Two

W hen they got to the bar, Griffin pulled the staff together and shared the terrible news about Shari. Annie saw genuine shock and emotion in every face. She noted that Griffin did not share information about his past or the trouble heading their way but simply told his concerned employees that they would be shutting down the bar after lunch service and would remain closed for a few days while they improved security and made sure everyone—both staff and customers—would be safe.

As Vinnie and Griffin moved into their office to interview each staff member individually, Annie sat down at the bar. There were only a few customers finishing up their lunch, and while she didn't think she was hungry, when Danielle brought her a turkey club sandwich and an iced tea, she simply said, "Thanks."

"No problem. You have to eat," Danielle said. "I made sure Griffin got some food, too. What the two of you have been through today is horrific."

"It was awful," she admitted, sipping her tea.

"I knew something was off with Shari, but she wouldn't

talk to me. I wish she would have said something if she was in trouble. I might have been able to help." Danielle paused. "Griffin said to tell you he's on the phone with the payroll people and it might be a while."

"That's fine. I need some time to catch my breath."

"Can I get you anything else?"

"No, this was really sweet of you."

"Don't worry about a bill; this is on the house. Boss's orders." Danielle gave her a smile. "I'm glad you've stuck around, Annie. Griffin needs someone like you."

"Someone like me?"

"Someone who can stand up to him. He's a lot of bark but not much bite. He's a sweetheart under all those hard edges, but not everyone sees that."

"I see it. He's a really wonderful man." She felt a wave of emotion run through her, and she drew in a deep breath. She could not break down now. She needed to hold it together for a while longer.

"Are you okay, Annie?" Danielle asked with concern.

"Just hungry," she said, taking a bite of her sandwich and blinking the tears out of her eyes.

"Well, then I'll let you eat."

She was happy when Danielle moved away to take care of another customer. She wasn't up for conversation at the moment.

After she finished lunch, she walked over to the tree and adjusted a few decorations, feeling sad that the tree might not be seen at all over the holidays. She wondered how long Griffin would keep the bar closed. This had to be such a busy time for them. They'd take a financial hit if they stayed shut down for too long.

Griffin finally made his way back into the bar, apologizing for having taken so long. Then they got back into the car and returned to the hospital. They sat by Shari's bedside for a good hour, watching her breathe in and out, but when the nurse confirmed that Shari would probably be asleep until morning, they decided to call it a day.

When they finally returned to her apartment, it was almost seven at night.

It had been a long day, filled with extreme emotions. While on one hand, it seemed like only minutes since she and Griffin had had breakfast together, on the other hand, it felt like ten years had passed.

"Do you want anything?" she asked Griffin, as she turned on lights, casting a cozy glow over the room.

"Nope."

He took off his coat and sat down on the couch, looking exhausted. He'd run his hand through his hair dozens of times during the day, there was a shadow of beard on his face, and his pallor was still off. She was worried about him. He was trying to do a lot of things at one time: taking care of his employees, making sure Shari was getting the best care, looking into updating the security system at the bar, checking in with Paul. She had a feeling at some point it was going to be too much.

She sat down next to him. "I want to help you. What can I do?"

"You're doing it," he said, taking her hand. "You're here."

"That doesn't seem like enough."

"Believe me, it's more than enough," he said, his gaze meeting hers. "You've been wonderful today, Annie."

"Just trying to hang in there with you."

He nodded, but he seemed distracted.

"What are you thinking about?" she asked. "It looks like you have something on your mind."

"I'm thinking that I need to do something I don't want to do."

"What's that?"

He pulled a phone from his pocket that she hadn't seen before. "Call my father and grandfather."

"Wasn't Paul going to do that?"

"He did speak to my father briefly, but I feel like I need to say something to them personally."

"That doesn't look like your usual phone."

"It's a burner phone, untraceable. I wouldn't want a call from me to jeopardize their safety."

"I don't think you ever told me how your family felt about what you did. Were they supportive?"

"My father was not. He thought I was throwing my life away, and in the end, his life, too. He was angry—justifiably so. My grandfather understood, but he almost died because of me, so I think he probably wished I hadn't done it, that he hadn't had to give up his bar, his friends, his home. I hurt them, Annie. I don't think I realized at the time how many people would be affected by what I did."

She was starting to see that the heavy weight Griffin had carried all these years hadn't been about himself, but about everyone else.

"I'm going out on the deck," she said, as she got to her feet. "There's a fire pit, couches, and lots of blankets. Why don't you join me after you decide what to do?"

"You don't have an opinion on whether I should make the call?" he asked with a frown. "That seems odd, Annie."

"I have an opinion, but it doesn't matter what I think, only what you think."

"Now you don't want to talk," he grumbled.

"It's your decision, Griffin. And you already know what you want to do." She walked into the kitchen to grab a bottle of wine, an opener, and two glasses. Then she headed outside. She set the wine and glasses on the table surrounding the fire pit, then lit the flame. The cool ocean breeze played with the flames, but within minutes, a warm heat was filling the air.

She opened the wine, poured herself a glass and then sat down on one of the couches in front of the fire and pulled a blanket over her legs.

Several deep breaths and a couple of gulps of wine later, she felt her body starting to relax. She had no idea what was coming tomorrow, but she was going to try not to think about it until then.

Her phone buzzed, and she saw it was Kate. *So much for not thinking about things.* "Hi, Kate."

"Hey, how are you doing?"

"I'm all right. Did you find out anything?"

"I just got off the phone with a Detective Baker. He said he spoke to you earlier."

"Yes, at the hospital."

"He gave me more details about the stabbing of one of Griffin's employees. You left a bit of that out."

"I didn't want you to freak out."

"I'm a federal agent. I don't freak out. Although, I don't like to think of my sister walking in on a scene like that."

"Now you know how we feel when you run into danger. At any rate, what else did the detective say?"

"He has one main person of interest, Kenny Taylor."

"Griffin mentioned him to me. He's the cousin of the cop who was put into prison."

"Yes. Apparently, he recently arrived at the Orange County airport."

She blew out a breath. "He's in town. That can't be a coincidence."

"He doesn't think it is. They're looking for him now. Detective Baker also mentioned that the knife used in the attack probably belonged to the victim. They haven't found the weapon, but they did find a drawer open in the kitchen with one knife missing that appeared to be consistent with the victim's wounds."

"It was Shari's knife?" she asked in surprise.

"She could have grabbed it to defend herself. We won't know for sure until the detective has a chance to speak to her, but it's interesting that she wasn't attacked with a weapon that was brought to the scene."

"Why is that interesting?"

"It suggests to me that there was an argument that escalated into a stabbing and that it might not have been a premeditated act."

"Does it matter? She was still almost killed."

"It matters in the sense that it plays into the motivation of her assailants. What were they doing at her apartment? There was no evidence of a break-in, so it appears she let them in or they had a key. They knew each other. So, what happened between the parties to change the dynamics of their relationship?"

"Griffin thinks that Shari might have refused to continue helping them."

"It's possible. There were unfortunately no witnesses. One woman on the first floor reported hearing a scream and a heavy thud, but she wasn't sure if it was on the TV."

"She couldn't tell the difference?"

"Detective Baker told me in that neighborhood people tend to look the other way, so apparently not. At any rate, Detective Baker is actively engaged in the investigation. He seems to be on it. I feel better knowing there's someone local involved and that he's competent."

"He's not bothered that Griffin went against his former partner?"

"He told me he's only interested in finding the person who attacked Shari Carlan, and I believed him. Now, let's talk about you."

She sighed, knowing what was coming. "I'm not leaving him, Kate."

"Are you in love with this guy?"

"Maybe," she admitted.

"Oh, Annie."

"What? He's a great person. You would like him."

"He sounds like he has a lot of baggage."

"Devin had baggage when you fell for him," she reminded her sister. "And you were in danger, too, as I recall."

"That was different. I'm a trained agent. You're an artist. This is not in your wheelhouse."

"I get that, but I'm sticking with Griffin."

"I don't want you to get hurt, Annie. And I don't just mean physically. You have a big heart, which can also be a big target."

"I appreciate your concern, but it's too late. I've already

jumped off the cliff."

"Does Griffin feel the same way about you?"

"I think he does. He's got a lot on his plate right now, but we've gotten really close."

"So, I have one more question. Once this is over, what do you think Griffin will do?" Kate asked. "Is he going to remain Griffin Hale? Or does he go back to being Michael Payton? And where does that leave you?"

"That's not one question—that's three." She let out a sigh. "I don't know, Kate. But I really want this to be over, so I can find out."

———✦✦✦———

Griffin must have stared at his phone for a good fifteen minutes before he finally punched in the number Paul had given him. It was his grandfather's number, not his dad's. He wanted to start with the one person who had always understood him better than anyone else—George Payton.

An older, raspy voice came on the line a moment later, and the familiar tone made his stomach turn over. This was the voice of the man who had really raised him, who had taught him how to be a man, to do what was right.

"Hello?" his grandfather said impatiently. "Is anyone there?"

"It's me," he said quickly, not wanting him to hang up. "It's—Michael." It was hard to say the name he'd used for the first thirty years of his life, but not the last four. He certainly didn't feel like Michael Payton anymore.

"Michael," his grandfather breathed. "I can't believe it's you. Are you all right?"

"I'm okay, but my new identity and location have been discovered. Someone is messing with me, and while I'm on the other side of the country, I didn't want you to be blindsided. I don't think anyone will come after you or Dad, but I can't guarantee it."

"Safety is never a guarantee, but I appreciate the heads-up. I'm sorry this situation has come back to haunt you. I was hoping it would never do that."

"I was too, but that was unrealistic."

"How have you been, Michael? What have you been doing? I've thought of you often these past years, wishing I knew where you were, if you were healthy, happy. I hoped for a call every Christmas, but I understood why you couldn't make contact."

"I thought it was best to make a clean break so that no one would ever hurt you again." Memories of his grandfather's beating still haunted him.

"I appreciate that, but I still miss you."

"I miss you, too. By the way, I opened a bar. It's not as good as yours, but we get a good crowd."

"No kidding. Isn't that something? You always did like working in the bar."

"I probably should have done that instead of becoming a cop."

"Well, maybe now is the right time. You married?"

"No."

"Don't want to let anyone get close to you?"

"I didn't want to let anyone get close, but recently I have." His gaze moved toward the windows. He couldn't see Annie, but he could see the glow from the fire pit, and he couldn't wait to join her under the blankets. He just wished that they weren't surrounded by danger, that they could just be normal, free to be together if they wanted to be.

"Is she good for you?" his grandfather asked.

"She makes me smile."

"Then she's exactly what you need. You had it rough growing up and worse after what happened; you deserve to smile."

"I feel like I need to cut her loose, though, keep her safe. But she's reluctant to go."

"Then she must care about you, too. Does she know everything?"

"She does now. She has been standing by me."

"Now you know what that feels like. Your grandmother always stood by me, no matter what, no matter how hard things got. That Paige, she wasn't worthy of you."

"Yeah, well, we don't need to talk about her." He cleared his throat. "How's Dad? Is he sober?"

"He is. He and his second wife are actually over in Italy right now."

"That's good. But does that mean you're alone?"

"No. I actually moved into a new apartment in a complex with some buddies. We play cards, go fishing, charm the single ladies. It's all good. I'm enjoying my retirement."

"I'm glad to hear it. Keep your eyes open."

"Don't worry about me. Take care of yourself, Michael, or whatever your name is."

"I will. I'm going to try to end this thing, Grandpa. I wasn't looking for more trouble, but now that it's here, I'm going after it. No more running. This needs to stop."

"I have every confidence in you. Don't wait another four years to call me."

"I won't," he promised. "Bye."

As his grandfather said good-night, he ended the call and let out a breath. Then he went to join Annie on the deck.

She opened up her blanket, and he slid in next to her.

"Want some wine?" she asked.

"I'm good for now. This is nice."

She gave him a smile. "It is nice. How did the call go?"

"Better than I thought. My grandfather sounded great. He's happy. He's living with friends. My dad is in Italy with his second wife. Everyone is good."

"That should make you feel a little less guilty about ruining their lives."

"A little." He gave her a thoughtful look. "You seem to have a way of knowing exactly how I feel. You see past my defenses."

"Sometimes. But you've built some fairly solid walls, Griffin."

"I had to do that."

"I understand now. But I'm glad some of them have come down between us."

"Me, too."

"I spoke to my sister Kate again. She had a long conversation with Detective Baker."

"Oh, yeah? I'm impressed he was willing to share his information with a fed. Cops can be territorial."

"I'm sure. But Kate has a way of getting what she wants."

"Did she learn that from you?"

Annie smiled. "Maybe. Anyway, she gave me two important pieces of information. Kenny Taylor arrived at the Orange County Airport sometime in the past few weeks."

His gut clenched. "She said that?"

"Detective Baker told her they're looking for him."

"That's huge news," he said. "It has to be him. He has to be the one calling the shots."

"It would seem so. At least we have a name now, someone to start with and maybe end with."

He pulled out his phone. "I'm going to text Paul."

"Maybe he can help locate this guy," Annie said.

"The more people looking, the better." After finishing the text, he set down his phone. "You said there were two pieces of information."

"Yes. There was a drawer open in Shari's kitchen and a knife missing from what appeared to be a set. The assumption is that the weapon used against Shari came from her kitchen and wasn't brought to the scene."

"She must have pulled the knife in self-defense, and they used it against her."

"Hopefully, she can tell us tomorrow."

"Hopefully." He let out a breath. "Well, your sister has definitely gotten us some good information. I'm glad you brought her in."

"Me, too. And I'm glad you called your family. You needed to reconnect."

"It did feel good to hear my grandfather's voice," he admitted. "I told him about the bar. I think he was proud I followed in his footsteps."

"I'm sure he was proud." She gave him a tender smile. "You're an amazing person. I knew it the first second I met you, when you rescued me from the sharks. We might have had the craziest first meet of all time."

"I'd have to agree with that. One of these days I'm going to get you back in the water. You can't let a shark or two scare you away from the big, beautiful ocean."

"I would not count on that."

"But you love the beach, Annie."

"I like it from up here. Isn't this cozy?"

"I have to admit it's not bad."

"We could make it better," she said, a hint of mischief in her eyes.

"Really? We're going there? With everything that's happened today?"

"Why not? It's been a rough day. We both could use a break. Live in the moment, baby."

He laughed. "My grandfather asked me if you were good for me."

"You told him about me?"

"Not your name, but I mentioned I was involved with someone."

"Involved. I like that word. What else did you tell him about me?"

"Wouldn't you like to know?" he teased.

She gave him a playful swat on the arm. "That's not fair. You know I'm a curious person."

"Well, you could try to get it out of me, but I don't know if you would be successful."

"Oh, I think I would be successful."

She made a sudden move, throwing one leg over his, so she was straddling him, turning his body instantly hard. She leaned down to kiss him, her silky hair brushing his face as her hot mouth invited him in. He only got one tantalizing taste of her tongue before she pulled back. His senses were screaming for more, and she knew it.

"Want to tell me what else you said now?" she asked.

"Not yet," he managed to get out, despite the fact that blood was racing out of his head, and he could barely think.

She pulled her top over her head. "What about now?"

He cupped her breasts with his hands as she kissed him once again, and her soft curves just about killed him.

"And now?" she asked.

"I said you make me smile," he conceded. "Are you happy?"

"Not yet, but I'm getting there. Why don't you help me out?"

"Love to," he murmured, pulling her back to him.

Twenty-Three

Griffin woke up to the sun streaming through Annie's windows on Monday morning. Turning his head, he saw her curled up on her side facing him, the sunlight casting a warm glow on her creamy skin and the light dusting of freckles on her nose and shoulders. Her hair fell about her face, her lips parted, her breath peaceful and relaxed.

He wished he could keep her like this: happy, carefree, not worried about anything. But as soon as she opened her eyes, all that would change. Her sweet, sometimes innocent, nature might be exposed to some really dark things, and there wasn't anything he could do to stop it.

He wished he could put her somewhere safe, but he was afraid that if they split up, he'd just be making Annie an easier target, someone to get to in order to hurt him. He had to keep her close.

Slipping out of bed, he went into the bathroom and took a shower, then dressed and headed for the kitchen. They still hadn't had time to shop, but after riffling through Annie's cupboards, he found pancake mix and some syrup. After whipping up the batter, he heated the grill and made pancakes. When he had a couple of good batches, he put some turkey bacon in a pan and fried up.

"I smell bacon," Annie said, as she came into the kitchen.

Wrapped in a soft, pink robe, she looked deliciously sleepy and sexy. She walked over to him and gave him a kiss that took him right back to the love they'd shared the night before.

"Breakfast again? You're going to spoil me," she added.

"It's not much, but it's something. Sit down, it's ready." He took out the plate of pancakes he'd stashed in the oven and put it on the table.

"Wow, these are all perfectly golden. You didn't even burn the first pancake. That's a feat, one I have never accomplished."

"You just have to get the griddle hot enough before you start."

"Maybe you should be doing the cooking at the Depot and not Vinnie."

"I can't even come close to his skills." He sat down across from her and helped himself to some pancakes.

"What are we doing this morning?" she asked, as she put a piece of bacon into her mouth.

"We need to stop in at the hospital, and see if Shari is talking. Vinnie was going to call our security company this morning. If he can set up a meeting today, I'd like to be there. What about you? You have class this afternoon, don't you?"

"Actually, I don't. It's finals week and since mine is an art class, the students just have to turn in their final project a week from today. I will not have to put you through the torture of babysitting me at the college."

"I would be happy to do it. When you talk, I am never bored."

She wiped her mouth with a napkin, and he wished she hadn't moved quite so quickly, because he wouldn't have minded licking that bit of syrup off her bottom lip.

She gave him a questioning look. "Something wrong?"

"Nope. All good."

She stood up. "I'm going to take a shower, and then we can get going."

"Sure." After Annie left, he took the plates to the kitchen, rinsed them off and put them in the dishwasher. Spying a couple of coffee mugs on the dining room table, he went over to grab them.

As he moved by the corner of the table, he accidentally knocked Annie's tote bag on to the floor. A dozen items fell out, including a file folder filled with sketches. Squatting down, he started to pick up the pages, frowning as the cartoon characters seemed to be familiar.

A bad feeling ran through him as he moved through the pages.

What the hell?

He picked up the pages and spread them across the table. Three of the sketches appeared to be him in some superhero form with bulging muscles and sharp features. He was riding a motorcycle, a surfboard, and serving drinks in a bar.

The bar was the Depot. All the details were there, but they were exaggerated symbols of the old train station. She'd drawn Vinnie, who wore his apron almost like a cape, Shari who looked like a gothic bird, and Justin, as some kind of boyish hero.

He couldn't believe she'd used him and his friends and the bar without telling him.

There was even a woman who looked like Megan.

Annie had started these sketches the first time she'd come into the bar.

He felt sick to his stomach. He'd thought she was so honest, so transparent, so guileless...

"I left my brush in my bag," Annie said, coming into the room in her bathrobe, her hair still wet from her shower. She stopped abruptly when she saw her sketches on the tabletop. Then her gaze met his. "Griffin, I can explain."

"What's to explain? You were using me. You were using all of us. That's why you were hanging out at the bar so much."

"No. I mean yes. Partly." She waved her hand in the air. "The first night I came to the Depot, you were rude to me. I was curious about you. Then I saw Paul bring Megan in, and you whisked her upstairs. There seemed to be some kind of mystery. My imagination kicked in. Later, when I started thinking about pitching a new movie idea, I thought about the bar, all the characters there. I didn't know what you were up to with Megan, so I made it up in my head. And I couldn't seem to stop drawing you or the others. I didn't know what I was going to do with the sketches. I was just drawing. That's what I do. I'm an artist. I express my feelings through my art."

He shook his head, not wanting to get sucked in by the plea in her eyes. "You lied to me."

"I didn't lie to you; I just didn't tell you."

"It's the same thing," he said harshly.

"I was going to tell you about it."

"Yeah? When? You've had plenty of time to bring this up. We've been together every minute for the last few days."

"There have been a few other things going on," she pointed out. "Look, I was going to say something after the interview, but then things were happening so fast, and you were distracted, and it didn't seem that important. I haven't done anything with the sketches, Griffin."

"You showed them to the people you interviewed with, didn't you? Do you know how much jeopardy and danger you could have put me in? And not just me—Megan is in there, too."

"I didn't pitch the Megan character in the meeting. I didn't show her sketch, because I knew her story by then, but I still didn't know about your past, Griffin. I had no idea you were hiding out under an assumed name."

"Would that have made a difference?"

"Of course."

"I don't know if that's true. You need this job. And you don't have any other ideas, do you?"

"Not at the moment, but I'll come up with something, or I won't get the job. Nothing was going to go any further without your knowledge. You have to believe me."

"I'm not sure I can."

Hurt filled her green eyes. "Griffin, I wasn't trying to cause you problems. It was just a lark in the beginning. I let my imagination go when I'm in interesting places, and the bar was fascinating to me—a train station turned into a kind of underground railroad for people in trouble, heroic figures taking care of the wounded or the endangered. It felt like an interesting plot. And you're a hero. You saved my life. You saved Megan's life and God knows how many other people."

"I'm not a cartoon character. This is not a movie."

"I know that. I'm sorry I didn't tell you."

"You didn't tell me, because you knew I wouldn't like it."

"I did know that," she conceded. "But I thought if they were interested, I could make you see that the characters wouldn't really look like you or anyone else in the end. This is just the seed of an idea. It gets changed a million times."

He shook his head, so much anger running through him, he didn't know what to say.

He walked through the door leading out to the deck and slammed it behind him. He really wanted to go farther than just the deck, but how could he leave her now? She might have lied to him, but she could still be in danger.

He paced back and forth along the railing, wishing he could be out on the ocean, riding the waves, forgetting about his problems, but that wasn't an option.

He'd told his grandfather last night he was done running. He had to find whoever was after him and then he had to decide what to do about Annie.

Until fifteen minutes ago, he would have done anything to try to keep her in his life. Now he didn't know if he wanted her in his life for another five seconds.

Annie came out onto the deck, obviously still wanting to defend herself.

He turned, putting his hand up. "I need a minute," he said tersely. "Can you give me that?"

"No. We need to talk this out," she said stubbornly. "I'm

not letting you go back into your shell."

"Is there really more you have to say?"

"Yes," she said, a fire in her eyes. "There's a lot more to say. Let's not forget that you lied to me, too, Griffin. And your lies were way worse than mine. You slept with me before I knew who you really were. How do you justify that?"

He ground down on his teeth, his jaw tightening. "I can't justify it."

"I forgave you for that. I stuck by you." She paused. "After you saved my life, you were a hero in my head, but I didn't even know your name. I couldn't stop thinking about you, so I started to draw your face. That's how it began. Everything else came later. I told myself that I was coming back to the bar to get story ideas, but that wasn't true. It was you. I had a freaking crush on you, and I couldn't forget about you."

There was an undeniable passion in her voice. She believed what she was saying and he wanted to believe her, too. But could he really trust that she wouldn't have used the sketches in the end, wouldn't have put her career goals before his privacy?

"Griffin? Say something."

"I need to think. I want to storm out of here. I want to put a few miles between us."

"But?"

"I can't leave you unprotected. You're still in danger; that hasn't changed."

"I can take care of myself."

"No, you can't."

She frowned. "What do you want to do then?"

"What we were going to do before. Get dressed. I want to leave as soon as possible."

She drew in a breath and let it out. "All right."

He turned his back on her as she went into the house. He put his hands on the rail and stared out at the sea. He'd been looking for a reason to break away from Annie, and he finally had one. *But did he really want to use it? And was he a*

*complete hypocrite for calling her a liar when he'd hidden his
entire past from her?*

His phone vibrated in his pocket. Pulling it out, he saw
Vinnie's name on the screen. "What's going on?"

"I have a new security guy coming over in a half hour.
Can you be here for that?"

"I was going to stop at the hospital."

"Shari is still asleep; I just called."

"I thought she'd be up by now."

"They want her to rest as long as possible. I was assured
that she's still in stable condition."

"That's good."

"Something that isn't good—I was going over the
security footage from last night. I saw a figure by the back
door. He blended into the shadows, but he was definitely
looking for a way in."

"When was this?" he asked, his nerves tightening.

"Around four a.m."

"I'll be over there as soon as I can." He hung up just as
Annie stepped out on the deck. She'd put on tight black jeans
and a turquoise sweater, her hair gleaming in the sunlight, her
face somber but as pretty as ever. *How the hell was he going
to cut her out of his life?*

But he couldn't be worrying about that today. There was
too much else going on.

"Who were you talking to?" she asked.

"Vinnie. He has a security guy coming over to the bar in
thirty minutes and Shari is still unconscious."

"I'm sorry to hear that."

"Me, too," he said tersely.

She frowned. "How long do you think you're going to be
mad at me, Griffin? Is this a forever kind of anger or maybe
you'll get over it in a few days or weeks?"

"We'll have to see," he returned. "But for now, we need
to find whoever attacked Shari and stop them before they hurt
someone else."

Twenty-Four

───➤➤◄◄◄───

Griffin didn't talk to her on the way to the Depot. Annie wasn't surprised. He didn't talk a lot even on good days, and today was definitely not a good day. She'd been mentally kicking herself ever since she'd seen him looking at her sketches. *Why hadn't she told him about the drawings?*

She knew why she hadn't said anything in the beginning, but that was before she'd gotten to know him, before they'd become friends, gotten intimate, explored each other's bodies with great enthusiasm, and certainly before she'd fallen in love with him.

Maybe that was it. She'd been afraid to fess up because she'd known he would use it to push her away, and whatever they were building together would be destroyed.

She snuck a quick glance at him, but his hard profile, the grim set of his jaw, and his extreme focus on the road ahead told her he was not in a forgiving mood yet.

While she understood his reaction, she hoped he would come to realize that they had both made mistakes. She might have taken his private life and drawn some cartoon characters and created a fantasy world, but he'd actually been living a lie. She'd forgiven him for the deception. He should forgive her, too.

What if he couldn't forgive her? What if it was over?

She wanted to fight for them, but she needed him to fight, too.

As much as she wanted to press for that, there was too much else going on. She needed to give him some time, as difficult as that was to do. She hated the uncomfortable awkwardness between them, but she had a feeling she would have to deal with it for some time to come.

Griffin drove into the parking lot behind the Depot. She saw Vinnie's car in the lot, as well as a work van labeled Sloane Security Systems.

Griffin shut off the engine. "I don't want to discuss your drawings in front of Vinnie," he said.

"I understand."

They got out of the car and walked through the back door. She could see Vinnie and another man in the office. She was debating whether she should sit in the bar or go upstairs when her phone rang. The number for the production company flashed across her screen.

Last week, she would have been thrilled to get the call. Now, she felt torn.

She needed to tell them she was interested in the job, but that her idea was off the table. She had a feeling that would be the end of any possible job offer, but it was the right thing to do.

Griffin stopped abruptly, pulled out his keys and handed them to her. "If you need to call someone back, you can use the apartment."

He gave her a pointed look, and she had a feeling he knew exactly whose call she'd missed.

She wanted to tell him what she was going to do, but Vinnie was calling his name, and he was already walking away. She needed to just do what she needed to do and then tell him it was done.

She went up the stairs and entered Griffin's apartment. It

looked exactly the same as when she'd been in it a few days earlier. She paused in the doorway to the bedroom, thinking back to the first night they'd spent there together, how happy she'd been. The next day had only gotten better when Griffin had whisked her away to celebrate her birthday.

How she wished they could be carefree and happy, no dark past hanging over Griffin, no secrets between them. Could they get there again? She really hoped so.

Sitting down on the couch, she pulled out her phone and called the production company. The HR person, Heather Baines, answered.

"Hello, Annie, thanks for calling me back so quickly," Heather said. "I have great news. They want to bring you back for a second interview. They're hoping you can come in on Wednesday. What's your schedule?"

"I can probably make that work, but I need to talk to you about something. I pitched an idea and some drawings for a superhero-themed movie, and I'm not going to be able to use that idea or those characters. Unfortunately, they were inspired by some real-life people, and I'm going to have to protect their privacy. I should have gotten their permission first, and I didn't."

"I'm really sorry to hear this. I know David and Rita were very excited about your ideas. You definitely cannot use them? There's no way we can get a release?"

"No. I'm sorry. I have other ideas, but that one is a non-starter. I wanted to be up front about it."

"Well, let me talk to the group and see if they're still interested in meeting. I'll get back to you."

"Thanks. I would love to work with them on other projects if that's a possibility."

"I'll be in touch," Heather said.

She ended the call and tossed her phone down on the table, feeling frustrated, angry, and disappointed in everyone, most especially herself. She wished she could leave, put some distance between herself and Griffin, because it was so hard to see the anger in his eyes, to know that she'd let him down

like so many other people in his life had let him down. She'd
wanted to be the person he could trust, the one he could count
on, but she'd blown that big-time, and she had a feeling that
earning his trust back would not be that easy, if it was even
possible.

Picking up her phone again, she decided to call Kate. She
didn't want to get in Griffin's way, so she'd hang out here until
he was done.

But when Kate answered, she didn't even ask about the
investigation, because what she really needed was some
sisterly advice.

"I screwed up with Griffin," she said.

"What? How?"

"I lied to him. He hates me, Kate, and I—I think I love
him." Her voice broke as she said the words.

"Oh, Annie, I'm sure he doesn't hate you."

"I wish you were right."

"First, tell me if you're safe," Kate ordered.

"Yes, I'm safe."

"Okay, then tell me what happened with Griffin, and
don't leave anything out."

—➤➤◄◄—

"Are you listening to me?" Vinnie asked.

Griffin started, realizing he hadn't heard a word Vinnie
had said to him since the alarm guy had driven away. He'd
been thinking about Annie, wondering if she'd agreed to
another interview.

He'd seen the guilt flash through her eyes when her
phone rang, and he was quite certain it was the company she'd
interviewed with. They probably wanted her to come back for
another interview, and he knew how much she wanted the
job.

*Was he being callous and unreasonable about the
sketches?*

They'd been a shock at first, but she'd said they were just

seed ideas, that the characters would grow and develop and move beyond her inspiration. *Was that true?* And even if it wasn't true, wasn't it about time he gave up on the idea of living an undiscoverable life when clearly he'd been discovered?

"All right. I'm going to go," Vinnie said. "You need to talk to Annie."

"Actually, I don't need to talk to her."

Vinnie gave him a sharp look. "Is something going on with you two?"

"It's a long story, but she hasn't been completely straightforward."

"About what? Does she know something about what happened to Shari, or what's been going on here at the bar?"

"No. No," he said quickly. "It's nothing like that."

"Then what is it?"

"She's been drawing us. Making cartoons with you and me, Justin and Shari, turning us into some superhero team."

"Seriously?" Vinnie asked in surprise.

"Yeah, she pitched a movie idea with us running an underground railroad through the bar. She said she did it before she actually knew about our arrangement with Paul, that she was just using her imagination and making a story up in her head. But all this time she was drawing me and she didn't tell me about it. I don't see how I can get past that. How can I trust her?"

"Well...I don't know what to say." Vinnie paused. "I actually do know what to say. Are you crazy? You've been living a double life and lying to everyone you've met the last four years."

"I had a good reason. That was different."

"What's Annie's reason?"

"I don't know. She said something about artist's block. She was having trouble coming up with an idea until she came into the bar. The train décor and the people inspired her."

"What did I look like?"

He frowned. "Does it matter?"

"Yeah, I want to know if she made me, you know, good-looking."

"You had bulging tattooed muscles from what I recall."

"I like that."

"You're not taking this seriously, Vinnie."

"And you're taking it way too seriously. I don't think she meant us any harm, and she didn't know what we were actually doing until she almost got run over."

"I know that. It's just…"

"What?" Vinnie asked.

"She let me down."

"Is it that? Or are you falling for her and looking for an excuse to end it?"

Vinnie's words hit close to home. "You told me to get rid of her days ago."

"That was before I knew how much you liked her and before I realized she was already in trouble. To be honest, I think Annie is great. And if she wants to make me a superhero, I could probably live with that."

"It would blow our cover."

"We're already blown, Griffin."

"Well, I can't think about it right now. I have to focus on finding Shari's attacker and the person or people who are trying to destroy me." As he finished speaking, his phone rang. It was Paul. "I hope you have good news," he said.

"I do," Paul said." I just got off the phone with Detective Baker. They picked up Kenny Taylor at the airport."

Relief flooded through him. "That's a huge break. Is he talking?"

"At the moment, he's rambling. The detective said he's high as a kite, but he keeps telling them to make him an offer, so I think he will talk eventually."

"I want to speak to him."

"Don't go down there, Griffin. Let the police handle this for now. You'll have your turn, but let's figure out if there's anyone else involved first."

He knew Paul was right, but he was itching to take action instead of always playing defense.

"I'm heading out your way," Paul said. "I'll probably be in town later tonight. I'll give you a call."

"I appreciate you getting involved in this."

"You've done a lot for me. I'm happy to help. By the way, there's a very eager FBI agent who's butting her nose in, too. Says she's Annie's sister."

"Kate Callaway," he said. "Annie called her."

"Well, she's got Baker on his toes, so it's a good thing. I'll call you when I get into town."

He let out a breath as he hung up. "They caught Tom's cousin, Kenny Taylor. He is high on drugs but wanting to make a deal. They found him at the airport. He must have been about to skip town."

"That's good news," Vinnie said. "Maybe he was done."

All evidence pointed to that possibility, but it didn't quite ring true. "I'm not so sure."

"He could have panicked after he stabbed Shari. Decided he'd gone too far," Vinnie added.

"That's possible. I really want to talk to him. I need to know if he was acting alone."

"But Paul said to stay out of it, right?"

"Yeah."

"You going to follow his advice?"

"For the moment."

"Do you think we should open the bar up today now that they have him in custody?"

"No. Let's stay closed until we talk to the police—just to be on the safe side. We don't know if Kenny was working alone, but hopefully we will have more information soon."

"Sounds good, although I'm itching to reopen. It's a busy time of the year. We lose a lot of cash every hour we're closed."

"I completely agree. I'd say tomorrow looks good, but let's wait to make a final decision until we can talk to Shari and the police.

"All right. Don't forget to take a look at the security footage from last night. Maybe you'll recognize Taylor," Vinnie said.

"I'd almost forgotten about that."

"To be honest, I couldn't make out more than a vague figure, who looked a little like the guy who slashed Annie's tires, but we definitely need better high-definition cameras."

"And fewer problems," he said. "I feel like I should be apologizing to you, Vinnie."

Vinnie shrugged. "You've always been straight with me. I knew what I was getting into. We've built a good business, and this is just a small obstacle in our path."

"When did you turn into Sally Sunshine?" he asked with a small smile.

"When you turned into Debbie Downer," Vinnie retorted. "One of us has to be optimistic. At any rate, I'm heading to the hospital. What about you?"

"I'll be there soon. I need to talk to payroll and look at the cameras."

Vinnie paused in the doorway. "I'm just going to say one last thing, Griffin. Don't let the anger between you and Annie fester. Have it out with her if you need to, but don't lock yourself up again. It was good to see you come out of your shell the past few days. You deserve to have a full life. Maybe this is your chance."

"Maybe," he said, wanting exactly what Vinnie had suggested—a life that could be lived in the light of day, no more shadows, no more hiding, no more running—and a woman, unlike any other.

Annie came out of the bathroom after rinsing her face with cold water and dabbing at her tear-swollen eyes. They were still a little bloodshot and the last thing she wanted was for Griffin to think she'd been crying. Not only did she not want to show that weakness, she also didn't want to distract him from the bigger picture, which was finding out who was trying to hurt him and possibly herself. That was really the only issue they should be dealing with right now.

It had felt good to talk to Kate, even though she felt a little guilty for dumping all of her problems on her younger sister, but Kate had reminded her that this was probably just a bump in their relationship, that if it was as strong as she thought it was, they would get past it.

As she moved into the bedroom, she sniffed, wrinkling her nose at the very strong stench of gas. The bedroom door was closed, and she didn't remember closing it.

Her body went on high alert, every muscle tightening, every nerve tingling.

She moved across the room and turned the door handle. It didn't open, but it wasn't locked, because the lock was on her side of the door. Someone must have pushed something up against it, because she couldn't get it to budge even an inch or two.

What was going on? She'd been sitting in the living room less than ten minutes ago. Someone had to have come into the apartment while she was in the bathroom and barricaded her inside the bedroom. *Why would they do that?*

With the smell of gasoline starting to make her feel sick, she had a very bad feeling in her gut. She couldn't call anyone, because her phone was in the living room.

She ran toward the windows. Unfortunately, the view from the bedroom also faced the old train tracks. There was no one in sight to flag down for help.

She opened the window to let in some cleaner air, but it only went up about six inches. There was no fire escape, but there was a narrow ledge about four feet down. It was barely a foot wide if that, but it did extend across the entire building. Ten feet away, there was a pull-down fire escape ladder, located next to the window for the second apartment.

If she could get the window all the way up, she might be able to climb out and get onto the ledge. But once she let go of the window frame, there wouldn't be anything to hang on to; she'd be walking a balance beam two stories above the ground, and she'd never been good at gymnastics.

Thoughts of her foot slipping and visions of her plummeting to her death ran around in her head, paralyzing her from taking action.

She turned away from the window, pacing back and forth at the end of the bed, trying to come up with another plan.

The smell of gas was getting stronger. Someone had to have doused the living room with gasoline, which could only mean one thing.

They were going to start a fire. They were going to burn down the bar.

Think, she told herself.

She was a firefighter's daughter. There was no smoke coming under the door yet, but it was probably only a matter of time.

She ran into the bathroom, soaked a towel in water and then went back into the bedroom and stuffed it under the door crack.

Then she looked for something she could use to break the window, but there wasn't much furniture in the room—a bed and a dresser and Griffin's guitar. The guitar would probably break before the window.

Fear raced up and down her spine. She didn't want to panic, but she was coming close.

Where was Griffin? Was he still in the office with Vinnie? Was he as trapped as she was? Or had something happened to him?

It was too damn quiet.

She opened the closet door and to her shock saw a baseball bat and a glove resting in one corner. Just what she needed.

She grabbed the bat and went back to the window. She hesitated for one more second.

Would breaking the window bring more danger?

It was a risk she had to take. Because there was no way she was going to die in this room without a fight.

Twenty-Five

Griffin spent more than twenty minutes on the phone with payroll, his second call in two days, and it was once again a frustrating experience. He really needed to change services. It should not take this long to make adjustments. When he was finally finished, he set down his phone and turned on the computer to look at the security footage from the night before.

Sure enough, there was the same hooded figure he'd seen slashing Annie's tires several days earlier. He appeared to be lurking around the back door. And then he disappeared.

His gut tightened. *Was that person Kenny Taylor?*

He remembered Kenny as having broad shoulders, a stocky build; this figure seemed shorter, thinner. But no matter how many times he looked at the images, he couldn't see any identifying characteristics.

What had the man been doing outside at four in the morning? Had he been trying to break in? Or was he using the key that Shari had given him?

He should have asked the police to check if that key was still in her possession. Not that it mattered; she could have made a copy. It was still difficult to believe she'd sold him out. But while he was angry, he was also worried for her. Ultimately, this whole situation was on him. He'd brought the danger to San Clemente. Hopefully, today, with Kenny in custody, they could figure out who else had been involved and put an end to everything.

His optimistic outlook ended abruptly when a loud crash overhead sent him to his feet. As he drew in a deep breath, he was assailed by the strong odor of gasoline.

A bolt of fear sent him rushing to the door. Annie was upstairs—alone. And it had sounded like the crash had come from his apartment.

Dammit! Why had he left her on her own?

He threw open the door and was only a few steps down the hall when a hooded figure came out of the bar and stepped in front of him, a gun pointed at his face.

"Stop right there."

He was shocked by the sound of the female voice. Then her hoodie slipped off her head, revealing thick, dark-brown hair, furious brown eyes. His heart stopped. He couldn't breathe. He couldn't believe it.

It wasn't possible!

"What?" he stuttered. "You—Paige?"

She gave him a hard, unforgiving, hateful gaze.

"You're not happy to see me, Michael?"

"What's going on?" He suddenly realized the floor was wet, soaked in gasoline, and there was a large gas can by the bottom of the stairs. "What the hell are you doing?" He started to move toward her.

"One more step, and I will shoot the floor and ignite a firestorm."

He froze, wanting to take her down, needing to get upstairs to Annie. God!

Had Paige already been upstairs? Had she hurt Annie?

"We're going to have a little chat before this place blows up," Paige said. "I'm sure you must have some questions. But if you're not interested in answers, I can shoot you right now.

Just remember…if you die, you won't get to her in time."

Which answered his question about Annie. "What did you do to Annie?"

"Annie," she said with a sneer. "Nothing. She's alive…for now. But she can't help you."

"I can take that gun away from you, Paige."

"You can try. But I'm a good shot. You know that."

He did know that. Her father had taught her to shoot when she was barely a teenager, and there was nothing she loved more than going to the firing range. "Why are you doing this?"

"Because you have to pay. You destroyed my life and Tom's. Now, you need to lose everything."

He heard the raw pain in her voice, and it seemed deeper than it should have been. "What happened to Tom was his fault, not mine. I didn't set him up. He did what he did. I just told the truth."

"You didn't give him a chance to make things right. You weren't loyal to your own partner, a man who had saved your life. You put him in that prison. And now he's going to die. If you hadn't turned on him, he never would have been there. He never would have been attacked. It's time you paid for what you did."

"Did Kenny get you into this?"

"Kenny hates you as much as I do, but he's too stupid to figure anything out. I only brought him along because I needed the muscle, and he's easy to control. All I had to do was keep him high enough not to ask too many questions."

He was stunned by her cold, calculating words. *Where was her heart? Where was her compassion? Where was the woman he'd once cared about?* She certainly wasn't this woman.

"Kenny stabbed my friend. He almost killed her," he said. "Was that part of your plan?"

"She came at him with a knife. It was self-defense."

"You were there? You watched it happen?"

"We weren't going to kill her. All she had to do was give

us the key to your apartment; it was very simple, but she suddenly got cold feet, despite the large amount of money we'd already paid her. She got herself into trouble. She fought with Kenny. I had nothing to do with it."

"You were willing to let a woman die for revenge against me? What happened to you?"

"You happened," she said fiercely. "You hurt me, and you hurt Tom, the only person who ever gave a damn about me. You took him away from me."

There was something off about her words. Paige had never been with Tom; she'd been with him. She'd been his girlfriend. *But Paige was acting like…*

"What are you saying? Were you in love with Tom?"

"Yes. I loved him," she cried. "And not just as a friend."

"When did that happen?" he asked, once again stunned by her words. "Was it after he went to prison?"

"No. It was before that—when you were partners, when we were all spending time together."

"Then why were you with me?" he demanded.

"Tom always said he was too old for me. But we had a connection that was very strong, very real. He understood me, the real me. He was fun. He wasn't all dark and moody like you, expecting me to guess your every thought."

"Did you sleep with him?"

"I wanted to, but he turned me down. He didn't want to screw you—his partner, his friend. And what did you do? You turned him in. You ruined his life and mine. And now you're going to pay."

"Why didn't you tell me how you felt about Tom? Why not be honest with me?"

"Because I wanted you to change your mind about testifying. I didn't think telling you I was in love with Tom would help that cause. Not that it mattered in the end. You did what you wanted. You destroyed a really good person. Tom did one bad thing—"

"Tom did many bad things," he interrupted.

"You made half of them up."

"I didn't."

"And now he's going to die," she cried again, her voice filled with anger and despair.

"I never wanted him to die, Paige."

"I always knew it would end like this. Tom and I would pretend that one day it would be all right, that we'd get married when he got out, that we'd have kids. He had only a few years left on his sentence. I thought our future could happen. But now it can't. Tom's life is over. And so is yours. Once my friend, Tracy, saw your picture on social media saving that woman from a shark, I knew it was time to make you pay, to make you suffer, to force you to lose everything."

"I lost everything once before," he reminded her. "My family had to move. I had to change my name. I couldn't be a cop anymore."

"So what?" she said scornfully. "You weren't in prison. You've had a life. And you've obviously had women, like the one you've been fooling around with this past week."

"What are you going to do, Paige? You're going to burn down the bar, try to kill me without killing yourself? Then what? The police already arrested Kenny at the airport. You know he'll sing like a bird. If you don't die today, you're going to end up in jail."

"I don't care what happens to me anymore. I've spent the last four years waiting for my life to start with Tom. But that's not going to happen now. I'm going to be alone. I might as well be dead."

As she started to feel sorry for herself, her hand wavered ever so slightly.

He saw his opening and took it, rushing straight toward her.

He thought he could get to her before the gun went off; he was wrong.

The blast knocked him backward, a searing, soul-shaking pain ripping through his shoulder. He fell to the ground, knowing the next shot would be through his heart.

Paige took a step toward him, the gun pointed directly at

him. "I told you not to move."

"Don't do this, Paige. Just walk away. Disappear. Have a life."

"No. My life is over and so is yours. But I'm not going to kill you with a bullet. That is way too easy. You need to suffer." She took several steps backward, keeping her gun on him. Then she turned.

Seeing the gas can behind her, he knew what was coming. He stumbled to his feet, lurching toward the office, the only room not covered in gasoline.

He wasn't fast enough. The gun went off and the hallway exploded in a tidal wave of fire. He instinctively covered his eyes as he flung himself through the office door. He thought he heard Paige scream, but all he could do was roll around on the floor of the office, batting sparks off his clothes as he tried to get to the window.

The wound in his shoulder was gushing with blood, but he couldn't think about that. He had to get out of the building. He had to get to Annie.

Terror ran through him. He had no doubt that Paige had doused the entire building in gasoline, including his apartment.

He shoved up the window and pushed out the screen, managing to get up and over the sill and then dropping to his feet. He ran around the corner and down the back of the building, screaming, "Annie! Annie!"

She had to be all right. She just had to be!

⭢ ⯈⯇ ⭠

Annie forced herself back into consciousness. The explosion had knocked her off her feet and bounced her head against the wall. There was a ringing in her ears, but along with that came the sound of someone yelling.

Was she dreaming? Was that *Griffin?*

She hoped it was him, that he was still alive. Blinking her watery eyes, she moved onto her knees. Despite the wet towel she'd stuffed under the door, smoke was starting to come into the room, and she could feel an intense heat blasting through the walls that she doubted would hold up much longer.

She finally made it to her feet and got to the window that she'd broken with the bat just minutes before. Thankfully, there was no screen.

She stuck her head out and saw Griffin down below. "I'm here," she yelled, realizing there was blood covering his shirt. "You're hurt."

"I'm okay. We have to get you out of there."

"How? Did you call the fire department?"

"I don't have my phone. Hopefully someone nearby called."

She hoped so, too, but she didn't hear any sirens yet.

She turned her head as the door to the bedroom blew open and chunks of wood flew across the room. She ducked as the flames came into the room with a shocking heat.

"Annie," Griffin yelled again, panic in his voice.

She put her head back out the window, more terrified than she'd ever been. "The fire is inside."

"Climb out, Annie. Get onto the ledge."

She looked at the narrow ledge and panic flooded her mind. "I can't. I'll fall."

Griffin ran over to the ladder next to the other apartment. He pulled it down and climbed up to the level of the ledge. "Climb out, Annie. You can hold onto the sill while you put your feet on the ledge."

She wanted to wait for the fire department. Surely, they would be here soon. But the fire was coming after her with relentless purpose. Her lungs were beginning to burn, and she knew that smoke inhalation could kill her before the fire even got to her. It was now or maybe never.

Somehow, she found enough courage to climb onto the windowsill. With every limb shaking, she swung one leg over the edge, her foot searching fearfully for the ledge below. When she felt it, she tentatively put one leg down, then the other, until she was all the way out, her fingers on the sill, her body pressed against the building. She turned her head to Griffin. He was at least six feet away.

He held onto the ladder with one hand, then stepped onto the ledge, extending his hand, which cut the distance between them to about three feet. It wasn't enough.

"You can do this, Annie. Don't look down. Just hug the wall and move your feet."

She wanted to do what he said, but she couldn't.

"I can't let go," she cried. "I can't do it. I'll wait for the fire department."

Even as she said the words, flames came out of the window, licking at her fingers. She moved her hands slightly out of the way, but not before feeling a searing pain.

"There's no time," Griffin told her. "Look at me," he said, drawing her gaze to his. "You can do this, Annie. You have to do this. You're a Callaway, remember. Callaways don't quit."

"I'm not as brave as the rest of my family."

"Yes, you are. Trust me, Annie. I won't let anything happen to you. I'm a superhero, remember."

"If you were, you could fly over here and get me."

"You're a superhero, too. I saw you in the sketches."

"That was a fantasy."

"A couple of feet, Annie, and then I'll take your hand, and I won't let go. You're not going to fall. But you have to do this now."

He was right. The fire was coming for her, and there was nowhere else to go. She moved her left foot a few inches, then her right, still hanging on. Then she managed to pull one hand free and press it against the wall.

"Good job," Griffin encouraged. "Keep moving along the ledge, hands on the wall. You're almost here."

She didn't think she was almost anywhere, but as another flame flew out the window, she let go of the sill and pressed both palms against the stucco, her body trembling with fear.

Terrifying thoughts and images raced through her head. *Damn her big imagination!*

But Griffin was talking to her. His voice was bringing

her back.

"That's it," he said. "Take little steps. Go slow. You can do it."

Her legs felt incredibly heavy but she managed to move again and then again, inching her way along the wall.

"Give me your hand, Annie."

She drew in a deep breath, her gaze clinging to Griffin's. "Don't let me fall."

"Never," he vowed.

She let go of the wall with her left hand and reached for him.

His fingers closed around hers and with his help, she made it all the way to the ladder. The steel rail in her hands made her feel immensely better. She went down first, and Griffin quickly followed.

When they reached the ground, he pulled her into his arms in a hard, tight hug. She clung to him for a long minute. She didn't want to ever let him go. But as she felt a growing wetness against her chest, she pulled back and saw that his shoulder and chest were covered in blood.

"Oh, my God, Griffin. What happened?"

"It's just a graze," he said, holding onto her arms.

"Someone shot you? I thought I heard a blast, but then everything exploded, and I think I was knocked out for a minute."

"It was Paige."

Her jaw dropped in shock. "Your Paige?"

His lips tightened as his face turned even whiter. "She was never in love with me. It was Tom. It was *always* Tom. I didn't know. I thought they were friends."

He was starting to ramble, and she realized that he was now hanging on to her more than she was hanging on to him. His eyes were starting to roll back in his head. The adrenaline and fear for her life was probably what had gotten him this far, but he was hurt, and she didn't know how badly.

"Griffin, lean on me," she said, finally hearing the sirens coming closer. "Help is coming."

"I—I think I'm going to pass out. We gotta get out of here, go to the front..."

"We will." She held his hard body against hers as they stumbled down the back of the building. She didn't really know how she was keeping Griffin on his feet, but somehow, they made it past the dumpster and into the employee parking lot as a fire engine pulled up next to them. She could see two other trucks in front of the building and there was also an ambulance—thank God!

A firefighter came running toward them, calling for the medics. "Is there anyone else inside?" he asked.

"Maybe a woman," Griffin said, jerking back to consciousness. "She doused the place with gasoline and started the fire; I don't know if she got out."

"Anyone else?" he asked.

"No."

The paramedics pulled Griffin away from her, and as she followed them to the ambulance, she glanced back at the Depot. It was engulfed in flames. If Paige hadn't gotten out, there was no way she could have survived.

She felt a wave of righteous anger and vindictiveness. She'd never wished for anyone's death, but if Paige didn't make it out, she wasn't going to cry. The woman had hurt Griffin and had tried to kill them both.

But her anger turned to pain as she watched Griffin's dream burn down. He was losing everything—again. He'd worked so hard. And Vinnie had, too. They'd both had a new start in life and now it was gone.

But they were all alive. That was what mattered.

She turned away from the fire and hovered nearby as the paramedics got Griffin into the ambulance. She didn't know how he'd climbed a ladder and talked to her so calmly while suffering so much pain and blood loss. It had to have been a rush of adrenaline. Either that, or he really was a superhero.

"You're going to be all right," she told him, wanting to give him the same reassurance he'd given her.

"Come with me," he said. "I don't know what happened

to Paige. She could still hurt you."

"You can come with us," the paramedic told her.

"Thank you," she said, happy not to have to leave Griffin. She hopped into the back of the ambulance and held Griffin's hand all the way to the hospital.

Twenty-Six

An hour later, Annie sat with Griffin in an exam room as the orthopedic surgeon on duty told Griffin that the bullet had blown through his shoulder, and he would need surgery to repair the tendons. It wasn't the greatest news, but compared to what could have happened, she was counting them both to be extremely lucky.

As the doctor left to get an operating room set up, Annie gave Griffin a reassuring smile, and took his hands in hers, happy to see the color returning to his face. He was more alert now than he had been in the ambulance. They'd cut off his shirt. The bleeding had stopped and his shoulder was now immobilized but she could still see the ashes in his hair and smell the gasoline and smoke clinging to his skin as well as hers.

"I told you it was going to be okay," Griffin said with a weak smile. "A few stitches, and I'll be good as new."

She thought he would probably need a longer recovery than that, but she was just happy that he would completely recover.

"You were right," she said. "And you gave me the

confidence to climb out that window and get away from the fire. You saved me again, Griffin."

"I didn't save you; you saved yourself. I was proud of you, Annie. You were incredibly brave."

She blinked back the tears that had been threatening to fall since they'd arrived at the hospital, as she was losing grip on her exhausted emotions. "I guess I do have a few Callaway bravery genes after all."

"More than a few." He paused, his gaze turning serious. "When Paige confronted me, when I realized you were upstairs alone, I was terrified. Why did I ever let you go up there by yourself?"

"You didn't let me. You offered me your apartment so I could make my call, and after I did that, I actually called Kate and had a little heart-to-heart with her. Paige must have come in when I was in the bathroom, because I didn't see her. When I came out, the bedroom door was barricaded. She must have shoved the couch in front of it. I could smell the gas, so I stuffed a wet towel under the door, and I used your baseball bat to break the window, but that was as far as I got before everything exploded."

"Smart girl on the towel."

"Firefighter's daughter. What happened downstairs?"

"I heard a crash. It must have been when you broke the window. I was in the office by myself. Vinnie had left to go to the hospital. I ran down the hall, and Paige came out of the bar with a gun. I thought I could overtake her before she shot me, but I wasn't successful. I tried to get into the office when I saw her move toward the back door. She shot out a gasoline can. I think she thought she had enough time to get out but I'm not sure she did. I could have sworn I heard her scream."

She squeezed his hand. "She didn't get away, Griffin. I spoke to Detective Baker while you were being examined. They found her body by the door. She's dead."

"Good," he said harshly. "What about Kenny Taylor?"

"He's in jail, and he told Baker everything. Paige was apparently the mastermind, but he was happy to get revenge after he saw Tom in a coma. He also confessed to stabbing Shari; he claimed it was an accident, that he was just struggling to get the knife away from her. Oh, and Shari confirmed his version of the story."

"She's awake?" he asked in surprise.

"Yes, Detective Baker was actually interviewing her when we arrived. She's going to be all right, Griffin. She told them everything, too. She took cash to let Kenny and Paige know what you were doing, where you were going, when the bar would be empty. She put the matchbook in the bar to gaslight you, I guess. She got her blonde friend to show up and ask if you were Michael. She gave Paige access to your computer. But then they wanted the key to your apartment, and she started to realize their requests were never going to end, so she said no, and they didn't like it."

As Griffin drew in a shaky breath, she realized most of what she had to say could probably wait. "We can talk about this later."

"No, tell me the rest. I need to know."

"Kenny admitted to being high most of the past week. After Shari got stabbed, he realized he'd crossed the line. He said he told Paige to leave, but she refused. She said she wasn't done yet; you hadn't suffered enough."

"That's basically what she told me, too."

"Kenny also said that Paige was the one who slashed my tires. She wanted to use me to hurt you."

"That makes sense. Now that I know it was her, I'm surprised I didn't realize the figure was a woman."

"She was in disguise."

"Because she knew exactly what she was doing. She grew up in a family of cops; she knew how to avoid security cameras, and she knew how to shoot a gun." He paused. "Paige was so cold when I was talking to her. She had no conscience, no nothing. She was operating on pure hate, and she couldn't see anything else beyond the fact that I had ruined her life. It was like she'd completely lost herself."

"I can't believe she was in love with your partner."

"Me, either. Apparently, Tom thought he was too old for her back then, but after he went to jail, they got close. She said she was going to marry him when he got out. When she realized that wouldn't happen after Tom was attacked in prison, she had to get even with me. She didn't care who got hurt along the way." He gave a bemused shake of his head. "I never imagined she could be like that. Maybe I thought she was a little spoiled, a little selfish, but in my wildest dreams, I wouldn't have predicted that she would do any of this."

"I'm sorry, Griffin."

"No, you are not apologizing to me, Annie. I'm the one who's sorry, not just for letting you go upstairs alone, but for reacting the way I did when I saw your sketches. It was stupid, and I shouldn't have reacted with so much anger. I know you drew the characters before you knew about my past. You thought you were making up a story; you had no idea how close you were to my secrets. How could you? I was leading a double life."

"That is the truth, Griffin. I pitched the idea before I knew you were Michael Payton. But just so you know, I told the production company that I couldn't proceed with my story idea or the characters, that they were too close to real people who would not be interested in signing releases."

"So, you didn't get the job?"

"They said they'd think about it and call me back, but I'm sure it's a no. They wanted the idea more than me. It doesn't matter. I will come up with something else that doesn't hurt anyone, and hopefully I'll find a company who wants to do a project with me. We don't have to talk about that now. I'm more concerned about you. The Depot is..." She couldn't bring herself to say the words.

"I know," he said heavily. "It's gone."

"Do you think the landlord will rebuild?"

"I don't know." He frowned. "Damn! The party for the kids, the fundraiser for Hamilton House. It's on Sunday. I'm going to have to find another location."

"I'll help you," she said, seeing the worry in his eyes.

"It will be hard to find a place so close to Christmas. And there will be a lot of expenses—"

"Stop. We'll figure it out. For now, you need to rest and get through surgery. That's all you are going to think about. I'll start coming up with a plan for the fundraiser. I'm sure I can find some space that someone will donate for the kids. I can be pretty persuasive."

He gave her a faint smile. "Don't I know it."

She smiled back at him, but then she turned serious. "There was a moment today when I thought I'd lost you, that I might die, and I wished I'd said something to you. I love you, Griffin. I know you think I was blinded to your flaws because you saved my life, and that I have this idea that you're a superhero. I'm not going to deny that I am incredibly proud and amazed at what you've done to help people in need and to save people's lives, including my own. But I don't love the superhero; I love you. I love the man who's passionate and tender and kind. The man who listens to me ramble on and makes me laugh and gives me courage and makes me happy. I love talking to you and making love with you and even arguing with you. Neither of us is perfect, and that's good, because then we can just be ourselves." She blew out a breath. "And once again, I am talking way too much."

"I love listening to you, Annie. And I love you, too." He paused. "But Paige said something to me, and it hit home. She said that I was dark and moody and that I took her down. That was before I turned into a ghost. I don't want to do that to you. I know I can be too quiet, that I push people away, and to be honest I was doing that long before I changed my name and ran for my life. I grew up alone. I've always been more of a spectator. Opening the bar was a way for me to be part of a scene without really being part of it—which you already guessed."

"I did guess that. I'm not worried about you being too dark. I know you need your space, your solitude. That is totally fine with me. But when you're ready to talk and play, then I'm there."

He winced as he adjusted his position.

"Be careful," she said quickly. "You should be resting. We can talk about all this later."

"It's all right. I'm fine. I like talking to you."

The nurse came into the room. "We're going to take Mr. Hale to the OR in a moment."

She nodded and got to her feet as the nurse stepped out of the room. She leaned over and gave Griffin a long, emotional kiss, feeling an immense rush of love for him. "I'll be here when you wake up."

"Good. Because we have a lot more to talk about, and I'm going to do at least some of the talking."

"I'm looking forward to that."

After Griffin was whisked away, she walked back into the waiting room, and realized it was full of not only employees from the Depot but a lot of their customers. She doubted Griffin had any idea how much he was loved.

Vinnie came over to her, concern in his eyes. "How's he doing?"

"He's going into surgery. But he'll be all right." She included everyone in the room with her comments. "He wants us to work on finding a place for the fundraiser. He's worried about the kids not having their Christmas party."

"That sounds like Griffin," Vinnie said with a nod. "He almost gets himself killed and he's worrying about a kids' party."

"I told him we'd work on it. We'll find another location and we'll make it happen, not just for the kids, but for Griffin, too."

"I'll help," Justin offered.

"Me, too," Danielle said, followed by a chorus of others, all willing to pitch in.

"Thanks," she said, starting to feel a little teary-eyed again at the swell of support. "I know Griffin is worried about all of you being out of work for a time, but he's going to try to do right by you."

"He just needs to get well," Vinnie said. "The rest will

sort itself out. Can I speak to you, Annie?"

She nodded and followed him away from the crowd.

"How are you doing, Annie? Did you get yourself checked out?" he asked.

"I was given oxygen in the ambulance. I'm okay, a little dry throat, but nothing terrible. I was really lucky. If Griffin hadn't come around the back and gone up the fire escape, I never would have had the courage to get on that ledge. Frankly, I still don't know how I did it. But when fire is licking at your fingers, it's a little easier to let go."

"There was a fire escape by Griffin's apartment, too, but it broke a year or so ago. The landlord took it down but didn't replace it." He frowned. "We should have made sure he did."

"I'm sad that beautiful old building is gone."

"Yeah," he said heavily. "Me, too. The landlord is flying in tomorrow."

"Do you think he'll rebuild?"

"I don't know, but if Griffin is up for it, I hope we'll reopen the bar somewhere."

"I'm sure that's exactly what he wants to do."

"Did you and Griffin work out whatever was bothering you both today?"

She smiled. "We did. There's nothing like a life-and-death moment to get your priorities straight. I love Griffin, by the way."

Vinnie grinned. "That isn't news, Annie. I've known that since about the first day you showed up."

"I didn't love him then. He was not at all welcoming that first day."

"But he grew on you."

"He did," she admitted.

"You're good for him, Annie, and I told him that earlier today." Vinnie paused. "Griffin said that you made me into a superhero? I really hope I'm the handsome one."

She laughed. "You're very handsome in my drawings. Your muscles are huge, and your apron is really a cape."

"I like that."

"But I'm not going to show the public my work. I will show you sometime, if you want, but that's as far as it goes."

"Listen, I know Griffin doesn't want to be famous, but I'm okay with it. You can use my likeness any way you want."

"I appreciate that."

"You had anything to eat or drink?"

She couldn't even remember. "I have no idea. This day has been a blur."

"Then let's get you fed. Because I know the one and only thing Griffin would want me to do right now is take care of you. I hope he told you he loves you, too, because he does. He's not always the best with words, you know?"

"I know, but he did say the words, and I am not letting him take them back."

"I don't think he's going to want to do that."

When Griffin woke up, the sun was coming through the window of his hospital room. Annie was sitting in a chair next to the bed, but she was resting her head on her arms on the mattress next to him, and she was fast asleep. Her beautiful, reddish-blonde hair, was still streaked with some ash from the fire, but her creamy complexion was rosy from sleep and there wasn't a scratch on her. For that, he was truly grateful.

He'd lost a lot yesterday, the bar and the business he'd built the past four years, but it didn't even matter, because this woman was all he needed. He wanted to wake up next to her for the rest of his life. And it was almost shocking to realize he could do exactly that.

There was no one else to run from. He could live his life in the open, in the sunshine. He didn't believe anyone else would come after him now that he knew it had been Paige and Kenny behind the attacks. They'd been the closest to Tom. And Tom was never going to wake up. It was amazing how the actions Tom had taken had changed the course of so many lives, most of all his own.

Annie murmured something in her sleep, and he smiled as he gently stroked his fingers through her hair. Even in sleep, she had something to say. He didn't think he would ever get tired of listening to her.

She drew in a deeper breath and then shifted position, finally lifting her head. She blinked the sleep out of her eyes as he ran his fingers down her face and gave her a tender smile.

"Good morning," he said.

"You're awake. How are you feeling?"

"Honestly? Never better."

"The drugs must not have worn off yet."

"I don't think it's the drugs. I think it's you. When I woke up and saw you next to me, all was right with the world."

"I think that's the nicest thing anyone has ever said to me."

"Well, get used to it, because I plan on saying a lot of nice things."

"So, now that you're talking, there's no stopping you," she teased.

"You got that right."

"But how are you really? Are you in any pain?"

He shook his head. "Not much."

"Would you tell me if you were?"

"Maybe."

"That's a no."

"Has anything else happened since I went into surgery?"

"No. Your entire staff waited until the doctor came out to tell us you did great and would make a full recovery, and then they went home. I told them we're going to hold the party somewhere next Sunday, and we'll let them know where as soon as we know. Vinnie talked to Deb at Hamilton House, and they were more concerned about your welfare than the party, but he assured them we were going to make the fundraiser happen. I'm planning to get started on all that this morning."

"I can help."

"You're going to rest and do what the doctor says."

"I'm not going to rest here, no matter what anyone says. I do not need to stay in this hospital." He paused. "However, it occurs to me that I'm homeless, unless a pretty redhead would like to invite me home?"

"Oh, you are definitely invited to my home, and we have several more months before we're going to get kicked out." She smiled. "We're quite the pair—unemployed and no permanent address."

"And yet amazingly happy," he finished.

"Amazingly," she agreed.

"Although..."

"What?" she asked warily.

"It's been a really long time since you kissed me."

"Are you sure you're up for that?"

"I only injured my shoulder; the rest of me is working just fine."

She stood up and gently put her hand on his chest. "Your heart is beating awfully fast."

"Because you're killing me with anticipation."

She gave him a wicked smile. "The wait is only going to make it that much better." She slowly leaned over, letting her hair tickle his chin, letting her breath warm his lips before her mouth touched his. It felt like the first time and the last time and all the times that would come in between.

When she lifted her head, she said, "You better get well really fast."

"Why don't you find the doctor and tell him to sign me out of here? Because I'm going to rest a lot better in your bed."

"I don't think they call that rest," she said with a laugh.

"There will be rest...after."

"When you put it like that..." She kissed him again and then headed out of the room.

He felt like a foolish idiot, grinning at the ceiling. He

didn't know what this crazy feeling was that was running around inside him, but he thought it just might be happiness. And he couldn't wait to get started on the rest of his life.

Epilogue

➤➤❮❮ ❮

 The party would be starting soon, and as Annie looked around the rec room at the Shoreview Senior Center just before three on Sunday afternoon, she felt proud of all she'd accomplished. Five days earlier, they hadn't even had a venue for the holiday fundraiser, but now they had created a winter wonderland. She'd been working on the room since nine o'clock in the morning, and with a lot of help from the Depot employees, the room had been decorated with holiday wreaths, garlands, lights, and, of course, an enormous Christmas tree.

 Now, the caterers had set up a buffet and were whipping up hot chocolate and hot cider drinks in the kitchen, while a few seniors came in early to grab a seat at one of the round tables before all the commotion started.

 The senior center had graciously offered their rec room for the party, believing, as she did, that a multi-generational event would bring joy to everyone.

 It had certainly been a whirlwind of activity the past few days.

 They'd plastered newly redesigned flyers all over town

and posted on social media to get the word out about the change in venue. The price of admission for the event was one wrapped toy with a label designating the age of the intended recipient and whether the item was best suited for a boy, or a girl, or was gender-neutral.

To make sure they had enough toys, Vinnie and Griffin had sent Justin and Danielle to the local toy store to pick up even more presents. In addition, cash donations to Hamilton House were also going to be welcomed, and all donors would be eligible for a raffle with the grand prize being a three-night stay at a very fancy and luxury hotel in San Diego.

"Wow," Griffin said, coming up next to her.

She gave him a happy smile, pleased by his reaction. She'd managed to keep him out of most of the work, wanting him to rest and heal, but he hadn't been the best patient, taking a lot of meetings with Vinnie and the landlord to discuss rebuilding and reopening the Depot. "You like it?"

"It's spectacular," he said. "You did all this in such a short time. No wonder I haven't seen much of you."

"I had a lot of help from your employees, who all seem to have vanished at the moment, but I guess they went to their homes to change before everyone gets here."

"They'll be back. Everyone did a great job. The kids are going to love it."

"And so will the seniors."

"I still can't believe you got the senior center to agree to a party for a bunch of at-risk kids."

"It's a win-win for everyone. The older folks get to enjoy all the young energy, the holiday spirit, the music that will be starting shortly, the great food donated by the wonderful people at Carmichael's Seafood Restaurant, the photo booth donated by Sonny's Surf Shop, and the video arcade games on loan from Game Systems, Inc., that will create even more fun. I hope I've thought of everything."

"I'm sure you have. It's perfect, Annie." He put his good arm around her shoulder, his other arm still resting in a sling. "This is better than what we would have had at the bar."

"I don't know about that, but as a nod to the Depot, did you notice the incredible miniature train working its way around almost two hundred yards of track?"

"I did notice that," he said with a grin. "Maybe we can find a place for it when we open the new Depot."

She gave him a curious glance. "Have you come to a decision?"

"We have. Vinnie and I are going to buy the property from our landlord. He has moved out of the area, and he doesn't want to rebuild, so he has decided to sell it to us."

"That's great. Is it a lot of money?"

"Yes," he said, but not looking too upset about it. "And the construction will be more money, but we've been putting cash aside the past two years, in case we had the opportunity to buy the building, so we have enough for a down-payment. We're also taking on a third partner—Danielle."

"Danielle?" she asked, surprised that the forty-something widowed waitress would have cash for that kind of investment. "Danielle has money?"

"Yeah, we had no idea. She got a settlement after her husband died, but she was bored doing nothing at home, so that's why she came to work for us. When she heard our plans, she said she'd be interested in investing if we wanted another partner."

"That's great. I think she'd be very easy to have as a partner." She paused. "Although, I think she might have a little crush on Vinnie."

"Oh, it's more than a little crush," Griffin said. "And apparently it's reciprocated. They've been seeing each other for months; they just didn't tell anyone."

She laughed at his disgruntled expression. "Imagine that. Someone else had a secret besides you."

He nodded, then dropped his arm from around her shoulders as he checked a text on his phone. She was a bit puzzled by his sudden distraction. "Everything okay?"

"Yeah, it's all good."

"Hey, I thought we tell each other everything now."

"Don't worry," he said reassuringly. "I just have a little surprise for you."

"Now I'm curious."

"You're always curious." He leaned over and gave her a sweet, hot kiss, that instantly made her toes curl. There had been a lot of those kisses in the last week and yet not nearly enough.

"Griffin. Not in front of the seniors," she said with a laughing protest.

"Don't mind us," an elderly woman said as she walked by. "It's been awhile since I saw a good kiss like that."

She flushed a little, then tapped her fingers against his chest. "No more of that until we're home."

"Hey, I just got rave reviews," he said with an unapologetic grin.

She liked how happy and carefree Griffin was now, and she was enjoying getting to know his lighter side. "I give you rave reviews all the time."

"Yeah, but that's because you just want more of the good stuff," he teased.

"That's true."

"But…" Griffin began, checking his watch again. "I have to go. I will be back in a few minutes."

"Do you need any help?"

"I'm good. I think it's time for you to open the doors, Annie."

"I think they're already open," she said, as a group of young kids came walking and skipping into the room, immediately crowding the food tables, racing across the room to see the train and the tree, and exploring the video arcade games they'd set up by the stage.

The children were followed by teenagers and a few parents as well as volunteers from Hamilton House.

She spent the next ten minutes welcoming everyone inside, a little worried that her fellow helpers were nowhere to be found, especially as the room filled up.

Danielle was supposed to be selling the raffle tickets.

Vinnie had promised to organize the toys that were brought into the party, and Justin was supposed to get the band going.

An uneasy feeling ran down her spine. Something was going on.

Griffin had mentioned a good surprise. She hoped it had something to do with that. She was still a little gun-shy after almost losing her life in the Depot.

As she glanced toward the front door, her entire mood lifted. She could not believe the group walking into the room: Mia and her husband, Jeremy, and their daughter Ashlyn, as well as her sister Kate and her boyfriend Devin.

When Kate and Mia saw her, they gave a little squeal and broke away from their guys to run toward her. She threw her arms around both of them in happy delight. After a happy hug, she said, "What are you both doing here?" Before they could answer, she turned to their men. "It's good to see you two as well. And you, Ashlyn," she added, smiling at Mia's daughter.

"We wanted to support you," Mia said.

"And we wanted to make sure you were really okay," Kate added. "Devin and I decided to fly out a few days early and spend some time with you and Mia before heading up to San Francisco for the family Christmas. I assume you're coming to that, Annie."

"I am definitely going to be there."

"With your mystery man?" Kate asked.

"Griffin will be there, too," she said, happy he was excited to meet her family. "I know you're going to love him."

"We better love him, after all he put you through," Kate said. "He better be worth it."

"He is—trust me."

"Where is he?" Mia asked curiously, looking around the room. "We really want to meet him."

"They actually want to vet him," Devin put in with a grin.

"And grill him," Jeremy added.

"I don't actually know where he is. He said he had a surprise, and I'm waiting for him to come back. In the meantime, is all well with you, Mia? Baby is good?"

"Baby is great," Mia said, patting her barely noticeable bump. "And I'm not throwing up anymore, so I'm happy about that."

"I'm really glad." A commotion near the entrance drew her gaze, and she couldn't believe her eyes for a second time.

"What on earth is this?" Mia muttered.

"Looks like a team of superheroes," she said, a smile spreading across her face as Griffin entered the room, wearing a muscled superhero outfit that somehow incorporated his sling as well as a cape and boots. He was followed by Vinnie, Justin, and Danielle, almost exactly the way she'd imagined them. "I can't believe they did this."

The team of superheroes ran through the room with drama and flair, handing out colorfully wrapped presents to all of the kids. And then Griffin stepped up to the microphone.

"I want to welcome all of you to our party. We are celebrating the great work of Hamilton House and also this wonderful senior center for hosting our event. We have music coming up, more presents, a raffle you won't want to miss, and plenty of food. But before we do anything further, we want to thank the woman who put all this together, the absolutely amazing Annie Callaway."

Applause followed Griffin's announcement, and she dabbed at her moist eyes.

"I know you're not shy, Annie," Griffin said, motioning her forward.

She walked up to the microphone and gave him a loving look, then said to the crowd, "I had a lot of help from the superheroes in this room. But our main goal is for you all to enjoy yourselves. And don't forget to buy a raffle ticket."

She stepped away from the microphone as the band took over, launching into the first of many holiday songs to be played that night.

—➤➤◄◄—

Griffin saw the tears in Annie's eyes and hoped they were happy tears. "I couldn't get the costume exactly right, but what do you think, especially since I had to work around my sling?" He flexed his one good bicep, which moved his fake muscles up and down.

"I think you're incredible and a little crazy. Why did you all do this?" she asked, as Vinnie, Justin, and Danielle crowded around them.

"You guys want to tell her?" Griffin asked.

"We want you to use us as your superhero team," Justin put in. "Griffin showed us the sketches, and we're all on board. But I also wouldn't mind if you remember this when you grade my final project next week."

"I'll be sure to do that," she said with a laugh.

"We'd love to be the inspiration for a movie," Vinnie continued.

"And I like the way you made me sexy. My boobs were huge," Danielle added with a big laugh.

"That's so nice of all of you, but I—I don't think I have that option anymore," she said. "I didn't get that job."

"Actually…" Griffin began.

She gave him a wary look. "What?"

"I went to the production company on Friday."

"You did what?"

"I went into the production company and I told them that you were wrong about not having our permission. They said they were happy to hear that because they really wanted to work with you. They also said they'd called you, but you hadn't called them back. Why not?"

"I thought they were just going to say no," she murmured. "And I was really busy."

And she hadn't wanted to be rejected, he thought. "They want you, Annie, with or without the idea. They told me that. They thought you were the best artist they'd spoken to in months. All you have to do is pick up the phone on Monday and call them."

A light came into her eyes. "They really want to hire me?"

"They really do. They'd be fools not to."

"Thank you—all of you. I promise I will do right by each and every one of you. You'll see sketches all the way along, and there's no guarantee that anything will ever come of it, but you never know."

"You're welcome," Vinnie said. "Now let's go have some superhero fun, gang."

"I'll join you all in a second," he said, as he took Annie's hands in his. "I know I interfered in your business. Are you angry?"

"No. I'm happy, and I'm in love with you. I can't believe you did that for me."

"You deserved it. And I wanted to have your back, the way you've had mine."

"We're a good team."

As he leaned in for a kiss, he heard a deliberate clearing of someone's throat. He lifted his head to see two very attractive blonde women giving him assessing looks. Behind them were two guys, who both seemed curious as to what was about to happen, as well as a little girl, who had big eyes and a big smile.

"Griffin, I want you to meet my sisters," Annie said. "Mia and Kate. And these are their significant others, Jeremy and Devin, as well as my beautiful niece, Ashlyn."

"I didn't know you all were coming," he said. "I'm kind of regretting the superhero costume now."

Kate was a very fit looking woman with short blonde hair and sparkling blue eyes and Mia was a softer version of Kate with longer blonde hair and blue eyes. While they weren't identical, they were clearly sisters, and shared some of Annie's features as well.

"We wanted to surprise Annie," Kate said. "And I wanted to meet the man who got my sister into all kinds of trouble and made her cry," she added pointedly.

"You're going to be the tough one, aren't you?" he said lightly.

"I am," she agreed. "I'd kick your ass if my sister wasn't so crazy about you."

"I believe you would."

"Keep that in mind for the future," Kate warned.

"It's nice to meet you, Griffin," Mia put in. "And while I don't do a lot of ass kicking, I can get my husband to help, so don't assume I'm a complete pushover."

"I wouldn't dare," he said with a laugh.

"I hope you know what you're getting into," Devin said with a dry smile, offering him a handshake.

"Although their bark is worse than their bite," Jeremy interjected, as he shook hands with him as well.

"I'm really glad you came," he said, seeing the happiness in Annie's eyes. "I know Annie misses you a lot."

"I do miss all of you," Annie admitted, slipping her arm about his waist. "And it means a lot to me that you are here."

"We're family. That's what family does," Mia said.

"I hope you like big family gatherings, Griffin," Kate said. "Because Christmas is going to be a blowout. And then there will be our brothers' double wedding. Did Annie tell you that Dylan and Tori and Ian and Grace are tying the knot together in February?"

"She mentioned something about that," he said.

"Good luck remembering everyone's name," Devin said. "I still get the cousins mixed up."

"Griffin will have plenty of time to remember everyone's name," Annie said.

"A lifetime," he agreed, looking into her beautiful green eyes.

"I think things are going to get mushy," Kate said. "Let's get some food."

"Are things going to get mushy?" he asked Annie, as her family headed to the buffet.

"Very," she said, a promise in her eyes. "I love you, Griffin."

"I love you, too. I want to be part of your family, and I want you to be a part of mine. I was thinking sometime this winter we might head down to Florida."

"I would love to meet your dad and your grandfather."

"Good."

"And I'm thrilled that I'm getting my own personal superhero for the rest of my life. So how about giving me a superhero kiss?"

"Here? In front of the children and the elderly?" he teased.

"Here, there and everywhere."

"I'm going to make you happy," he vowed.

She gazed into his eyes. "You already have."

THE END

—➤➤◄◄◄—

If you love romantic suspense, don't miss out on Barbara's new *Lightning Strikes Trilogy*:

Beautiful Storm (#1)
Lightning Lingers (#2)
Summer Rain (#3)

—➤➤◄◄◄—

About The Author

Barbara Freethy is a #1 New York Times Bestselling Author of 65 novels ranging from contemporary romance to romantic suspense and women's fiction. Traditionally published for many years, Barbara opened her own publishing company in 2011 and has since sold over 7 million books! Twenty of her titles have appeared on the New York Times and USA Today Bestseller Lists.

Known for her emotional and compelling stories of love, family, mystery and romance, Barbara enjoys writing about ordinary people caught up in extraordinary adventures. Barbara's books have won numerous awards. She is a six-time finalist for the RITA for best contemporary romance from Romance Writers of America and a two-time winner for DANIEL'S GIFT and THE WAY BACK HOME.

Barbara has lived all over the state of California and currently resides in Northern California where she draws much of her inspiration from the beautiful bay area.

For a complete listing of books, as well as excerpts and contests, and to connect with Barbara:

Visit Barbara's Website:
www.barbarafreethy.com

Join Barbara on Facebook:
www.facebook.com/barbarafreethybooks

Follow Barbara on Twitter:
www.twitter.com/barbarafreethy